LYLE NICHOLSON

PIPELINE KILLERS

vinci
BOOKS

By Lyle Nicholson

Bernadette Callahan Series

Polar Bear Dawn

Pipeline Killers

Climate Killers

Caught in the Crossfire

Deadly Ancestors

When the Devil Bird Cries

The Suspect from Berlin

Suspects and Liars

Vinci Books

vinci-books.com

Published by Vinci Books Ltd in 2025

1

A CIP catalogue record for this book is available from the British Library.
Paperback ISBN: 9781036703622

Chapter One

Detective Bernadette Callahan was speeding. The single-lane asphalt highway shimmered in the August heat. Cresting a small hill, she felt the Jeep Cherokee's chassis rise. She let off the gas a little. Jeeps were built for rough terrain, not high speeds. She reminded herself of that, and slowed down to 120 kilometers per hour.

The investigation she was speeding toward had not yet been classified as either an accidental death or a homicide. The chief of detectives from the Royal Canadian Mounted Police Serious Crimes Division wanted her take on it. There was, "something strange about the body," according to Jerry Durham, RCMP Chief of Detectives. He needed her eyes on the scene.

A body had been found under a pipeline that crossed a stream just outside of Red Deer, Alberta. Bernadette did not think of what caused the death. She never thought of victims until she saw them. Usually the way a victim laid or looked would give a clue as to what happened moments or days before. They always told a story. Either Bernadette would figure it out or the Crime Scene Investigator would. The CSI would painstakingly plod around the scene in hot polyester coveralls, detailing mountains of evidence. Bernadette was glad she was a RCMP Detective and not a CSI. She hated polyester.

Bernadette was mid-thirties, 5-foot-8, with a mildly athletic build that showed constant efforts in the gym mostly nullified by a diet of junk food with a focus on donuts and double cream, double sugar coffee. She had short-cropped brunette hair with highlights of red showing that were not Miss Clairol, but real Irish roots blended with Dene First Nations. Her green eyes were set against her slightly beige complexion, where her Irish roots again battled for dominance, showing up in freckles that fought for space on her arms and face.

The asphalt highway turned west toward the Rocky Mountains, the hot, glaring sun causing Bernadette to don her dark aviator glasses. She took another swig of her now cold coffee, grimaced as the tepid sweet fluid drained down her throat, and reminded herself to bring her coffee thermos cup next time. She would forget the reminder.

A large German shepherd named Sprocket was sitting alert in the back seat, checking the clouds, the trees, and the cows as they shot by. He never barked. He knew better. He was obedient enough for that. Sprocket was a dropout from RCMP dog training school. Not attentive enough. No spunk, they said. No killer instinct.

Sprocket was the perfect dog for Bernadette. He was a good running companion, a good listener—for a male—and never judgmental when she consumed pizza and boxed red wine. She often wondered if she could find Sprocket's traits in a man.

A large oil service truck appeared in the distance.

Bernadette's Jeep came up behind it, overtook and passed it. The road dipped, and then turned a bend. A black mass appeared ahead. Bernadette began to slow, glancing in her rearview mirror to locate the truck she had just passed. It was gaining on her.

The black mass started to fly. A flock of crows feasting on roadkill. A sea of black wings took to the air, cawing their displeasure at being chased from their afternoon meal. One bird did not fly; it hopped and then started to flap. Too slow. The Jeep's grill made first contact. The bird bounced from the grill onto the hood and did a cartwheel past the window.

Bernadette saw the bird was a hawk. "You son of a bitch, that serves you right for feasting with crows . . . you dumb ass." Bernadette fumed as she resumed speed, not wanting the large oil truck to rear-end her. She was shaken by the incident, and mad at the hawk. "Damn thing is supposed to be a hunter, not a scavenger," she muttered over her shoulder to Sprocket. She was pissed at killing the hawk.

Sprocket did not move from his seat. His tongue flicked out, did a long circuitous route around his nose before hanging out. One of his eyebrows twitched. The large bird hitting the windshield was a shock to him as well, but he dared not bark. Bernadette did not like barking in her Jeep. The dog went back to staring out the window.

The turn Bernadette wanted came up on the right. She braked hard, dropped the Jeep into four-wheel drive and followed a gravel road that turned into a dirt track. There were numerous fresh tracks. The other patrol cars would be there. And oil service trucks. Bernadette had been told this victim was in the middle of an oil spill. Oil spills were bad. In cattle and farming country near a river they were especially bad, and that's what Bernadette had been told this was.

The town of Red Deer, where Bernadette's RCMP Detachment was based, was home for hundreds of Canadian oil companies that sent their rigs and men hundreds of miles in all directions to drill and service oil wells. Red Deer was also rich farming and cattle country. The farmers and ranchers did not always get along with Big Oil, especially when the oilmen were careless.

The dirt track led through a field of tall wheat, their heads full and leaning with the weight of their grain. In a few more weeks, the threshing machines would be mowing these fields. Right now they bathed in the sun.

The road came to a stand of trees that lined a creek. A fleet of oil services trucks parked at different angles circled two RCMP cruisers. The oil trucks flashed yellow lights; the RCMP cruisers flashed red and blue lights. Like the circus dropped just beside the creek, and someone forgot to put out the announcement.

Bernadette parked, stepped out, and opened the back door for Sprocket to go for a run. She gave the dog strict instructions to stay close to the Jeep, and not chase gophers. The dog looked up, cocking one eye and one ear in her direction, and took off into the field. Bernadette shook her head and headed down to the creek bed.

The creek was deep; a winding path led down to the creek bed. Large poplar trees rattled their leaves in the light breeze. With each step downward in the rich dark earth, the temperature lowered from the scorching afternoon heat of the wheat field to the coolness of the creek below. The smell of oil assaulted Bernadette's nostrils and burned the back of her throat. Descending the path, she could see a small army of oil workers laying absorbent booms around the spill and mopping up any oil that escaped. They looked defeated by the large task at hand.

Black oil glistened on the rocks. It oozed down the creek, slowing the water into thick molasses. Low hanging branches dragged their leaves in the thick morass and became black paintbrushes hanging ever lower, sucking the acrid oil into their roots.

The pipeline was elevated on a trestle that carried it from one side of the creek to the other. Bernadette stopped halfway down the path and surveyed where the victim lay. The pipeline on the trestle was cut in two, and one end was bleeding oil through hundreds of porous openings. *Like the whole pipe had developed a bad case of Swiss cheese*, Bernadette thought. She was told the oil in the pipeline had been shut down, but the oil had gushed for hours before being discovered.

Two crime scene investigators wandered around a yellow tarp that lay half submerged in the creek, the legs in blue coveralls rested in the creek and the boots, with toes pointed upwards, glistening with oil. Bernadette ruled out drowning. She gazed up at the height of the pipe to the creek bed. It was perhaps 4 meters. A height usually good enough for broken bones, unless the person did a header—fell headfirst. She looked up and down the stream and continued her walk down the path.

She recognized the two CSIs as she approached. One was a short, round Filipino named Basilio, whom everyone called Bas. The other was a tall, wiry older guy nicknamed Angus for his habit of eating beef at almost every meal. He was from Hungary, not Scotland, and his real name was Antal, but his friends swore he consumed an Angus cow a month, so the nickname stuck.

Bas and Angus turned to Bernadette as she crunched on

the stream bed toward them. Angus raised a hand that held a clear bag of evidence he'd been collecting, "Hi, Detective, glad you could make it."

Bernadette walked up to Angus before responding. She didn't want the oil workers listening in on their conversation. "What's so important about this vic that I needed to drop out on this fine day? This kind of has industrial accident pasted all over it, if you know what I mean."

Angus smiled. His somewhat crooked teeth looked like weapons he used to consume his daily beef quota. "I called your chief because this vic looked way strange, as we say in the technical sense, and I wanted you to see it." He flashed another smile at his CSI humor and motioned for Bernadette to view the body.

Bernadette crouched over, and Angus pulled back the tarp to reveal the victim. A skinny, sandy-haired kid, no more than mid-twenties, lay underneath. He wore blue coveralls, with an oil logo emblazoned on one side of the chest, and the name "Nathan Taylor" on the other.

"So, what do you figure for cause of death and time?" Bernadette asked, as she looked the body over.

"Well, that is the question. There are no outward signs of trauma or injury, other than a small gash on the right arm." Angus held up the victim's skinny arm to point out a small rip to the coveralls. "You see here, a 4-centimeter tear in the fabric, and a 3-centimeter tear in the epidermis. The depth of the cut to the arm is maybe .158 centimeters."

"So, we're talking about a cut maybe a one-sixteenth of an inch deep, that doesn't sound life threatening. What time did our victim die?" Bernadette asked. Bernadette still hated metric, and converted everything to the old school measurements when she could.

"Interesting question, and I could normally nail that for

you with body temperature. Only the victim has been lying partially in the creek, and the cold water skews my estimate," Angus admitted while gazing at the slow-running creek. "Now, my other method would be liver temperature, and I got a problem with that . . ."

"So, what's the problem?"

"From what I can see of this body, we are light on some organs."

"Light on organs? What are you saying? How can this body be missing organs? I thought you said there was no external trauma other than the small cut on the arm." Bernadette knelt down to look more closely at the body.

"There isn't. Not another mark on him." Angus opened the victim's coveralls, and Bernadette saw that his abdomen was shrunken, exposing the telltale contours of the spine. "But see, this is where we should have the stomach, liver, kidneys, and I feel nothing. Gone . . . vacant . . . nada . . . as in not here."

"Is this kid an alien, or some kind of freak?" Bernadette pulled the tarp further back to examine the body more closely. The kid looked normal, very skinny but normal.

"No, I don't believe we have an alien, but we do have a strange victim," Angus said, and covered the body back up. The oil workers were edging closer. He didn't want them seeing the remains.

"Any idea how long this body was here or who discovered it?" Bernadette asked as she looked around the scene. The oil workers went back to mopping up the oil in the creek. They made like they weren't trying to eavesdrop on Bernadette's comments.

"The farmer up there on the ridge said he found the body this morning around 10 a.m., and the kid's boss standing next to the farmer said he sent him to this location at 8 a.m., so we have maybe a two-hour corpse tops. Bodies don't lose their organs that fast. Organs may shrivel inside a cadaver over time, but this feels like they're missing. I have a rush put on this with the coroner's office, but I wanted you to see this before we sent the vic there." Angus stood up and stretched, his tall frame blocking the afternoon sun, and throwing a shadow over the yellow tarp.

"What's in the evidence bag?" Bernadette asked, pointing her boot toward the plastic bag containing a small Plexiglas carrying case with several vials.

Angus pointed toward the top of the bank, "No idea, maybe the oil guy at the top of the bank knows what it is. We found several of these vials around our body; most of them were broken open."

Bernadette glanced up to the top of the bank. Two RCMP constables were in conversation with oil company personnel, and a very loud farmer. The words of the farmer rolled down to them. He was pissed his creek was defiled with oil. "This shit was never supposed to happen—god damn it—you said you had a shit load of checks and balances—and what I see is a shit load of oil in my water."

The farmer's words echoed into the deep creek. The black oil had silenced the rushing creek water, and only the anger of the farmer was giving voice to the disaster that was in the creek bed.

Bernadette walked up the bank and joined the group. Constable Stewart was on the edge of the crowd. Bernadette stood by his side and quietly asked, "So, what do we have here?"

Constable Stewart looked all of 19, blond, short-cropped hair, blue eyes set off by the still-pink hue on his cheeks. His body was that of a brawny weightlifter; his biceps bulged out of his shirtsleeves. No one dared call him youngster.

Stewart nodded at Bernadette. "Hi Detective." Stewart pulled out his notepad and read his notes quietly to her. "The victim worked for the pipeline company. His boss is the one the farmer is yelling at. What we have ascertained so far is the victim was here to do some routine inspection on the line. How this catastrophic failure in the pipeline began is unknown, nor do we know how the victim met his death." Constable Stewart snapped his notebook shut and placed it back in his breast pocket.

"Sounds like the usual bizarre case." Bernadette walked into the group and tapped the farmer on the shoulder. "Excuse me sir, Detective Bernadette Callahan of the RCMP Serious Crimes Division. Might I have a word with this gentleman for a moment?" She motioned to the oil company exec the farmer was berating.

The farmer took a breath, "Hell, I'm not done chewing out his ass yet."

"I completely understand your anger at the oil spill; however, we also have a death of this person's colleague to consider. I'll bring this gentleman back as soon as I'm done." Bernadette managed a small look of consolation towards the farmer. The man was more concerned about the death of his stream, than the body of the young man. The farmer scowled and backed away reluctantly. There was enough anger in him to fuel at least another hour of shouting at the oilman. Oil was smelling up his stream, destroying his water supply, his precious wheat in jeopardy. No, he wasn't even close to done venting his anger.

Bernadette walked the pipeline man away from the group. He introduced himself as Steve Sawatsky, Quality Health and Safety Manager for Tamarack Pipelines.

"Thanks for getting me away from that guy; even a short reprieve is appreciated. How can I help you, Detective?"

"What exactly was this young man sent here to do?"

"He was doing what we call oil coupon inspection. Oil coupons are small pieces of metal that rest inside the pipeline and are used to judge the thickness of the pipeline wall. We pull them out and check them for wear. The kid was sent here to do that."

"The vials that were found around his body, are they part of the testing?"

Sawatsky lowered his voice, looked around to see who was in earshot, "Look, I have no idea about the vials. He was here on company business to pull a piece of metal out of a hole, make a record and move on to the next one." He moved closer to Bernadette, "If this kid put anything in the pipeline that caused this mess . . ." He stopped in midsentence as if the air had leaked out of his voice. "We were just lucky the pipeline came apart in the creek, and whatever caused this didn't go further. I've never seen a pipe become so perforated like it is here." Sawatsky moved further away from the group, "Look, between you and me, the kid wasn't supposed to be on the trestle over the creek. It looks like he opened a valve and then fell. I'm in all kinds of shit on this. The kid shouldn't have been working on his own today, but I was short staffed . . ."

"Did Nathan Taylor know he'd be on his own today?" Bernadette asked.

"Yeah, sure he did, I told him two days ago I'd be sending him out for testing, and he'd be going solo. He seemed all happy about it. So was the rest of my crew."

Bernadette scribbled in the notebook in her illegible handwriting. She called her scratches on paper handwriting; her detachment chief called them hieroglyphics. Bernadette looked up, "You think this young man was responsible for the pipeline breach?"

Sawatsky hitched up his pants, pursed out his lips and looked up at the sky for a second. "Look, this kid was a smartass university summer student, always mouthing off about how oil was causing all these problems. A real shit disturber with the crew, and a slack-ass son of a bitch who couldn't pull his weight. We put him on monitoring detail to keep him away from the crew, so as he wouldn't get his ass kicked. There was no one within miles of him."

"You can account for every one of your crew?"

"Absolutely, we were running pigs an hour's drive from here, and all my crew was signed in and with me for the whole day. We started at 0730 hours this morning, and like I said, I sent the Taylor kid off by himself to do some testing over this creek. He left on his own in a company truck. I got here when called out by our emergency response spill people at 1000 hours."

"What are pigs?"

"A sensor we use to check the pipes for weakness. We don't have to shut the oil flow down to use them. We've been running these checks all week.

"No one followed him?"

"No, I can swear to that. I had 5 guys on my crew, and they were all there, and I was on my cell phone for most of the morning with my office, so check the GPS on my phone if you want to check my whereabouts." Sawatsky threw out the last statement like a dare.

Bernadette just scribbled, *boys working with pigs*, and looked up, "You have the contact information for the next of kin for the deceased and his last known address in town?"

"I gave it to your young constable there. There was supposedly some girl he was rooming with in town, kept bragging about how tired he was from screwing her all night," Sawatsky smiled at Bernadette to accentuate the word screwing. "Is that everything? Because after that farmer gets done chewing on my ass, corporate in Calgary is fixing to get on it." Sawatsky stopped and put his head down, "Look I'm sorry if I sound like a hard ass about the kid. He was a pain in the ass, but no one wanted to see this tragedy. Deaths and injury are part of our business, but we don't wish it on anyone."

Bernadette smiled at Sawatsky and watched as he walked back over to the farmer, who immediately resumed yelling at him. She shook her head in mild sympathy and found Constable Stewart, "How about if we take a ride into town and visit the address of our deceased?"

"Sure Detective, not much more going on here. The other constable can wrap it up as soon as the body is sent to the morgue," Stewart said as he walked toward the parked vehicles with Bernadette.

They came out of the shade of the trees and back into the heat of the sun. Bernadette put her sunglasses back on. "Did you get what university this kid was from?"

Constable Stewart turned back as he was about to get into his cruiser, "Yeah, they said the University of Victoria, supposedly a chemistry major."

"Shit." Bernadette stopped in her tracks.

"You look like you've seen a ghost. What's up?"

Bernadette composed herself and laughed. "You know it's probably just a coincidence, but the reason I'm in Red Deer is because of someone from the University of Victoria."

"Long story?"

"Hell yeah, long story, probably a three beers and nachos story. It can wait." Bernadette smiled. She looked round, whistled for Sprocket, and moments later he came loping out of the high wheat covered in burrs. Bernadette cursed mildly, grabbed the pair of gloves she carried for this exact purpose and picked the burrs out. She poured a flask of water into a bowl, and watched Sprocket lap at the water with his large tongue, there seemed to be no apology for his misbehavior, there never was.

Constable Stewart pulled ahead, leaving a cloud of dust in the hot summer air. Bernadette followed in her Jeep. They reached the highway asphalt and sped off into town. Rounding a corner, Bernadette saw crows feasting on the dead hawk. She muttered to herself, "See what happens when you hang with the wrong crowd?"

Chapter Two

Nathan Taylor's apartment was just off downtown in an older section of town, dominated by mostly apartment buildings. The Red Deer River, now running slow in the summer heat, meandered just a few blocks away from the four-plex that was the apartment.

The buildings had seen better days, and probably better landlords than the one that owned it now. The outside was peeling yellow paint, with two brown wooden balconies hanging on for dear life. One enterprising tenant had placed a piece of two by four against the sagging balcony to keep it from dropping off the side of the building. A lone kitchen chair bleached by the sun and cigarette butts sprouting from a coffee can were evidence that someone lived there.

Constable Stewart pulled up ahead of Bernadette, popped his trunk and put on his armored vest that made his massive weightlifter chest even more defined. Bernadette averted her eyes. The constable was way too young for her.

But those pecks of his were eye candy, and she couldn't help but peek.

Constable Stewart looked up at Bernadette as he closed the trunk, "Not wearing your vest, Detective?"

Bernadette laughed, "Hell no, I intend on standing behind you—you know I always got your back."

Stewart shook his head in mock disapproval, "I think the apartment's the one on the right side." He led the way as they walked across the broken cement walkway that stretched over the parched brown lawn. A dog barked from the lower unit, a face appeared at a window next door and quickly disappeared. "*No one really likes to see the RCMP,*" Bernadette thought.

Constable Stewart pounded on the metal door of Unit 4, disregarding the doorbell that hung from a single wire, dangling in disrepair, but daring someone to use it anyway. His heavy fist made a thumping sound that echoed into the quiet neighborhood. The dog next door stopped barking.

Bernadette rested against the back of the peeling porch rail, hoping it would hold. "What do you think? We go get a search warrant and come back?"

Stewart held up his hand, "Wait, I think I hear some movement inside."

A shuffling sound was followed by a door lock being turned. The door came open a crack, and a sleepy female voice said, "What do you want?"

"RCMP, we need to speak to you about Nathan Taylor, please open up," Constable Stewart said to the door. He placed one hand on the doorknob.

The door opened fully to reveal a disheveled young blonde clad in tight-fitting t-shirt and panties. She was cheerleader pretty, full bosom, wide hips, and portioned like a beer ad for Coors or Miller Lite. The only blemishes were metal rings on her nose and above her eyes. The young lady shielded her eyes from the bright sun, "What'd you want with Nathan? He's still at work."

Bernadette stepped from behind the large frame of Constable Stewart, "Sorry to inform you Miss, but Nathan Taylor was found deceased out on a pipeline this morning."

The young lady stood back from the door, dropped her hands to her side. "Oh . . . that kinda sucks."

"Were you and Nathan Taylor not close then, Miss . . .?" Bernadette asked. The answer to this was obvious but she thought she'd ask the question.

"The name's Chandra Rice . . . no, God no, we were just roomies . . . my girlfriend moved back to Toronto, and I needed help with the rent. Nathan Taylor answered the ad, he looked harmless, and so he took the other room. I work nights at Cowboys' Bar and Grill. I hardly saw him."

Bernadette took out her notebook. "Oh? I have a note here from his boss where he says you two were quite an item." She looked back from her notes, staring down the young blue eyes with her own steely green.

"Yeah, he wished," The young girl flipped her hair; the other hand massaged her tummy.

"So, there was nothing between you?"

Chandra pursed her lips, looked down at the floor while examining a pink toenail, "You know you . . . could say there was something. The little guy was some kind of a perv; he liked to watch me when I had guys over. I'd be doing it with my boyfriend, and the little jerk would be at the bedroom door with a camera."

"You knew this?" Bernadette asked. She noticed Constable Stewart's eyes widen.

Chandra bowed her head. Her long hair covered her

eyes. "Yeah, I knew it got him off, and I figured what the hell . . ."

"Sounds like it got you off as well," Bernadette countered.

Chandra flipped up her hair; a knowing smile edged her lips. She forced it back. She shrugged her shoulders. "You can come in if you want . . . I've got nothing to hide."

"Obviously. How about if you put a shirt on Chandra. I need my constable's full attention," Bernadette nodded towards Constable Stewart as they walked into the dark apartment.

Chandra flashed her eyes and smiled at Stewart and whirled to walk back to her bedroom. Stewart's eyes stayed glued to her ass as she walked out of view.

"Easy, Constable, they say you can go blind from watching that." Bernadette smiled in Stewart's direction.

"Yeah, but if I had that seared into my retinas, it might not be so bad," Stewart laughed.

Chandra returned wearing a shirt, her long legs still catching the constable's eye, and flicked the lights on to the main living room and kitchen. The place was a disaster of empty pizza boxes, beer cans, and fast-food cartons. The smell that rose up as they closed the door was stale pizza and beer. Bernadette smelled young hormones as well but thought better than to comment on it.

"Nathan's room is down this hallway," Chandra motioned to them. "Look, I have to shower and get ready for my shift, so look around, ask me whatever, but I gotta be outta here in an hour . . . okay?"

"Sure," Bernadette said as she followed Constable Stewart down the hallway.

Nathan Taylor's room had the same design as the rest of apartment. Empty pizza boxes and beer cans, half-consumed cans of beans with a spoon stuck at half-mast, with clothes scattered about the room. A laptop computer sat in the center of the room on a small desk with a chair that looked like it had been rescued from a garbage bin. A Sony video camera was plugged in beside it, and one Post-it Note stuck to the side of the laptop. The Post-it Note said, "Today is the Day."

Bernadette turned to Constable Stewart, "How are your computer skills?"

Constable Stewart stood over the laptop, his large fingers hovering over the keyboard. "You know we can't access this unless we have a warrant or permission from his next of kin."

"Uh-huh, sure I know that. I'm up on my law. Did you by any chance reach the deceased's next of kin?"

Stewart shrugged, "Ah, no, I placed a call to the number I got from the pipeline company, but I got no answer . . . I left a message."

Bernadette squared her shoulders, as if about to make a speech, and turned to face Constable Stewart. "Constable, I believe that on this computer we will find evidence that will lead us to who killed one Nathan Taylor, therefore no warrant or permission is required."

Stewart lowered his large frame onto the desk chair, as he powered up the laptop, "Okay, that's a bit on the fringes of the law, but that works for me, Detective."

The laptop was still powered up, with no password protection required. Stewart got onto the videos and documents site, and the first thing that came on was Chandra. Chandra in low lighting straddling atop a male with his hands on her thighs . . . the volume was on high, and the loud sounds of Chandra's enjoyment were obvious. And then . . . Chandra turned her head toward the camera and winked.

Constable Stewart's head lurched back. "Damn, these two had one hell of a kinky relationship."

A voice behind them said, "Am I in trouble?"

Bernadette turned to see Chandra standing at the door, "No, videotaping sexual acts between consenting adults is not a crime . . . It would seem from your actions . . . the wink you gave to Nathan that you were aware of the taping. Whether this makes you as perverted as Nathan, well I leave that up to you."

Chandra looked away and left the doorway. Bernadette looked back at the computer. "Constable, can we look over another file, as I am quite sure our victim did not die of this . . . though he may have turned himself partially to stone . . ."

Stewart's face turned visibly red, "Sure, sure . . . I'll access some of his recent places on the Internet."

They viewed a few more sites, and then came to the PLK website. The site was populated with a graphic from Star Trek, and various planets bounced around. Then four young men came into view. "This looks like a video conference our victim saved," Bernadette said.

A tall blonde kid sitting at a table spoke first. "Nathan Taylor, your mission, should you accept it, is to strike a blow for all Humanity. To avenge the wrongs done to our former leader, Professor Alistair McAllen, and show the world that we . . . these gentle nerds here, and I . . . have more power than anyone in the world. By tomorrow, they will no longer fear Al Qaeda; they will fear us, the Pipeline Killers. I, your commander, Paul Goodman, command you to go forth and do battle. Our fellow warriors, Bill Hirschman, Martin Popowich, and Jason Campbell will monitor your feats, and will go forth to do battle once your attack is successful. Live long and prosper."

The video ended with a Star Trek Voyager space vehicle streaking across the sky, and music playing in the background. Bernadette stood back from the laptop "Damn it, this is as bad as it gets."

"What's as bad as it gets?" Stewart looked up from the computer, "This looks like a bunch of university kids doing a spoof on Star Trek."

"Yeah, it would be if they hadn't mentioned Professor McAllen . . . look, grab the laptop, and meet me back at detachment headquarters. I need to meet with our chief and make a call to a guy I know at the Canadian Security and Intelligence Agency."

Bernadette headed outside. The strong light of the late afternoon hit her as she walked down the steps and got into her Jeep. Her mind was flashing through all the possibilities of what was about to hit the oil industry this time. The first time McAllen surfaced he almost put Alaskan Oil and Fort McMurray Oil Sands into mothballs. His lab creation called polywater could have suspended production for years if she hadn't figured it out. But what the hell was he up to this time?

Chapter Three

Bernadette was about to drive directly to the RCMP detachment, until she looked at Sprocket. To keep the dog cool, she'd left him in the Jeep with the a/c on and the windows rolled up. Someone had once tried to steal her Jeep with the big dog in it once and found themselves on the pavement and looking at a set of snarling teeth. But she would never leave the big dog in the Jeep for any longer than she had to.

She was 10 minutes from her home and another 10 minutes back to the detachment. She could spare the time and drop off the dog. Her chief was a fan of dogs, but RCMP trained dogs, not untrained like Sprocket.

Traffic was light, and she drove up to her duplex a few minutes later. The dog bolted from the Jeep toward the house as soon as she opened the door.

"So that's the thanks I get for taking you on a road trip," Bernadette yelled to Sprocket. Sprocket raised one ear in response and scratched at the door.

The door opened in the adjoining duplex, and Harvey

Mawer poked his head out, "Hey Bernie, you back already? I heard there was a big oil spill, and a dead body out west of here."

"Damn, news travel fast in this town," Bernadette said as she waved at Harvey.

"Hey, I'm still hooked into the Oil Patch, you know old wives and oilmen, and we're about the same for good gossip. You got time for a coffee?" Harvey walked toward her door, standing there, waiting for her reply.

Harvey was a great next-door neighbor. Retired for the third time from different careers in what was called the "Oil Patch," which meant the oil business. Harvey was crowding his 70s with bad arthritis that kept him from a fourth run at the oil business. He looked out for Bernadette, watered her lawn, and mowed it, shoveled her snow in the winter, and looked after Sprocket when she worked late, which was often.

"Sorry Harvey looks like I'm the one investigating the dead body, and I need to get back to work. You mind watching Sprocket a bit, maybe walk him a little?"

Harvey walked over, scratched Sprocket behind the ears, and let him lick his hand, "You know I never mind. I got some new dog treats he'll like. What time you expect you'll be back?"

Bernadette shrugged and blew out her breath. "Who knows? This latest one's got all kinds of things piled into it. I'm hoping by early evening. You can leave Sprocket inside my place after."

"Oh, heck no, I got the whole series of World War II CDs, and I'm making some firehouse chili. Sprocket and I can watch those till you get back."

Bernadette hugged Harvey, "Thanks Harvey. God, I'm

glad you're too old for me, because I'd be hitting on you all the time."

Harvey stood back from Bernadette, "Hey, easy young lady, you'll make my new girlfriend jealous."

Bernadette let Sprocket into the house, got him some water, and then headed back to the Jeep. She really would love to hang out with Harvey and Sprocket on the back porch, it was Friday night, but there was something there, something in the recent video from the so-called Pipeline Killers she needed to deal with. All of it made her feel unsettled, queasy inside, like right after she'd eaten a large Monte Cristo sandwich.

The RCMP Detachment was the usual beehive on Friday night. The late-night bars in Red Deer would be busy as young people with too much money from the oil fields were ready for a good time. Their ability to have fun would be fueled by massive quantities of alcohol and drugs, and from midnight to 2 a.m. the officers would be busy sorting out the mess.

Bernadette found her Chief of Detectives, Jerry Durham, in his office. She liked Jerry. He was a fair guy who worked hard at his job, and hard at his relationship with his family. A straight up guy in his mid-40s with 20 years of marriage and two teenage kids and enough ambition to keep the higher-ups in Ottawa happy. Jerry tried to keep in shape, but the job showed the strain, a small paunch showed on his mid-weight frame, and his hairline was receding far beyond his ability to deal with it. He wasn't about to do the close bald shave, not his style, not yet.

"Hey Detective Callahan, I got this laptop that Constable Stewart dropped off, which I made him fill out an evidence report for." Jerry called out. He added a small frown in Bernadette's direction. "Now I assume that you've cleared the viewing of this computer with the deceased's next of kin?"

"Yeah . . . about that, Chief," Bernadette dropped into the chair in front of him. "I was in pursuit of the possible suspect or suspects who may have been involved in the murder of our victim." She threw a weak smile with the words, and then watched to see if they worked.

The chief dropped his head in his hands. "You know Detective; I wonder why I have any hair left at all with some of your procedures."

"Chief, did you look over the video that Constable Stewart and I viewed today?"

"Yes, I did, and I saw what looks like a Star Trek spoof, just like the constable mentioned. How can this be something that could have put our victim in harm's way?"

"Because they mentioned Professor Alistair McAllen," Bernadette leaned forward placing her hands on the desk.

"Detective, I know you had some history with this guy, but I doubt if he can cause more mayhem from wherever he's hiding. You think that maybe you're just a little paranoid where he's concerned?" the chief asked as he reached for his ringing phone.

"No, I don't think I'm paranoid at all, I'd like to be ready for him this time . . ." Bernadette's words trailed off as the chief raised his hand and put his ear to the phone.

Bernadette sat there in an uneasy silence. She could hear the chief talking with the coroner. The coroner had a loud Scot's Brogue. He'd been in Canada for 45 years and still sounded like he'd walked out of the Scottish Moors yesterday.

The chief dropped the phone in the cradle, his face looking a slightly whiter color. "The coroner says we've got to get to the morgue right away, there's something he wants to show us."

The morgue was quiet. At 6 p.m., most of the staff was gone. The security guard let them in. Their shoes squeaked on the linoleum tile as they walked down the long hallway. The smell of formaldehyde hung in the air. Someone once told Bernadette they thought it was the cologne of the dead. It was all always there. It would linger in your clothes after you left the place. It enveloped you like a glove when you walked in, assailing your nostrils first, then the back of your tongue, and then the stuff would slip down your throat until you were forced to swallow it. Gagging was optional.

They walked down the long hallway in silence, pushed through a set of double doors that sighed softly as air pressure was released, and found Dr. Keith Andrew. The Doctor was a mass of long grey hair, bushy eyebrows, and four days of five o'clock shadow on his face.

Bernadette could never get over not seeing pants under his white smock. Dr. Andrew wore a kilt both summer and winter. If you asked, and if you knew him well, he would take you aside, and confide that it was, "So the boys could breathe." Bernadette realized he meant his balls.

"You made good time," Dr. Andrew yelled to them in his rich brogue. He drew the words out like a poem from Robert Burns. The cadence was there, it sounded the same to Bernadette. Dr. Andrew was an abnormality for a coroner who was actually a doctor, and his fame for dropping his medical opinions into his reports was legendary in the small city.

"Doctor, what are you in such a hurry to show us?" Chief Durham asked.

"Oh, aye, the most recent body is quite the sight. I don't believe in my many years I've had the opportunity to view something as amazing as this." Dr. Andrews' eyebrows rose as if a conductor was motioning for the orchestra to begin.

Andrew motioned them towards the body, and drew back the sheet, "You'll notice there are no contusions on the body that suggest bruising or blunt force trauma."

Bernadette scanned the naked Nathan Taylor from the top of his head to the bottom of his feet. She had to agree, there was not a mark on the kid. "What killed him?

Andrew's eyebrows rose in unison, "Ah, now that is the fascinating question. Here we have a corpse that we think is missing organs, but it's not."

"The CSI told me he felt no organs in the abdominal cavity," Bernadette said, leaning closer to the body.

"Yes, it would appear that way, but look," Andrew said as he removed a small cover that was covering the intestines in a tray beside the body. "You can see they are here but flattened and perforated. It looks like something ate into them."

Bernadette's head shot back at the sight. "What does that?"

"Interesting question," Andrew said. "Now, in my travels in South America, I came upon this in the Amazon. Corpses literally eaten alive from the inside, something the Portuguese called the *Candiru* or vampire fish, which is a tiny parasitic fish. It had the locals so scared men would tie a string around their penises before they went swimming, they believed it protected them from the fish crawling up their . . . you know what I mean . . ." Dr. Andrew examined the faces of both Bernadette and Chief Durham to see if they were getting his explanation.

Chief Durham touched his crotch, as if warding away the evil of the vampire fish. He looked up, realized where his hand was and quickly moved it, "Really, you think this kid was eaten inside by a vampire fish?"

"Absolutely not, just pulling your leg, telling you bit of lore. No, Canada is far too cold for these fish; the streams freeze in winter. The things would die. Now then . . . . I reasoned that something must have entered our victim's blood stream, and this is where I found our culprit," Andrew said, his smile widening at his captive audience, and loving the joke he'd played.

Chief Durham relaxed visibly. The vision of a tiny vampire fish swimming up a man's penis was slowly vanishing from his brain, "So, what thing have you found?"

"Things, my good man. Things," Andrew said. "I realized that something attacked this man through his blood stream from the tear in his arm, and I needed to examine his blood. There was very little in him. The human body should have about 5 liters of blood. This body had a tenth of that."

"Now, what little blood he did have I had analyzed, and found something very significant." Andrew paused. Only the sound of the air conditioning could be heard in the room. "Our victim had an extreme case of Hemochromatosis."

"Hemo . . . what? Bernadette asked.

Dr. Andrew's eyes widened. "This essentially is a buildup of iron in the body. I won't bore you with the entire prognosis of this disease, but from my analysis, this victim had quite the advanced stages of the disease, which is exactly why he was attacked."

"Attacked by what?" Bernadette asked with exasperation in her voice. The merry-go-round of vampire fish to an iron disease in the blood was getting tiring. She wanted answers.

"That, I must show you," Dr. Andrew motioned for

them to come over to his counter where a microscope was set up. "Look in here and tell me what you see."

Bernadette adjusted the powerful microscope to her eyes. The viewer came into focus and a mass of small moving shapes came into view. They were white in color and looked like little sausages. "What am I looking at?"

"From my tests, we are looking at a microbe that consumes iron. Industry has been working on this technology for years. I recently read a study from a company that wanted to engineer a process called *bioheap leaching* with microbes that would live on sulphur and iron the way we live on protein and carbohydrates," Dr. Andrew said. He swayed side to side as he spoke. His kilt made a gentle swishing sound.

Chief Durham looked into the microscope. "You think this is what killed our victim then?"

"Aye, I do, and from what I heard of your pipeline spill out west of here, I believe this young man, now a victim of his own means, tried to inject these microbes into the Pipeline, and they attacked him as well when he cut his arm. Let me show you my other experiment." Dr. Andrew motioned for them to follow him to another counter. The counter had a glass case with a small pipe inside.

"Now watch this," Dr. Andrew said as he drew a small eyedropper from the microscope glass and dropped a bit of liquid on the metal pipe. He snapped the case shut, smiled, and looked down in anticipation.

At first, there was nothing, just the pipe as Bernadette watched, her eyes staring hard, waiting for a change, something, or anything to prove the Doctor's hypothesis. Then, there it was, parts of the pipe became lighter. Then holes appeared. "That is exactly what happened to the pipeline west of here." Bernadette turned to Chief Durham. "Now do you believe me when I tell you we need to be worried about the video on the laptop?"

Chief Durham's face changed color. His normal off-beige had morphed into a pasty white. "I think we need to get Canadian Security and Intelligence Service involved in this. This reaches beyond Red Deer."

Bernadette pulled her cell phone out of her pocket. "Chief, I know an agent with CSIS in Edmonton, whom I worked with on something like this before. He'll want to be in on this, and he knows just the people to call." Bernadette had Anton De Luca on speed dial. He picked up on the second ring.

"Hey, Detective Callahan, long time since I've heard from you, what is up in your little city," Anton asked.

Bernadette loved Anton like a younger brother. He was 26, a well-educated, good-looking Italian Canadian. They had worked hard together to try and capture Professor Alistair McAllen a year earlier when he'd invented a threat called polywater that made water too heavy to force oil to the surface in oil fields. His invention had threatened both Alaskan and Canadian oilfields. They stopped the threat of polywater, but never captured McAllen.

"Anton, great to talk to you, and I need to get to the point. We found a microbe that attacks pipelines; we think Professor McAllen is behind it. I'm going back to the detachment and send you a video of some University of Victoria students we think are involved."

"Bernadette . . . you said McAllen?" Anton asked after a pause.

"Yes, I did, if what I just saw in this lab is real on a large scale, then someone has developed a microbe that can attack pipelines." Bernadette looked over at Dr. Andrew, who was nodding in agreement.

"Send me the file. I'll talk to you soon," Anton said.

Soon did not come until just before midnight. Bernadette returned to the detachment, sent the file, completed her reports, and returned home. She rounded up Sprocket. Harvey's door was open. Both Harvey and the dog were snoring on the couch while the Allies stormed Normandy yet again, but this time in color on Harvey's big screen TV.

Bernadette walked the dog back to her place, and he lay on his dog bed and was back to sleep in seconds. She rummaged for food, found some recognizable leftovers in the fridge and some red wine, and curled up on the sofa for her usual Friday night . . . alone.

The cell phone rang. It was Anton, "Hi, Bernadette, sorry it took so long, but the guys in Ottawa can move slowly."

"How unusual," Bernadette said in her sarcastic tone.

"So, here it is . . . once they understood the threat, all kinds of higher ups and government officials got excited by this case. The defense of oil is one of their main agendas. We've already called CSIS in British Columbia. They contacted City of Victoria Police and three of the young men on the video tape have already been taken into custody."

"My god, that was quick," Bernadette said as she took a gulp of her red wine.

"Well, here's the other part. I need you in on this case. And we need to be in Victoria tomorrow morning for the interrogation."

"You want me in on this?" Bernadette almost inhaled her wine.

"Yes, I'll fly down to Calgary, and we'll catch the 11:25

direct to Victoria. I can brief you on what we have in the morning. Sleep fast, Detective. I'll buy breakfast tomorrow."

Bernadette looked at her watch; it was midnight. She needed to send an email to her chief telling him she was going to Victoria, pack a quick bag for who knew how long, and get up early for the hour and a half hour drive to Calgary to be there by 10:25 a.m. She drained the last bit of wine in her glass, washed it in the sink, and started on her preparation.

Chapter Four

Bernadette backed out of her driveway at 6:30 a.m. and made it to the highway going south in 15 minutes. Saturday morning traffic was light. A few transport trucks were her company. The sun, already high in the eastern sky, threw a long golden light on the wheat fields. The Rocky Mountains to the west provided a border, a definition point that the prairie ran up to and stopped.

The morning air held onto the cool crispness of night. The day would be hot by afternoon. Bernadette left the window open a crack, and let the cool air hit her face. She picked up her large double cream, double sugar coffee at the Tim Horton's drive through on the south end of town. As she waited in line she sent a text message to Harvey Mawer. She asked him to pick up Sprocket and take of care him of him for a few days.

She knew Harvey wouldn't mind. Matter of fact, he'd spoil Sprocket rotten by the time Bernadette returned. They'd watch more war movies together, and Harvey would encourage the dog to bark at the Nazis while they feasted on

Bratwurst and Hamburgers. Sprocket would pass nasty farts for days.

It took Bernadette at least two days to bring Sprocket back into acceptable canine behavior after his "boys" weekend with Harvey. She smiled as that thought of Harvey and Sprocket came to her. She hit the accelerator and joined the highway on the road south.

The airport was crowded. Passengers on business, on pleasure, on whatever, were flying somewhere on an August weekend. Bernadette had checked in online before she left home and made her way through security with her one carry-on bag.

She saw Anton De Luca waiting for her on the other side of Security. He was holding a large coffee and a small bag that would be her breakfast sandwich, to which he added his charming Italian smile. People who walked by could not help but notice him. Curly black hair, dark brown eyes, and dark skin complemented by a tall athletic body would stop traffic anywhere. Bernadette loved the looks she got just being near him.

"Hey Bernadette, I got your usual," Anton laughed as she approached. He gave her a welcoming hug, a kiss on the cheek, and coffee. "Hey, this is almost like old times."

"Let's hope not. Last time we failed to catch McAllen, we had numerous politicians trying to fashion us a new rear end. I could do without those old times." Bernadette took a sip of her coffee, savored the caffeine, cream and sugar mixture to see if it was just right. It was perfect; Anton knew her mix.

Anton smiled, "Let's walk to our gate, and I'll fill you in our progress so far."

Bernadette fell into step beside Anton, "Progress, what

kind of progress could there be from midnight to 9:30 a.m.?"

"The fast-moving wheels of the Canadian Security and Intelligence Service. I thought you knew we were a razor-sharp, fast-acting agency." Anton threw a wink in with the words.

"Please . . . what did you stumble on is more like it."

"Ha, Bernadette, you nailed it again, I am always amazed at how quick you pick up on things. We picked up three of the university students on the videotape you sent us. They have been in interrogation since 1 a.m. this morning, and quite frankly, they could not get their stories out fast enough."

"How good is their story and does it implicate Professor McAllen?"

They reached the gate and found two seats away from the other passengers. Anton turned to Bernadette, "They claim this Pipeline Killer Bug they invented was a class project from Professor McAllen. He challenged them to reinvent the nanites that were in some Star Trek episode."

"Nanites? What the hell are nanites?" Bernadette took a long swig of her coffee.

"I see you were never a Star Trek fan?"

"Nope, just didn't take. I'm more of a Matrix kind of girl, but only because Keanu Reeves is so cute," Bernadette blushed as she admitted it.

Anton winced in mock embarrassment for her. "Okay, the short version of nanites and Star Trek is the nanites were a fictitious life form of submicroscopic robots that went rogue from their intended use and began cannibalizing the starship Enterprise."

Bernadette said, "Okay, fictitious, cannibalizing . . . got that part."

Anton looked around to ensure no other passengers could hear him, and then lowered his voice, "Well, okay, so they didn't invent robots, but they invented a cannibalizing organism, or Bio Bug, as they like to call it, that has an appetite for iron. They claim they thought their little invention would be just a minor annoyance to pipelines; you know make a hole or two and get some notice. I don't think they knew it would kill Nathan Taylor."

Their flight was announced. Bernadette drank the last of her coffee, and realized she did not have enough time to pick up another. She frowned at the information from Anton, and the empty cup. "Did the students say if they are still in contact with Professor McAllen, and what they, or he intended to do with their Pipeline Killer, the Bio Bug they created?"

Anton picked up his carry-on bag and computer case. They joined the back of the line shuffling its way onto the plane. "Well, there our investigators ran into a dead end. Seems the three students we picked up were not in contact with McAllen. The one that was, Paul Goodman, was supposedly tight with the Professor, but he is missing at present."

Bernadette's head jerked around, "Missing? What do you mean by missing?"

"Let's say just not located. His friends have not seen him since they made the video for Nathan Taylor a few days ago. He was not in his room and looks like he hasn't been there for a day or two. The local Victoria Police Force is trying to track down his girlfriend, some Russian exchange student they said he was hanging with."

Bernadette hung back as the last passengers boarded, "Wait a minute, did you get a picture of this girlfriend of Goodman's'?"

Anton grabbed his cell phone out of his pocket, and scrolled down to a picture, "Yeah, right here, the other students had a group picture of her . . . quite the good-looking girl."

"That's not good," Bernadette said looking at the photo.

"What's wrong?" Anton looked over at Bernadette. The airline attendant looked at Bernadette with concern as well. They were stopped just before the entry of the plane.

"You don't see it, do you?"

"See what?" Anton's puzzled look turned to a grin of amusement.

"This girl is drop-dead gorgeous. A total 10 and Paul Goodman is two and a half tops. I got a bad feeling about this. We better find this guy soon." Bernadette gave the phone back to Anton as they entered the plane and found their seats.

Bernadette reclined her seat as they leveled in flight and watched the expanse of the Rocky Mountains glide by underneath. A pattern was forming. The death of Nathan Taylor was linked to an invention by students at the University of Victoria. They were linked to Professor McAllen. The next few hours would determine were the next links would lead. Bernadette did not like the feeling it gave her. Bile rose in her stomach. It wasn't from the bad airline coffee. It was the fear of what Professor McAllen was up to.

Chapter Five

A light rain fell as the aircraft touched down on Vancouver Island. Bernadette peered out the airplane window and could just make out the terminal as a fog rolled in off the ocean. The neon sign for Victoria International Airport started to disappear into the fog.

Bernadette had been on this island only once before. She was eight years old and travelling in a van with her mother and father. The band was Callahan Country Expression. Her father, Dominic Callahan, was the lead guitarist and her mother the lead vocalist. Her mother was beautiful, with long black hair, deep brown eyes, a smile that could light up a stage, and a voice that reminded people of Emmylou Harris.

They toured the entire island from one smoky bar to another back in the days when everyone smoked in bars, and second-hand smoke was what billowed out the tavern door. Bernadette slept amongst all the musical equipment in the back of the van, wrapped in a sleeping bag. Her mother would check on her between music sets. She was never happier. It was her fondest memory of her parents.

The airplane door opened. Cool moist air filled the airplane cabin and Bernadette dropped back into the present. Anton led the way, and they followed the other passengers out of the airport terminal. Standing straight, as if too attention, a young brunette dressed in navy blue jacket and pants waved at Anton as they arrived.

Anton introduced agent Samantha Graves. "Detective Bernadette Callahan, this is Agent Samantha Graves . . . the very reason that Canada is safe from terrorists is because Samantha is here on the West Coast."

Samantha laughed and gave Anton's arm a small punch, "Detective, as you can see our agent is the best storyteller in the Canadian Intelligence Agency."

Bernadette instantly liked Samantha. She had an open style about her, and ready smile and she didn't have the problem of taking herself too seriously. "Yes, I admit, I have been subjected to the great Italian storyteller."

Anton looked in mock surprise. "Ladies, you wound me deeply." He walked with Samantha as they proceeded to her car. "Have there been any more developments since we last spoke?"

Samantha turned towards Bernadette as she was opening the trunk of the car, and Anton placed their bags in the back. "From the interrogations, it seems that Martin Popowich was the one working closely with Paul Goodman. The other two, Hirschman and Campbell, were mostly drinking buddies who thought the project was a joke. They stood by to make the video for Nathan Taylor, but claim they knew little about what they were up to."

Bernadette sat in the back while Anton folded his long frame into the front of the mid-size car. They pulled away from the parking lot and joined the highway for the half-hour trip into the city of Victoria. "Has anyone located the missing Paul Goodman?"

Samantha glanced into her rearview mirror to look at Bernadette. "We have the Victoria Police Force working on it. Goodman was last seen with his girlfriend, a Natalya Smirnoff, two days ago, and hasn't been located."

Bernadette asked, "What do you have on this Natalya Smirnoff?"

Samantha looked back as she passed a car on the highway. "No such person. That's a fake identity, and right now we are processing her facial recognition through all North American data bases."

Bernadette reached forward in her seat and tapped Anton on the shoulder. "See, there you go, the moment I saw her picture next to Goodman's I knew we had a problem—and really—with a name like Smirnoff?"

Anton looked over his shoulder, "What, you don't believe in the power of love, or that an ugly man can attract gorgeous women?"

Bernadette looked out the window and said, "Sure, I believe in the fairy tale stuff all the time. But in real life—no. Real life says gorgeous babes go after men with money or good looks. What do you think, Samantha?" Bernadette turned and looked in her direction.

Samantha laughed. "Well, I remember the old saying you can love a rich man just as well as a poor man, but I'm with Bernadette—good looks carry a lot of weight." She smiled in Anton's direction. Her eyes did a quick tour up and down his handsome frame.

Anton, slide down in his seat. "You know, you ladies are a disgrace, and here I thought you had a higher moral code."

Bernadette shifted more upright in her seat. She decided to change the subject, "Samantha, have you been able to access our university boys' laptops and cell phones yet?"

Samantha slowed behind a motor home in the afternoon traffic, and looked only briefly into the review mirror as she focused on the road. "We have court orders for all their computers, cell phones and any documents in their dormitories, and we have all of them except Goodman's. There's already several defense lawyers at the law courts building trying to make any information we obtain inadmissible, but we doubt they'll get far with that."

"How so?" Bernadette asked.

"The heads of the Canadian Intelligence Agency in Ottawa have decided the only way the students could have devised this virus that attacked the pipeline was by using university computers. They have thrown section 342.1 of the Criminal Code at them, which makes it an offense to use a computer to commit a crime," Samantha said. Her eyes widened as she threw out the criminal code.

"Doesn't that sound a bit thin?" Bernadette countered.

Samantha laughed, "I know, but it'll hold them for now. A team of Crown Prosecutors is in the process of issuing a Security Certificate, which will have the Defense Lawyers worked into a lather when they file it."

"Isn't that only used on foreign nationals or foreigners who've become permanent residents who are suspected of committing terrorist acts?" Bernadette said.

Anton turned his head towards Bernadette in the back. "The security scare over Canada's oil has escalated the use of Security Certificate measures into a wider range. Al Qaeda has scared the oil industry with their announcement they wanted to shut down Canada's oil supply to affect American

Industry. An anti-terrorism squad was set up in Alberta back in June, called the Integrated National Security Enforcement Team, or INSET. Of course, environmentalists and other groups are worried they can now be labeled terrorists," Anton smiled broadly as he added, "and it looks like they were right."

They said nothing more until they reached the Victoria Police Department Headquarters in downtown Victoria. Bernadette let a thought roll around in her head. The thought was of something else that surfaced. About a death here many years ago, but she submerged it; it was too painful.

They followed Samantha into Department Headquarters and were introduced to the person who had been leading the interviews of the three university students. Bernadette remembered the rooms being called Interrogation, but now the more politically correct "Interview Room" was used. The results were the same. "Keep them till they cracked," was the motto.

The lead interviewer was Agent Assad Mohammad, a slight, well-dressed man in his late 30s with well-manicured hands. Bernadette had never seen a man with such good-looking hands. He could have modeled rings for men in a jeweler's catalogue. She tried to remember the last time she had a manicure; she couldn't, so let it go.

Anton shook Assad's hand. "Assad, good to see you, we haven't crossed paths since training days back in Ottawa. Anton turned to Bernadette. "Assad here was one of the key interviewers who cracked the terrorist plot to attack Ottawa some years back. He looks smooth, but his powers of persuasion are legendary."

"Glad to meet you Mohammad, and good to know you're a force to be reckoned with," Bernadette said as she took his hand. *Hand lotion, Oil of Olay* . . . the thoughts bounced in her head as she shook his hand.

Assad said, "Detective Bernadette Callahan, I am delighted to meet you. I have heard some stories of your powers of perception. These are things that cannot be taught in school, but must be learned over time. Some never learn them at all."

Bernadette laughed, "You mean like most of our commanding officers and superiors?"

Assad was visibly shaken by Bernadette's comments, "No, no, I meant nothing of the sort . . . I just meant . . . the powers of perception . . . and intuition . . . how they must be . . ."

Anton nudged Assad. "Now you can see how Detective Callahan is a force to be reckoned with . . . she's just having fun with you, Assad."

Assad laughed, "Yes, quite right, I forgot how you people here in Western Canada like to make fun of your superiors. Not something we are used to in Ontario."

Bernadette was about to add a bit about the nature of superiors in Ontario and how they suffered from a condition called *tight ass* when a police constable approached them. He spoke quietly and briefly to Assad, and then left.

Assad looked at Anton and Bernadette, "They found Paul Goodman . . . or should I say they found his body."

"Where?" Bernadette asked.

"Just over the bridge in a place called Esquimalt, in an apartment building. The landlord was looking for rent from the tenant, and the body he found was identified as Paul Goodman from his driver's license."

Bernadette looked at Anton, "I think you and I need to go to the crime scene. I'd like to see if there is any sign of this Smirnoff, and where she went."

"You think she's gone?" Anton said.

"She is long gone and my number one suspect," Bernadette said as she saw Samantha approach. "Samantha, they found Paul Goodman very dead, and I'm betting the former beauty once known as Smirnoff was part of it."

Samantha stopped in her tracks. "I just got a hit on the facial recognition software. Natalya Smirnoff is Zara Mashhadov, a known Chechen Terrorist. The Russians have been looking for her for years. Zara is known for acts of terrorism in both Russia and Chechnya.

"Damn, we need to put out an all-points bulletin on her right now," Anton said.

Bernadette raised her hand. "You can put the bulletin out, but my bets are that this Zara is no longer in the country." She looked at Samantha, "You see how a women's intuition is always dead on? A good-looking woman, and especially with a name like Smirnoff—what was Goodman thinking?"

Chapter Six

Anton and Bernadette rode to the crime scene in a Victoria Police car with a young police constable. The apartment building was an older three-story walkup. A police constable guarded the door; tenants peered out of their doorways, and a man that Bernadette assumed was the building's superintendent was being interviewed by a Victoria Police Detective. Bernadette looked inside the doorway of the apartment and motioned for the crime scene investigator standing over the body to come over to talk to her. She could not contaminate the crime scene.

Covered in full white polyester coveralls with only his facing showing out of a white hood, the CSI approached Bernadette. He was mid-thirties from what showed of his face and missing a shave by one day. "How can I help you?"

Bernadette flashed her badge. "What do we have here?"

The CSI pointed his thumb in the direction of the corpse. "From our visual, we have blunt force trauma to the head. Looks like someone bludgeoned this guy to death with a cast iron frying pan we found close by. There's hair and blood on the frying pan, so no mystery there. We estimate time of death around 8 or 9 a.m. yesterday."

Anton turned to Bernadette. "Maybe she didn't want to make him eggs?" He added his devilish smile. "Back in Sicily they call it *un incidente in cucina,* or a cooking accident. It usually happens when an Italian man returns home early in the morning with the scent of another woman on him."

Bernadette shook her head. "You know, sometimes your Italian humor really does escape me—as in right now." Turning back to the CSI she asked, "Did you happen to recover a laptop in the apartment?"

"Yeah, my partner did. He's bagging it right now."

"Okay, can you have that processed ASAP for prints and sent to CSIS Agent Samantha Graves at Victoria Headquarters? This is part of a major investigation."

The CSI hesitated. "I don't know. I'll have to clear with my lead detective, and he'll have to clear with his section chief."

Anton pulled out his card and his badge. "Look, I hate to pull rank, but this is now a major investigation of national importance. Have your section chief call me, and I'll clear it with your detective."

"Sure, you know I just have to follow protocol. I don't want a damn lawyer reaming me out in court later saying I didn't follow procedure. Look the detective is in the hallway. You clear it with him, and it's fine by me," the CSI said.

Bernadette approached the detective at the doorway. He was writing notes and sweating in the hallway. He was late fifties, dressed in blue jeans, striped shirt and a badly worn sports jacket. A necktie attempted to make him look professional. And it failed. Bernadette introduced herself and Anton while they flashed their badges and cards.

The Detective looked at their cards. "Impressive, we

got a RCMP from Alberta and Canadian Security and Intelligence from Edmonton. What the hell was the deceased up to?" He stuffed his notepad in his pocket. "Detective Matt Letourneau, how long are you in town for?"

"Until we complete this investigation—this started with a suspicious death in Red Deer and has led us here. We believe the deceased invented something that killed a person there and has some potentially harmful implications for Canada's oil security—which is as much as I can say for now," Anton said.

"Well, thanks for letting me into the outer rings of the loop," Letourneau said. "If there's anything I can do to help, let me know."

"We need the laptop found in the apartment to be sent to Agent Graves at your Victoria Headquarters and a positive ID on who rented this apartment," Bernadette said.

"Sure, not a problem on both counts," Letourneau said, pulling out his notebook again. "The person who rented the apartment was an Adalina Torres. The building superintendent said she was a cute little girl who said she was a foreign exchange student from Spain, and the passport she showed him confirmed it."

Anton pulled out his phone and scrolled to the picture of Natalya Smirnoff with Paul Goodman. "Would you show this to the building superintendent, and ask him if this looks like Adalina?"

"Sure, just a sec." Letourneau took the phone and showed it to the superintendent, who was still standing down the hall, wondering when he could call in the carpet cleaners, so he could rent the apartment out again.

Letourneau returned the phone to Anton. "Yeah, he says the hair is different, never seen her as a blonde. Matter of fact, he said he only saw her when she rented the place about a month and half ago and hasn't seen her since."

Bernadette looked at Anton, "Well, there you have it. Smirnoff to Torres to Mashhadov, this girl does some nice changes. I bet if we check the airport, we'll find out which passport she used to leave town."

"You think she's already left town?" Anton said as he dialed Samantha Graves.

Bernadette looked back into the apartment, "Yeah, I think she's gone, and I think she got what she came for. Goodman—the poor bastard—had no idea what she was up to. I'll bet we find out that these university kids were posting themselves and their Pipeline Killer invention on Facebook or YouTube. They got interest all right. It looks like international interest."

Anton put up his hand as he speed-dialed his phone and connected with Samantha. "Hey Samantha, we think we have a travelling ID for Mashhadov. The apartment superintendent claims she was using the name Adalina Torres and claiming to be a Spanish National. Yeah, see if she left through the Victoria Airport. Thanks. We'll be back at Police Headquarters in 20 minutes. Any information on our suspects being interviewed?"

Bernadette watched Anton as he listened intently to Samantha; his face was going into contortions. "What've you got?" she finally blurted out when she couldn't take the suspense anymore.

Anton closed the phone and put it in his jacket pocket. "Samantha accessed Martin Popowich's laptop. He was hiding a mountain of cash in an offshore account in the Cayman Island.

"How big a mountain?'

"A half-million US dollars," Anton said back.

"Large Mountain, more than you and I'll ever see unless we win the Lotto. What's a third year university student doing with that kind of cash? Sounds like Mr. Popowich has some questions to answer," Bernadette said as she started down the hall, avoiding the two men pushing the coroner's gurney. A black body bag lay on top of it.

Anton followed her down the hallway. "I think Mr. Popowich is in this very deep."

"Yeah, this whole case is setting up to be another cluster of suspects behaving badly. I get a feeling that Mr. Popowich and his cash have lot to tell us," Bernadette said over her shoulder. They walked into the bright West Coast sunshine. Bernadette looked up at the blue sky with wispy clouds floating by. "You know it's a beautiful day about to turn ugly."

Chapter Seven

Bernadette and Anton arrived back at Police Headquarters and found Assad Mohammed waiting for them outside the interview room holding Martin Popowich. He looked somewhat tired. His trim suit was wrinkled and small lines forming around his eyes. He visibly brightened when he saw Bernadette, "I hear you found one of our students, dead unfortunately, but this helps to complete our equation."

"How do you figure that?" Bernadette asked, walking up to Assad.

Assad touched the side of his head, "We know where all the suspects are, and living or dead never matters to me, as soon the truth will be found."

Bernadette smiled, "I like your optimism. Have you questioned our Martin Popowich about the half million in his bank account?"

"No, I was just about to, and if you'd like to join me, I'd be happy to have you in the interview." Assad gestured towards the interview door.

Bernadette turned to Anton. "Why don't I sit in with

Assad, and you go see if Samantha has come up with anything new."

Anton nodded his approval and walked down the hall towards Samantha's office, "Hey, just remember at the end of this wonderful day, we need to find an Italian restaurant."

Bernadette shook her head in his direction. "That Italian is always thinking with his stomach." She turned to Assad, "What has Popowich given you so far?"

"Absolutely nothing. He claims he played along with Goodman's Star Trek fantasy and the idea of inventing a threat to pipelines. He says he was not involved in any with communications with Professor Alistair McAllen." Assad motioned for Bernadette to proceed into the interview room.

"Your average bystander, who just happens to have a large amount of cash in an offshore account," Bernadette said.

"Yes it would appear that is the case; would you care to take the lead in the interview? I would be happy to observe your techniques," Assad said.

"Why thank you, Assad, my technique is a little more on the unorthodox side . . . I make it up as I go." Bernadette smiled and entered the room.

Martin Popowich slouched and crossed his arms when they entered the room. He was early twenties, fair complexion with sandy brown hair. Adolescent pimples dotted his face. He wore khaki cargo shorts, a sweatshirt, and flip-flops. His eyes did a quick inventory of Bernadette and then his gaze returned to the table. The room was tiny. A fluorescent light accentuated the table and three chairs. White on white was the color scheme. Martin was behind the table, his back to the wall.

Bernadette's chair screeched as she pulled it back from the table. "Hi, I'm Detective Bernadette Callahan of the RCMP Serious Crimes Division." She sat across from Martin, their knees almost touching. "I'm working the case of your deceased friend, Nathan Taylor."

Martin sat up, unfolded his arms, and moved his knees away from Bernadette's. "Yeah, I heard about that . . . unfortunate . . . I didn't know him that well" His eyes went wide, showing defiance.

Bernadette moved her chair closer, their knees almost touching again. She leaned forward, "Well here's some more unfortunate news . . . your pal Paul Goodman . . . we just found him dead. Yep, head caved in by a frying pan in the apartment of his girlfriend . . . what's her name . . . oh yeah . . . Smirnoff." Bernadette leaned back to watch the news wash over Martin.

Martin slapped his leg and screwed up his face, "Ah shit, that really blows . . . Goodman, he was a good guy . . . this really sucks."

Bernadette leaned in. "You know what's worse, and now—here's where this really sucks—some of us here—yes right here in this room—think you had something to do with Goodman's death."

Martin's eyes bulged—his breath became erratic. "No way, no god damn way! I never touched him, I never seen him. He was with that Russian bitch the whole time. I had nothing to do with that shit."

Bernadette turned to Assad. "Now isn't it amazing how talkative and explicit they can be when trying to exonerate themselves?"

Assad took the cue from Bernadette. "Mr. Popowich, here is a problem that we are having with you . . . our investigator found 500,000 American dollars in an offshore bank account in your name." Assad read from a paper in his hand. "My source states this account with Barclays Bank in the Cayman Islands was set up a week ago."

"You know, I'm just a regular detective, who deals with mostly drug dealers and dead bodies," Bernadette said, looking into Martin's eyes, "But I have to say, a half million dollars—man—that takes a bunch of explaining—don't you think Agent Assad?

Assad nodded, "Yes, a large amount of cash like this has many questions attached to it."

Martin looked back and forth between Assad and Bernadette. His eyes squinted as if he was looking to find the truth, or whatever truth they would accept. "Look, this is explainable, easily explained . . ."

"Why don't you start with how you set Goodman up with this Smirnoff gal, who by the way is a known terrorist from Europe named Zara Mashhadov? Now, do you know what that gets you?"

"Look, I didn't set anything up . . . I . . ." Martin tried to speak.

"I said, do you know what that gets you?" Bernadette asked cutting him off.

"No . . . I have no idea . . ." Martin said. His eyes widened.

"It gets you to the front of the line in the Canadian Justice system. The most special treatment we can offer. It's what we offer all suspected terrorists." Bernadette leaned forward and winked at Martin.

Martin sat back, looked at Bernadette and Assad, and paused. A look of defiance came over his face. "You know what, you can get my lawyer, the one I've been asking for since I got here, and you know what else?" He slouched and spread his legs while looking at Bernadette. "You can blow me while I wait—bitch."

Bernadette turned to Assad "I wonder if you wouldn't mind giving Mr. Popowich and me a moment together, and if you would turn off the video recording." She threw a smile back at the suspect.

Assad rose from his chair, adjusted his jacket and tie, "Certainly, I'll give you two a moment to yourselves."

Martin smiled as Assad closed the door. He looked Bernadette in the eyes and was about to say something when the slap she landed on his face bounced his head off the wall. "Hey, you can't do that shit—that's police brutality—I got my rights . . ."

Bernadette leaned across the table. "No, that wasn't police brutality. That was me, reminding you, that you're in the presence of a lady, and you were rude. If you want to see police brutality, I will go outside, borrow a night stick from one of the officers and wale on this knee until it's the size of a basketball." She placed her hand under the table and squeezed his knee—he winced with pain. "Now *that*—would be—police brutality."

Assad returned to the room. "Ah, I see you've had your time alone, I hope it was successful." He smiled serenely as he sat down.

Bernadette turned to Assad. "I think that Mr. Popowich and I are on the same page now." Turning back to Martin she winked. "How about you? Can we continue, or should my colleague leave the room again?"

Martin Popowich held his hand to his face, and moved his body closer to the wall, he nodded his head.

"Now, you wanted to say that you had nothing to do with the murder of Paul Goodman, is that right?"

Bernadette asked. This time she looked over at Assad, who was taking notes.

"Yeah, absolutely, look I haven't seen Goodman since we made that video. He was hanging tight with the Smirnoff girl, she was always grabbing his ass, and running him back to her place . . . she wouldn't tell us where she lived . . . wouldn't let Goodman tell us either," Popowich said.

Assad leaned forward, pushing his note pad over on the table for Popowich to see, "This figure here of a half million dollars, how do you explain that?"

Popowich looked defeated. He sighed deeply, looked up to the ceiling and formed his works carefully. "I . . . okay . . . I sold my friends out . . . okay? I was contacted by some guy from the USA who said if this Pipeline Killer stuff was real, then they'd pay me a shit load of cash for it."

"Do you have names of these people?" Assad asked, making notes.

"Yeah, this guy called the group the Ghost Shirt Eco Warriors, and he kept rattling on about how our invention was going to cause a big stir in the United States. He kept laughing at his own joke about setting America back one hundred years."

Assad turned to Bernadette. "You ever heard of such a group?"

"No, but the Ghost Shirt Warriors refers to a group of Lakota Sioux that believed a shirt with magical powers would protect them from harm in battle. Unfortunately, somebody forgot to tell the white settlers with the guns. The poor bastards were shot off their horses." Bernadette leaned forward to Martin. "How long ago did you sell some of your ingenious product to these people?"

"Last week, some little guy came by, they did the wire

transfer after I gave them a demonstration of the Bio Bugs capabilities and then I gave them twenty vials out of lab at the university."

"You could ID this guy, do a sketch for us?" Bernadette asked.

"Sure." Popowich said. His eyes wandered back up to the ceiling. "But I can do better than that, we met in our lab, and we have our own CCTV camera in there."

Assad made a note. "I'll have the police pick up the camera."

"One other thing," Bernadette said. "Did any of your group know that some of these vials were missing?"

Martin lowered his eyes, "Yeah, Goodman knew. He did an inventory three days ago. I'd never seen him so mad. He asked me, and I swore to god I didn't know." He ran his hands through his hair. "The other two, Hirschman and Campbell, didn't have access to the lab where we stored the stuff."

"Who did Goodman think stole the vials?" Assad asked.

Martin exhaled deeply. "Smirnoff . . . he'd given her a key . . . she told Goodman she wanted to come to the lab at night and have sex with him when no one was around. She said she'd surprise him wearing some sexy clothes. I guess he bought it, because he gave her a key."

"Did you see Goodman confront her with this?" Bernadette asked.

"Yeah, it was bad . . . they were hollering and screaming in the lab. She pushed him and called him a jerk and a dumb ass. I think she was throwing some stuff because there was a mess when they left."

"Do you think Smirnoff ever suspected you, or Hirschman and Campbell—thought that you'd taken the vials and were blaming her?" Bernadette said.

Martin looked at his fingers and picked at a dirty nail. "You know I saw a look from her . . . it was accusing . . . a long stare. She never said anything, but I think she was hiding something else."

"What's that?" Assad asked as he made his notes.

"My laptop is missing the formula. The one Goodman used to make the Bio Bugs so viscous. Someone used a USB stick, downloaded it, and then deleted it. I think it was her, and I think after the vials went missing that maybe Goodman found out about it, because our laptops are networked."

Bernadette turned to Assad. "You know, maybe Mr. Popowich did get Goodman killed after all. He may have shown our Mashhadov, aka Smirnoff's hand before she was ready to steal the vials and the formula and beat it out of here."

Assad stood and straightened his tie. "I believe we have enough for now. How about you, Detective?"

"Yeah, I'm good. We have a lot to work on."

Martin Popowich looked from Assad to Bernadette. "When can I go? I've been cooperative, haven't I?"

Bernadette put her hand on his shoulder. "Yes, you've been very cooperative. And that will show in the report that Assad will write. But this is far from over and you will be a guest of the Canadian Justice system for some time. Now we don't have Starbucks or free wireless, but the room and board is free."

Bernadette followed Assad out of the interview room. They met with Anton and Samantha in the hallway. "Looks like Martin Popowich was more involved in this than he first let on. But then—we get that a lot."

Samantha looked up from a note she was reading on her

cell phone. “We found out the whereabouts of Adalina Torres, AKA, Zara Mashhadov.”

“Let me guess,” Bernadette said. “Somewhere far away from here?”

“She arrived in Barcelona on an Air Canada flight from Toronto at 0735 hours Barcelona time yesterday. We’ve sent an alert to Interpol, but it’s too late. She’s cleared customs there as Adalina Torres.”

Chapter Eight

Zara Mashhadov's stomach was in a knot as she stood in the line for Passport Control in Barcelona; she kept wiping her hands on her jeans to hide the sweat. The killing of Paul Goodman was a mistake, but necessary. She would have preferred to kill Martin Popowich. Goodman accused her of stealing twenty vials of Bio Bugs. But she hadn't stolen them—yet.

Zara was planning to steal all forty vials and saw twenty were missing from the lab. She was certain that little jerk Popowich had stolen the twenty, but she couldn't convince Goodman. The argument that started in the lab continued when they got back to her apartment.

She only intended to shut him up, cool him off, but the weight of the cast iron frying pan was more than she expected. Paul lay there dead, and she needed to run. Zara had gone back to the lab, taken the remaining twenty vials of bio bugs, and headed for the airport.

Barcelona was her destination, but she had wanted to fly through Frankfurt or Paris. Flying through those places could have covered her tracks. She would have taken Euro Rail from there to hide her destination. But all the transatlantic flights were full. The height of August travel season decided her route.

Victoria to Toronto, then the overnight flight to Barcelona had placed her in front of a Spanish Customs officer with her Spanish passport and Castilian name. Adalina Torre's passport said she had been born in Barcelona, and by rights would speak pure Catalonian with a lisping Spanish dialect.

Zara spoke Chechen, German, Arabic and a rudimentary Spanish from the two years of living in Barcelona. At Passport Control, she yawned sleepily, flashed her eyes at the slightly unshaven and handsome young man behind the glass, and was relieved when he stamped her passport and welcomed her home to Barcelona.

The airport was packed with tourists getting bags, meeting cruise ship agents, and milling about looking lost. Zara threaded her way through the masses with her one carry-on bag and took a taxi into the city.

The taxi dropped her off at a small hotel on the Ramblas, the busiest street in Barcelona, at 8:30 a.m. The street vendors were open—some of them had been open all night. Small tapas bars were serving breakfast to the North Americans and Europeans who did not understand the Spanish rhythm of late Breakfast, late lunch, and even later dinner.

Zara checked into the hotel as Adalina Torres. She did not have time to get another passport or credit card. She needed this identity for only a few more hours. The knot tightened in her stomach again as she spoke only a few brief words in Spanish to the desk clerk. *Would he wonder that her Spanish did not match the name on her passport?*

The desk clerk handed her passport back to her, smiled and wished her a pleasant stay. The desk clerk was Albanian, his Spanish was good, but his ear for dialects would probably not be. The knot in her stomach subsided briefly.

She entered her small hotel room and made a phone call. It was to the number of a close friend of the Chechen's. A voice answered the phone, "How may I assist you today?" The voice was English but with a Slavic accent.

"I need a ticket for La Sagrada Familia, but it must be today, I am leaving tomorrow to see my uncle in Madrid." Zara gave the coded message.

"I can't get something to you that fast; you'll have to go to my vendor on the Ramblas, go to the tourist stall in front of the Royal Ramblas Hotel, and ask for Antonio, he will have a ticket for you."

Zara hung up and walked out into the street; the stall was only one block away from her hotel. She found Antonio and told him she'd been sent by the *office* to pick up a ticket.

Antonio nodded, "The ticket is 35 Euros, do you need a map?"

"Yes, but one for all of Barcelona, not just the tourist areas," Zara said. This was the other part of the code.

Antonio handed her the ticket and the map, "The map is one Euro, and I think you will find the Ravel of interest . . . so few people go there."

Zara took the map and the ticket and headed back to her room. The map and the ticket together provided the direction of her destination. There was no way they could communicate this information by phone or text. The ears of the CIA, NSA, and Interpol were everywhere, listening to every call made. They were using old-fashioned technology of ciphers and codes to avoid the omnipresent electronic surveillance. The map had a slight indent on one street name, almost like Braille, and the ticket had a number in the middle that corresponded to an address.

Zara ran her hand over the map area of the Ravel and found the street. She then looked at the ticket and found the street number. She shredded both the map and the ticket and flushed them down the toilet. She was almost home. Now she just needed a disguise.

Zara waited for the shops to open at ten, made a few purchases at a clothing store, and returned to her hotel. She looked to see if any police cars were outside the hotel, or police lurking down the street. Only tourists arriving off a cruise ship crowded the lobby.

Zara went to her room, stripped off her clothes, and destroyed her passport and credit cards. This would be the last sighting of Adalina Torres. She put on a long brown abaya and a black hijab, covering her hair to just above her eyes.

Zara walked past the front desk, eyes down with one small bag under her arm, dressed as an Arabic woman. The tourists, exhausted from flights and cruises, made a path for her as she exited the hotel. She turned right out of the hotel and headed down the Ramblas toward the docks. Three streets down, and just before the large market, she made another right.

Zara, head down, only noticed briefly the boisterous Swedes downing Heinekens in the outdoor bar. Swedes, Finns, and Norwegians descended on Barcelona in the summer for long weekends of drinking and eating. Cheaper drinking prices drew them from their home countries.

Her journey took her deeper into the narrow streets of the district called Raval. Arabic, Indonesian, and Romanian replaced the sounds of Spanish voices. Shops no longer displayed the ubiquitous Spanish hams, but spices and foods common to Pakistan and East Europe. Zara melted into the sea of other women in similar Arabic dress.

At a small door, she knocked softly. The door opened a crack, just enough to identify her, and she glided inside. A young man, dark hair, dark skin, dressed in stained t-shirt and worn jeans, led her upstairs to a darkened room.

In the corner sat a man hunched over a table. A small crack of light showed his creased face, grey whiskers, and bushy eyebrows. Zara's heartbeat faster; she swallowed hard. She had not seen Adlan Kataev for three months.

"How is it with you, Zara?" Adlan asked, rising from his chair. His smile said it all to her. He was glad she was back.

Zara walked into his embrace, the first one in many months that meant something to her. "It goes well Adlan . . . it goes well . . . I have returned with enough vials to exact our revenge . . . God willing."

Adlan motioned for the other men to leave the room, "Zara, what did you bring?"

Zara set the small bag on the table and opened it up, producing a smaller pouch with numerous vials. "I put all of the Bio Bugs vials into these small cosmetic and shampoo containers, anything under 100 milliliters they do not check at security," she said, holding the vials up for Adlan's inspection.

Adlan took a vial from Zara, and held it up to the dim light in the room, "But how do we manufacture more? I intend to use all of these in the next few weeks. These will only be good enough for the start of my revenge."

Zara stood closer to Adlan. "Here, I have the formula I took from their computer . . . this is for the special catalyst Goodman told me makes these organisms aggressive. The vials I stole from the lab have been subjected to the catalyst." She handed him a USB memory stick.

Adlan took the small black memory stick in his large, gnarled hands. "So, this is the formula to make more of these little organisms. Excellent."

"Yes, they were smug about their formula. They said they had the only copy, and no one else could stop their Bio Bugs once they were linked with the aggressive gene. They even joked the gene was the wrath of God." Zara rubbed Adlan's large shoulders and put her chin against his chest.

Adlan moved away. "This is good, very good; I will distribute this to our fighters immediately." His eyes closed. When they opened, they shone wide, as if a vision had struck him. "We will prepare a special surprise for the world with half of these vials. The other half will be used to destroy pipelines in Russia."

Zara tried to move toward Adlan again, but he sat down and motioned for her to take the chair across from him. "What will you do with the other half of the vials?"

Adlan reached across the table and took Zara's hand. "It will be a surprise even for you . . . I do not want to spoil it." A broad smile spread across his face. He patted her hand, grabbed the bag of vials and walked toward the other room. "Have some tea; I will speak with you later."

Zara watched him disappear into the other room, the dark curtains waving in the doorway. She was used to watching him leave. He had found her in a burnt-out Chechen village back in 2000. Russians looking for Chechen separatists had pulled all the men out of the houses and shot them. Her mother hid Zara in a cellar.

Adlan's pockmarked and unshaven face against the harsh daylight was the first thing Zara saw after three days of hiding in the damp, bug infested cellar. The shooting had long stopped, the fires were out, but she dared not come out.

Adlan got her to come out. He coaxed her, told her she would be okay. He said he would take her into the forest, and he did. Zara at twelve years old remained in the forest, hiding and fighting the Russians for the next eight years. Then they had to run from Chechnya as Russian Federal Security Service closed in, and the price on their heads became too high for capture.

Zara fell in love with Adlan, but he returned little affection. The Russians murdered his family in the 90s. Somewhere in the Chechen war for independence they had tortured his wife and sons to give up his location. They never gave him up and died violent deaths.

At the age of eighteen, Zara seduced Adlan. She crawled into his bed one night, and forced herself on him. He cried during orgasm. The hurt and pain of his suffering poured into her . . . and she held him for hours afterward.

Their lovemaking was intermittent, sometimes there was passion, and mostly there was the release of anger. Adlan hated Russia; he hated the world for not coming to the aide of the Chechens. His hate boiled and simmered. Zara wondered what surprise he had for the world. She poured herself a cup of strong tea, added sugar and let the weariness of her long journey descend on her.

She knew the surprise that Adlan would have for the world would be equal to the hatred he had for the world. She sighed as she drank her tea. The next days and weeks would not be happy ones for those who were the focus of his wrath.

Chapter Nine

Bernadette eyed the sandwich with suspicion. Tuna with mayo on whole wheat was what the label said. She took the hard wrapper off, sniffed it once, then twice, and took an exploratory bite. Just as she expected, the taste was somewhere between sawdust and flavored paste.

She chewed it enough to swallow, then took a swig of her tepid coffee and hoped her stomach would recognize the offer of food. She turned to face the front of the boardroom table where Anton was giving a summary of the day's events.

Anton looked up from his notes, "So, we have made a positive identification on the man that Martin Popowich claims he gave the Bio Bug vials to." He looked down at his notes again and adjusted his shirt collar, "We have a Talbert Hensley, who is linked to the Eco Terrorists called the Ghost Shirt Society. He is an American citizen, formerly of Stockton, California."

Bernadette asked, "Is there any background on this guy?"

Anton gazed down the file. "Looks like some petty criminal. There were a few arrests for auto thefts and B& E, then an arrest at the Occupy Wall Street in San Francisco . . . then, wait a minute . . ." Anton turned a page on the report. "You'll never guess how this guy got fingered for a robbery."

Bernadette shrugged and looked across the table at Samantha and Assad. "Okay, we give up Anton. Tell us how much of a mastermind he was or wasn't."

Anton gazed around the table, pausing for effect. "The kid robbed a house, then crapped in a toilet and didn't flush. They had his DNA on file from some other break-and-enters . . . you could say the kid crapped on himself."

Bernadette pushed the sandwich aside. Bad food and bad humor where too much to take. "Tell me, if this kid had priors, how did he get across the Canadian border? Does Canada customs have any record of him entering, or where he entered?"

"Yeah they do, he entered through Blaine, Washington, by car," Anton read further down the sheet. "Looks like we have him on a special watch list, and we were asked to let him through by the FBI." Anton scratched his chin. "I need to speak to someone about why this guy is being given special clearance. In a case like this, it's usually because he's undercover . . . I'll have to check."

Assad tapped his pen on his pad of paper. He was listening, not writing. "Did Interpol find Zara Mashhadov in Barcelona?"

Anton glanced at his notes, this time going over to a second page. "I have a note here that Adalina Torres, our suspect aka Zara Mashhadov, checked into a hotel in Barcelona, and when the police arrived, she was gone. The Interpol guy said they scared the hell out of a busload of tourists but no Adalina, no Zara."

Samantha scribbled a note on her pad and put the pen to her lips. "Can I just get my head around few of the events?" She looked around the table, assumed consent and continued. "What I see so far are four university students who wanted to do a project to replicate something called nanites . . . that was on a Star Trek episode many years ago . . . am I correct so far?"

Bernadette nodded, "Sounds good so far—go with it."

"Okay, the students recreate the nanites, which they call a Bio Bug, or super bug that eats metal in pipelines, and somehow they received international attention from European terrorists, and an Eco Terrorist group in the USA —am I missing anything?" Samantha looked up from her notes, her own voice showed her doubt.

Bernadette tapped her own pad of paper. "Yeah, you're missing an important piece of this puzzle. The chemistry professor that they were doing this little project for, Professor Alistair McAllen was complicit in trying to damage oil production last year in Alaska and the Oil Sands. I think he's still part of this, maybe pulling some of the strings. I'm not exactly sure how he's doing it, but I think he's still in this equation."

Anton shuffled his papers and was about to say something. His phone buzzed, "I think I need to take this; it's my section chief Patterson." Anton rose and walked out of the conference room and into the hallway.

Bernadette shifted in her chair; Chief Patterson from the CSIS in Edmonton did not like her. She'd made him look bad when they were chasing McAllen the previous year. Her instincts had proven right; his had been so far off he'd looked foolish. She wondered if he'd forgotten that. As she watched Anton on the phone in the hallway outside through the boardroom window, Anton frowned in her direction. Obviously, Chief Patterson's memory was intact when it came to her.

Alistair McAllen watched a gecko climb the wall of the restaurant. Light green with small patches of brown, the gecko made slow progress up the wall, raised its small head, surveying the waiters and patrons as they walked by.

The evening was still warm, the adobe brick walls emanating heat from the day's sun. McAllen still wore shorts, sandals, and a linen shirt at eleven at night. He pushed the unfinished plate of food away and picked up his wine glass. Small rivulets of condensation streamed down the glass.

The waiter walked by and filled his water glass. McAllen thanked him in Spanish and picked up a small package on the table. The package was from Paul Goodman. It didn't say that. The return address was Emilo Sanchez, from Santa Fe. But that was the place Paul sent mail from. The package was addressed to McAllen's housekeeper who lived just outside of the center of Merida, Mexico, where McAllen lived.

McAllen already knew that Paul Goodman was dead. Three university students had sent texts and tweets about it in the past few hours. Of the students under arrest, McAllen only knew of Martin Popowich. Martin was a smart ass. He kept his grades just high enough to get by, but there was never any real spark there. He used Goodman to help him get by—everyone knew that—even the professors.

Goodman was McAllen's star pupil. He was brilliant, intuitive, and passionate about chemistry and biological sciences. The original idea for bio super bugs was McAllen's; Goodman had run with it. He wanted to reproduce the metal destroying super bugs to please McAllen. Goodman told McAllen he wanted to "give him something else for his arsenal, if polywater failed," and polywater had failed.

McAllen opened the package. A small USB memory stick fell out, with a note. He took the memory stick, rolled it in his hand, and picked up the note.

The note read:

Professor, things are getting a little crazy here. Not sure who to trust anymore. I'm sending you a copy of the formula for the super bugs. The password is the same one we set up.
Paul Goodman

McAllen looked up at the sky; dark clouds were forming. A small tear made its way down his cheek. He brushed it away. He wished he'd told Goodman to stop the project, but secretly he never thought Goodman would do it. He had done it. Now he was dead.

McAllen weighed his options. He had been hiding in Merida, Mexico, for several months. The only one in Canada who knew his hiding place had been Goodman. Goodman was dead. Did Goodman's killer know about the connection to him?

The gecko started its climb up the wall again, this time at a faster pace. It saw something, a bug perhaps, that would be dinner. It disappeared over the wall. McAllen watched it go, and knew he needed to leave as well, to disappear, but first he had to solve the riddle of what was in this USB stick. He needed his own lab, which was here in Merida. He was now playing a dangerous game. He'd gambled in the past with getting caught and won, but even a gambler knows luck can run out.

Anton came back into the boardroom. "I just received a report about Talbert Hensley. He is not working with the FBI; an undercover FBI agent is accompanying him. They requested that he be allowed through our border. He was coming to Canada to pick up the vials from Popowich."

"And they couldn't have arrested him with the vials he bought from Popowich?" Bernadette asked.

"They wanted the people at the top that Hensley works with," Anton said. "Some FBI chief told Patterson they've been trying to crack this group for months. Seems they're funded by some rich guy who remains anonymous and keeps putting up cash to fund this Ghost Shirt Eco Warrior Society."

"So where is this guy headed? For pipelines in Canada or the USA?" Samantha asked.

"Their reports say the USA, somewhere in Montana." Anton said.

Bernadette sat back in her chair. "Well, isn't this sweet? This thing starts here and ends up in the USA and Europe. All we have are the dead bodies to sort out."

Anton looked at Bernadette. "Ah, yeah, I need to speak with you in private for a moment." He motioned for her to follow him out into the hallway.

The hallway was crowded with City of Victoria Police officers about to change shifts for the evening. Anton motioned for Bernadette to follow him further down the hallway until they found a quiet area. "Look," he cocked his head to one side, and put his hand on her shoulder, "I didn't think Chief Patterson would come down so hard on me for having you on this case . . ."

"But he's being a real hard ass about it, is that what you really want to say," Bernadette said. She moved slightly closer to Anton as three police officers walked by.

Anton let out a breath, "Yeah, that's it exactly. This is my case, and I'm supposed to be in charge, but . . ."

"But he's your boss," Bernadette said. "Look Anton, I get it, your boss doesn't like me, and will do anything to get back at me for showing him up."

"It's more than that." Anton looked into Bernadette's eyes. "He said he found information that your father was a drug dealer here in Victoria before he died. He thinks your judgment in this is compromised . . . now don't even ask me how he put that together, but he's using that to get you off this case." Anton scanned Bernadette for a reaction.

"You know he's wrong about his information—my father was never smart enough to be a drug dealer. It's true he died here in Victoria, a wino, crack-head junkie—but no—he was never a drug dealer," Bernadette said.

Anton touched Bernadette's arm. "Look, I'm sorry about all this. I brought you into this case, and my boss has ordered me to take you out. How about if I buy you dinner tonight? I booked us all rooms over at the Marriott and found a nice Italian restaurant. How about if you relax tonight on the tab of the Canadian Security and Intelligence Service—think you could handle that?"

Bernadette put her hand on Anton's arm. "You know if you weren't so damn cute and didn't have such good taste in food and wine I'd turn you down—but what can I say—I can hang out here tonight. You can even fill me in on how you plan on solving this case without me." She turned and walked back with Anton to the conference room.

Chapter Ten

Sarah watched Talbert Hensley shove another large piece of steak into his mouth, and chew down with the part of his mouth that didn't hurt. The left side of Talbert's jaw was bandaged, and a yellow bruise ran from the gauze up to his eye.

The wound was from an altercation getting off the Car Ferry from Vancouver Island. Three men in a van swerved in front of them, jumped out and claimed Talbert had cut them off. Sarah was stunned as Talbert, ever the cocky little bastard, jumped out and argued with them.

She was the undercover FBI Agent who had made friends with Talbert to find out more about the Eco Terrorists, and now she had to defend him. She was trained in martial arts, and could have taken down all three men in a heartbeat. Instead, she kicked one in the shin, and stomped the other guy's foot.

One of the men got behind her, and drove his fist into her head, dropping her to the ground, and they commenced laying a beating on Talbert. Somehow, enough other cars stopped or slowed that the men left. Sarah had only a mild headache, but Talbert's jaw had suffered a major contusion with a broken tooth.

She patched him up as well as she could, bought some serious painkillers, and took the wheel of the rental car. They headed east along Interstate 90. Leaving Seattle behind, they passed Ellensburg, Moses Lake and Spokane before Talbert pointed out a truck stop diner and told her to pull over. Talbert gave Sarah directions one day at a time. She knew he still didn't trust her.

Sarah had been born in Baltimore, Maryland. She'd wanted to be in the FBI ever since she was ten years old. She watched reruns of the TV show, The FBI, with her dad, a sergeant in the Baltimore Police Force. She loved her dad, and every time they watched the FBI show, her dad would say, "Now Sarah, that's the force that catches the real criminals. We cops catch just the small fry—but those guys —that's the real thing."

Her Dad had been killed on the streets of Baltimore in the line of duty. One of the small fry, with a large gun shot him. Sarah never forgot what her dad had said. She made up her mind she would get into the FBI.

Everything in her life was geared to her goal. She had honors in high school, Bachelor's Degree in Criminal Justice with honors, and five years on the Baltimore Police force while completing a degree in computer science. All this effort was to make herself of value to the FBI.

Sarah Collins was accepted on her first attempt into the FBI, and brought to the J. Edgar Hoover building in Washington to work as a Special Agent. She was in. She loved it. The first three years.

Somewhere in the workings of the hierarchy of the FBI, someone, a very high up someone, decided they would form a special team of agents to get close to suspected terrorists. They would infiltrate the terrorist organizations to their very core.

Sarah would never forget the day she'd been summoned into her section chief's office. Chief Maynard Briscoe was considered to be an old pompous prick by the young agents. Everyone wondered when he would announce his pension plans and give them a break. Sarah would never complain about Briscoe. Her father had taught her to always be respectful of her superiors and work within the confines of the department. "Respect the department and those who work in it, and it will take care of you," her father had said.

But that day, a chilly February afternoon as light snow fell outside the J Edgar Hoover Building in downtown Washington D.C., Sarah stood to attention in front of Briscoe's desk. There was no chair. He liked Agents to stand in front of him.

Briscoe shuffled some paper, coughed several times, and regarded Sarah through bushy eyebrows. "Agent Sarah Collins, you are being considered for a special team, and I want to know if you're up for the challenge?"

"Yes, sir," Sarah said, eyes straight and focused on the picture of the President and the American flag behind Briscoe's desk.

Briscoe opened Sarah's file. "Agent Collin's, you have shown exemplary work as an agent, and that is why you were chosen for this assignment."

"Thank you, sir." Sarah allowed the beginnings of a smile to edge her lips.

"Now, you need to know that you will be getting quite close to some of our chosen terrorist targets, and you may have to perform some special . . ." Briscoe looked away from the file, and fidgeted with his tie. "You may have to perform some special functions."

Sarah's throat constricted slightly. "Functions, sir?"

Briscoe coughed again, and with his hand covering his mouth said, "Agent Collins, are you ready to sleep with terrorists to infiltrate their organizations?"

"Excuse me, sir?"

Briscoe dropped his hands to the desk. "We need to be able to get close to these people; our intelligence department feels this is the best way to do it. Are you ready for this challenge?"

Sarah looked at the floor; her hands began to sweat, "I never really thought of anything like this before sir. I knew I'd be putting my life on the line when I joined the department . . . I never questioned that . . . but this assignment . . . I'm not sure . . ."

Briscoe slide another file from underneath Sarah's, and as it came into view it gave her more of a shock than the assignment she'd been offered. The file was marked Jonas Ubani, and a bright red flag was attached.

Briscoe saw the tension in Sarah's face and the rapid movement of her eyes. It was exactly the reaction he'd been looking for. "I understand you know this individual?"

"Yes I do." Sarah answered. There was no way she could lie about it, the file would probably have everything about their relationship. "We met four years ago. Jonas was an intern in the emergency ward where I brought my police partner when he was shot in the arm . . ."

Briscoe raised his hand, "There's no need to go into the details—it's all here in the file." He leafed through the pages, "Yes, you met, you fell in love, and you managed to keep your arrangement secret. It seems you knew that FBI would question your affair with a known enemy of the United States of America."

Sarah stiffened, "Jonas Ubani is not a terrorist . . . sir. He is a good doctor at Mercy General in Baltimore. He left Nigeria because he was vocal about the government's corruption."

"Yes, that is in the file as well, but he claimed that an American oil company was part of the corruption. That is what got him the red flag." Briscoe said.

"Yes sir, I understand that, but . . ."

"No, there are no buts where the state department is concerned. You know as well as I do, that a person who is red flagged can be removed from our soil at any time. Your good Doctor Ubani is no exception."

"Yes sir," Sarah said. Her face was now visibly flushed. There was nowhere she could go with this argument. Her secret affair with Doctor Jonas Ubani was in the open, and her future with the FBI was on the line.

Briscoe closed Ubani's file and slid it back under Sarah's. "I know this is quite unfortunate that the good Doctor Ubani has been red flagged, and this may in fact be all a misunderstanding. But here is what I'm prepared to do. You accept this assignment, and this red flag disappears."

Sarah felt her knees almost buckle. She took a deep breath, there was no way out, "Yes sir, that is most generous of you . . . can you give me some time to think about . . ."

"You have until the end of the day," Briscoe said.

Sarah whispered a, "Yes sir," and walked out of the office. Her cubicle was down the hall, and she returned to it and slumped in her chair.

Her dilemma had no gray area. Accept the assignment, sleep with some terrorist, and get her lover Jonas red flag taken off his file, or not accept the assignment and see what Briscoe would do to ruin her life.

The sound of a golf ball bouncing out of a putting machine came down the hall. The sound was from Briscoe's office. Pock, pock, pock the machine sounded as the ball returned to Briscoe's putter again and again.

The sound infuriated Sarah. For the first time in her career, she doubted the wisdom of her superior. She marched back towards Briscoe's' office. She decided to accept the assignment, but they'd have to remove the red flag from Jonas Ubani's file first.

Under her breath as she stood in front of Briscoe's door, she muttered, "You pompous old prick."

Special training took place two weeks later. For two months she learned the culture of possible extremist groups. She was taught how to be submissive, walk behind a man, the customs of cooking and etiquette of numerous Asian countries. Her head was swimming with the possibilities of which group she would be chosen to infiltrate.

At the end of the training, she was ushered into a boardroom, and shown a series of photos of what looked like young hippies from California. A senior agent named Caulfield said, "This is your target. They're after America's oilfields and infrastructure."

"I'm protecting big oil?" Sarah asked.

"You're protecting America," Caulfield answered. His eyebrow did one arch. A motion that said, "*Don't question—just do.*"

Sarah had walked out of the room crestfallen. No, she would not be chasing some of the deadliest terrorists who were trying to blow up Americans. She would be chasing a group of American hippies who wanted to mess with American Oil. Perhaps if her assignment had been different, something to do with Al Qaeda, Sarah might have felt better about what she was doing to protect Jonas Ubani, but this assignment of protecting oil—only heaped the insult onto the injury. Jonas Ubani hated everything there was about oil, for what it had done to his country.

She had met intern Jonas Ubani, with the kindest eyes, the soft smile and lilting African accent mixed with his years in a London Medical school, and she was smitten. She'd asked him on a date. They'd been inseparable ever since.

Until she joined the FBI, when she found that Jonas Ubani had a file. The file was flagged. Jonas had led protests in Nigeria against the oil companies. The oil companies that took the oil and gave the profits to the government, and the government gave nothing to the people.

Jonas had left Nigeria before the Police came to get him. He had told Sarah, "They had a special name there. Officially they are called the Mobil Police Force of Nigeria. Their unofficial name is the Kill and Go. Because that is what they do."

Sarah knew Jonas would not like her new assignment. She shouldn't have told him. But she did. They met over dinner, a little Nigerian Café in downtown Baltimore. Sarah had Jollof of chicken and rice. It reminded her of a Jambalaya, but without the seafood, and more of a cinnamon and ginger flavor. Jonas had the Suya with Rice, the Nigerian take on a Kabob.

They shared a Mango Sundae for dessert. They both had a sweet tooth. Sarah remembered the look in Jonas's eyes as she told him her new assignment. She tried to put it into words that would be more palatable. Something that he could assimilate without coming to a conclusion of what her mission was. A conclusion she'd already reached.

"You're going to sleep with a man who's after American

oil Sarah?" Jonas asked. His voice came out a whisper. But it was a loud whisper.

Sarah grabbed Jonas' large hands in hers, "Look, the FBI thinks he's a threat, and—"

"Sarah, the FBI thinks I'm a threat. America thinks everyone who is against oil is a threat. Have I not told you the waste that oil has brought to my people? Nigerians live in poverty, while the oil is burned every day in the cars of America. Big oil prospers, while Nigerians go hungry—and every day the oil is sucked from beneath their feet.

"Jonas, I know it seems wrong, but it's what my agency, my government wants."

Jonas stood up. He was tall, athletic. He loomed above Sarah. "Sarah, I do not condone this. American oil companies can protect themselves. They have the money. They do not need you—my lovely Sarah— to prostitute herself for more riches . . ." He stopped, then, bit his lip. Tears formed in his eyes, and he walked out of the restaurant. Sarah watched Jonas walk down the street. She wanted to chase after him and tell him the real reason she accepted the assignment. It meant him staying in America; it meant her keeping her job in the FBI, and her promise to her father. There was no grey area, Jonas walked out into the black night and Sarah could see her path in bright lights before her. Sleeping with the enemy.

Now, seven months later, Sarah Collins, skilled in martial arts, awards in marksmanship, criminal profiling and forensic computer science, was eating barbeque in a café in off the Interstate in Montana. She'd met up with Talbert just after he was released from jail for his part in the Wall Street Occupation demonstrations in San Francisco.

The FBI orchestrated a "bump," for Sarah to meet Talbert. The bump was an accidental meeting. Her cover was a recently divorced woman with a hatred for corporate America, but a big enough alimony check to keep any man happy. It was all Talbert could ask for.

Talbert was all of 22, unkempt hair with a wispy beard and washed-out blue eyes. He was medium height and lean in a wiry way that belied a strength and nervous energy. His participation in the Wall Street Occupation demonstrations was somewhat sketchy at best.

Sarah observed him hang out with the demonstrators during the day, then slink off at night to sleep in a cheap motel nearby. The cold pavement and a sleeping bag were not his style. The FBI knew that Talbert had become involved with the Ghost Shirt Society through an old friend. They knew who that friend was, but not whom he reported to.

The FBI wanted Sarah Collins to become Rebecca Jones, befriend Talbert Hensley, and have him lead her and the entire FBI strike team to the heart of the Ghost Shirt Society Eco Warriors. That had all sounded so simple many months ago.

The months had rolled by; Talbert had fallen for the good-looking Rebecca Jones, a brunette with liquid brown eyes, easy smile and lovely figure. He wanted to sleep with her the first night . . . she put him off. After several more attempts, and when his interest was almost waning, Sarah gave in to the wiry and energetic Talbert.

Sarah needed to become Rebecca Jones that night with Talbert. Her cover was a committed activist to the Eco Warrior movement and groupie who followed the likes of Talbert Hensley around from one activist demonstration to another.

The first night she had sex with Talbert Hensley, she almost threw up. Talbert was horrible in bed. He had no idea how to please a woman, and all Sarah could think of while he moved on top of her was of Jonas back in Baltimore.

Sarah decided after the first night, if she was to succeed in this mission, she needed to bury Sarah Collins and become her cover of Rebecca Jones. She was told to do that by the undercover coach from the FBI, and she had to put it into practice. Her mental health was at stake. Talbert Hensley's life was at stake. If she stayed Sarah Collins, she'd kill the little jerk.

Now, all these months later, Sarah and Talbert Hensley had made their way from San Francisco, from one activist rally to another. A team of FBI agents was always close by, ready to pounce. But Talbert would only move from one city to another, getting his directions by word of mouth from other activists.

Talbert never used a cell phone, wouldn't go on the Internet, and went to thrift shops to exchange his clothes. He told Sarah he was afraid of having traces or GPS signals placed in his clothing if he wore them too long.

Sarah realized why the FBI needed someone to get close to Talbert; he could move like a shadow. One day they would be in a motel just outside of Portland for the night, and just around midnight, he would tell her they had to leave. They would head out the back door, and a car would be there to pick them up. It made the FBI team shadowing them crazy.

Talbert wouldn't use a cell phone or let Sarah use one. A GPS signal was in a microchip under her skin. She did not know what Talbert would do if he ever found out she was an agent. She could defend herself easily against him, but what about at night, while she slept beside him?

Watching him chew his food, winching with pain, actually gave Sarah pleasure. She often had visions of him choking to death on the big pieces of meat he chewed down, even right now, she wondered if she would perform the Heimlich maneuver on him, if it happened, or just watch to see if someone else knew it.

Talbert took the large knife with the serrated edge, and sawed off another piece of meat, getting it ready to stuff into his full mouth. Sarah eyed the knife. She saw a vision of herself grabbing it and slicing it quickly across his jugular vein . . . he would bleed out in seconds.

The waitress came by; she'd been at their table numerous times to fuss over Talbert. Rebecca was getting tired of the attention. "Did the poor boy need more water, another soft bun, and maybe some tapioca pudding for dessert?"

Sarah smiled at the waitress, "You know, I think he'll be just fine. He's a tough guy, aren't you honey?" She tapped the table in his direction. Both his hands were busy sawing the steak and getting more ridiculous-size pieces into his mouth.

Talbert made a wide grin, pieces of steak showing out of this mouth as he chewed. Sarah had already decided they would be in separate beds tonight. She would place a few crushed up sleeping pills into his warm milk that she gave him with his painkillers.

Chapter Eleven

Anton dropped Bernadette off at the Marriot Hotel in Victoria's inner harbor. He'd somehow managed to get them rooms at the height of the August tourist season in Victoria, with tour buses expelling passengers into the already packed lobby.

He even had her upgraded to the concierge level, with a quick check-in through the Gold Elite check-in desk. Bernadette's affiliations with hotel chains were usually limited to the Best Western and Motel 6, and she wasn't very high up in status with either of them.

Bernadette entered her well-appointed room with luxurious furnishings and views of the harbor and did what she always did in times of frustration—got changed for a workout in the gym.

Her small 20-inch carry-on bag always included three sets of workout outfits with a pair of runners, as well as her extra clothes. In the face of frustration with no sex and no chocolate, a girl could always hit the gym, and that is what she did.

The hotel gym was empty when she arrived at six o'clock. Hotel gyms were never well used, and it was fact Bernadette enjoyed. She hit the treadmill hard with intervals of power walking, jogging, and then wind sprints. A series of weights followed, and she hit biceps, triceps, and then legs with sessions back on the treadmill doing sprints to keep her heart rate up.

By seven-thirty, she was mildly exhausted and happy. Her frustration with being taken off a major case had ebbed, and the mess of her love life was only a distant nagging thought. She showered and changed into her standard going out for dinner clothes, a black pair of wool blend dress pants, a red blouse (that didn't show stains) and a black pashmina shawl that a girlfriend in Edmonton convinced her she had to have. She still wasn't sure about the shawl.

She added a pair of silver Navajo earrings and simple jade pendant with silver chain. She was just admiring herself in the mirror when Anton called from downstairs at eight-fifteen for dinner. "Yes," she thought to herself, "looking damn good . . . and going out with a work colleague."

As they walked to the restaurant from the hotel, a gentle breeze blew in from the harbor, cool and tinged with salt. Anton informed her that Samantha and Assad would not be joining them. Assad still had too much follow-up to be done on the interview of the suspects, and Samantha was deep into the computer files of the laptops that they had seized.

They walked along the Victoria Harbor, and then took a right along Wharf Street. Throngs of tourist in clusters—some in families and some in tour groups—crowded the streets. A crowd approached. Bernadette and Anton had to squeeze against the buildings as they passed. They were a tour group from one of the cruise ships, small stickers with the name of their ship plastered on their lapels. A smiling tour guide uttered an endless stream of useful facts about Victoria to those interested enough in the group to listen.

Bernadette always imagined herself going on a cruise ship sometime. She liked the idea of watching these people amble by, lost in their reverie of yet another port they would visit for only a brief few hours, and then leaving. It seemed like a tasting tour of civilization.

Anton took her arm and directed her down a small narrow alley where the restaurant was located. The place was packed with a large group outside the door waiting for their reservations. Bernadette wondered how long they'd have to wait for a table; Anton had told her he didn't have a reservation. Hunger was making itself known with a small growl in her stomach.

Anton smiled, "Let me see what I can do." He waded in amongst the people at the entrance and began talking quietly with the maître de.

Bernadette looked up and down the alley and wondered if they shouldn't just go to one of the pubs they'd passed on the way.

Anton was suddenly taking her by the arm. "They can seat us right away."

"How did you do that?" Bernadette's eyes were wide with both amazement and amusement at Anton's talents.

Anton smiled. "Hey, the maître de is from Sicily, and I'm from Sicily . . . and just like that . . . what can I say . . . we're in."

They walked past the other people waiting at the front door. A wave of mutterings and rumblings made its way through the waiting diners. Anton flashed his smile in their direction. A lady in a sequin track suit, with a tour label that proclaimed her as Agnes said, "You know I've seen him before . . . he's from one of those crime dramas . . . like CSI or maybe that True Suspect thing."

A woman beside Agnes, dressed in a purple velour suit with a name tag that stated she was Grace, "Na, I've seen that guy, he's been on that cooking show from Europe, the Italian Chef or something."

"You think that's him," Agnes said.

"Oh yeah," Grace said. She stood watching Anton disappear with Bernadette into the crowded restaurant. "What a doll."

Bernadette overheard the conversation as they walked by. "You know, Anton, you do seem to have an effect on women. You ever think of taking up acting?"

Anton waited as Bernadette was seated. "There are too many good-looking Italians looking for acting jobs." He took his chair across from Bernadette. "But how many have their chance to protect their country?"

A waiter filled their glasses with water; another dropped a basket of bread on the table and then filled a small bowl with olive oil and balsamic vinegar to dip the bread into. Bernadette took a piece of still warm bread and began tearing off chunks. "Anton, I don't believe in all the time we've known each other that you've told me your reasons for joining the Canadian Security and Intelligence Service."

Anton's face took on a frown. "Bernadette, to most people who ask, I give them the stock answer . . . but to you . . . I'll give you the truth."

Bernadette was about to place a morsel of bread into her mouth, freshly dipped into the olive oil and balsamic mixture. Instead, she put the bread on her bread plate, "I'm all ears, Anton."

"You know how I'm always joking with you about being Sicilian, but it's also a badge of honor to me and to my family. Sicilians are very proud and determined people who take their traditions seriously," Anton said.

"Yes, I always gathered that. I've seen the Godfather at least three times."

Anton allowed a small chuckle, "Yes, well, I think the Godfather set us back a few centuries, but you're not far off on my own history."

Bernadette leaned forward and whispered. "Your family is in the mob."

Anton's one eyebrow went up, and he looked to see if anyone was within hearing distance. "Well, it wasn't my whole family, it was my uncle."

The waiter came by and dropped off menus, told them the specials, and they were out of the scallops. They ordered the Zuppa di Pesce and Insalata Mista, and Anton ordered the seared venison while Bernadette chose the Beef Tenderloin with Gorgonzola cheese. Anton chose a Chianti to go with the dinner.

As the waiter left, Bernadette leaned forward again. "Is your uncle still alive?"

Anton picked up some bread, dipped it into the olive oil, and placed it in his mouth. He chewed and swallowed before answering. "No, he's been dead for ten years now, taken out by a rival gang back in Sicily. The only good thing about him was he stayed in Sicily."

Their waiter came by with wine glasses, uncorked the wine, poured some for Anton to taste, and then filled their glasses. Bernadette let the wine swill in her glass, breathed in its earthy nose and said, "So luckily none of his actions over there affected you over here."

Anton took a sip of his wine and put the glass down. It was if a cloud had passed over his face. "You know I wish that statement were true, but my uncle did something that did affect my family . . . it affected them to their very core . . . he murdered a priest."

Bernadette put down her wine glass and swallowed hard. "Oh my God, I felt a shadow pass over my mother's grave just then." She made the sign of the cross before she could stop herself. "So you entered the service for . . ."

"Atonement. Is that what you were about to say? Because that is exactly what it is." Anton took a large swallow of wine. "My mother wanted me to enter the priesthood to make atonement for the sins of the De Luca family, and I chose to be an analyst in the Canadian Intelligence and Security Service instead." Anton leaned forward. "And you know what is funny, Bernadette, is that I hate guns. I can hardly fire one without my hands shaking."

Bernadette placed her hand on Anton's. "Don't worry . . . I'm a freaking marksman when it comes to guns . . . I got your back, kid." There was a tear in her eye, as she looked at the handsome young man who had become serious with the revelations about his past.

The soups arrived, and Anton sat back visibly relieved, like he had been to confession. "So, Bernadette, I've just given you my sordid family history. What's yours?"

Bernadette put down her spoon and patted her lips with her napkin. "Mine is simple. My mom, a good-looking country girl who sang like an angel, meets an Irishman who plays music in a bar. They sing together, get married, have six children, and the Irishman goes back to playing music in the bars while my mother pines for him."

"How did he end up here in Victoria and dead?" Anton asked after a pause. The clatter of the restaurant became audible again.

"My dad, the famous Dominic Callahan, at least in his own mind, could never give up the party scene. He'd come back to my mom, stay awhile, leave her pregnant again, and off on the road he went again. The booze got to him, then the crack cocaine. I think he came to Victoria like a lot of addicts do because it's the warmest place in Canada to live on the streets."

"Sorry to hear that."

"Yeah, well, it's never a pretty story. My mother died shortly after news of my dad's death. The two were welded at the hip in sorrow." Bernadette let out a sigh. "God, look at us . . . two Catholic kids doing a confessional over wine."

They let the conversation rest as they dug into their soup of fresh mussels, tiger prawns and chunks of halibut in a tomato sauce and sprigs of cilantro. The waiter came back, filled their wine glasses, and Bernadette looked to Anton. "Well, has anything developed in the case?"

Anton rested his spoon in his bowl, dabbed his mouth with his napkin, "The FBI has a close watch on Talbert Hensley, who bought the vials of Bio Bugs from Popowich. They told Patterson he's in Missoula, Montana, right now, and they think he's headed for some of the big pipelines that cross from Alberta into Montana."

"Would that be the pipelines that bring oil from the oil sands?"

Anton sat back as the waiter removed the soup bowl, "Uh-huh, that would be the big fish they think the eco terrorists are after." He looked down at his wine glass, twirling the glass and watching it swirl. "There are two major rivers the pipeline crosses, the Missouri, and the

Yellowstone. If they hit that pipeline with the Bio Bugs, we would have a major catastrophe."

"Why can't the big oil companies just shut that pipeline down?" Bernadette asked.

Anton looked up from his wine glass. "It's not as simple as that. If they shut the pipeline down, then the eco terrorists might get wind of it, and know the FBI is on to them. Besides, it's just a guess; there is another pipeline in North Dakota they could hit as well."

The waiter placed the Insalata Mista in front of them and wished them a hearty, "Enjoy!" and left. "Is the FBI confident they can stop this Talbert before he injects the bio bugs into the pipelines?"

Anton poised his fork over his salad. "I was told that the FBI agent travelling with Talbert is posing as his girlfriend, and is keeping close watch on him . . . hopefully they have it under control."

Bernadette lowered her fork, and put it on the table, "Oh my god, you mean a female FBI agent in deep cover is actually sleeping with this guy?" She took a sip of her wine, "You know, I understand the Americans are serious about defending themselves from terrorists, but man, sleeping with the guy . . ."

"You find that objectionable for deep cover . . ."

"— I find it objectionable for any kind of cover." Bernadette picked up her fork again, and toyed with some of the greens in the salad.

Anton swallowed a mouthful of salad, "I agree with you, but these are dangerous times. I'm sure the Americans thought this was the only way to get close to the guy. We heard the guy won't carry a cell phone, moves around a lot, and trusts few people." Anton looked sideways for a second to see if any of the diners could hear them. "I just heard he got into some kind of altercation at the border, and he and the FBI agent are lying low until he recovers."

Bernadette dropped her fork, "What kind of an altercation?"

"Something to do with road rage just off the Car Ferry from Victoria. Three guys in a van laid a serious beating on Talbert and get this . . . the FBI agent had to defend him."

Bernadette leaned back. "And that doesn't seem odd to you?"

Anton said, "How should this be odd? The report from the FBI agent was that the vials were still intact in the car after the fight, and these guys gave Talbert a pretty serious beating . . . I know, I know . . ." Anton raised his hand, "You're thinking it was a diversion of some kind . . . the FBI already considered that."

Bernadette shook her head. "When will we ever learn to go with our instincts? If it looks like a diversion . . . it's probably a diversion."

Anton smiled. "Hey, Bernadette, relax, it's just road rage, happens all the time in America, and Canada has it too. My god, look at Vancouver, the traffic there . . ."

"Okay. Anton," Bernadette said. "Road rage, that's what the FBI and Canadian Intelligence have decided . . . works for me." She picked up her wine glass, and raised it in a salutation. "Here's to catching the nasty terrorists."

By the time they returned to the Hotel it was just past 11 p.m. Bernadette gave Anton a hug, wished him well with the case and headed to her room. She slipped out of her clothes and into a t-shirt, found a Pellegrino in the mini-bar, and watched the Harbor shimmer and twinkle with the lights from small boats.

A thought was tugging at her consciousness. The thought was about the man she was supposed to call. If she had called Chris Christakos, the RCMP officer she'd been having a relationship with even last week, it would have been fine. Now it was three weeks since she said she'd call.

She'd met the handsome Greek-Canadian constable while on the case chasing Professor McAllen. Christos, or Chris as he liked to be called, helped her locate McAllen. He'd been living on Galliano Island as the lone officer of the RCMP detachment. That island was 2 hours and 26 minutes away, with a ferry ride. She checked a Google map before she left home.

She was supposed to call him. Wasn't that the way they left it, to give an answer to a question he'd asked her? It was simple. "Do you love me?" He'd left it at that, in their last phone call.

She could have called him. She should have called him. But what could she say? Yes, I'm madly in love with you, but I'd have to leave the RCMP to be with you. *To become what?* Was the thought bouncing around in her head. The Island Chris lived on was full of artists in winter and tourists in summer. She'd have nothing else to do there but be his wife . . . and whatever else she could find to occupy her time.

Bernadette couldn't paint worth a damn, could barely write legible case reports, and most people annoyed her, so running a bed and breakfast was not a consideration. And then there was the other thing. Most relationships came with baggage. The handsome Constable Chris had a Greek Mother who hated Bernadette—she didn't even try to hide it.

Then there was Chris's sister, Lenia. She'd kept asking Bernadette about the life span of RCMP detectives, and how often they were killed or injured in their line of work. The inference was obvious. Lenia, wanted Bernadette very dead or at least maimed and away from her brother.

Bernadette hugged herself, let out a deep sigh, and crawled into bed. Her love life was long distance both in geography, and the span of culture between Chris and herself. She didn't know if she wanted love to find a way—or a way out. She closed her eyes and went to sleep.

Chapter Twelve

Bernadette caught the Airport shuttle bus on Sunday morning. She didn't want to bother either Anton or Samantha for a ride. They were deep into the case, and she was not. She welcomed the opportunity of the two-hour plane ride back to Calgary with just her thoughts for company.

The plane landed in a perfect blue-sky morning and she was in her Jeep in the airport parking lot when her cell phone rang. Bernadette smiled when she saw the caller ID. "Anton, you missed me. How nice."

"Hey Bernadette, of course, if my mother would agree, you'd be the one for me—you know that."

"Okay Anton, you smooth Sicilian, what's up? What'd you need?"

"Bernadette, if more of the RCMP was as sharp as you, criminals would give up—there'd be no money in it. Listen, I need a favor, all our guys are tied up—you know budget cuts and that stuff."

Bernadette started her Jeep and lowered her windows. The heat was rising from the asphalt. "Budget cuts sure, okay, cut the preamble and get to the point. You know I'm here for you."

Anton laughed. "I always forget that buttering you up never works with you . . . so here it is. The coroner, Dr. Andrew, sent a sample of the Bio Bugs to the University of Calgary to the Biological Science Building."

Bernadette rolled up her windows as a 747 took off. "What's that, you want to me to check a university?"

"No Bernadette, I need you to see a Doctor David Lim at the Biological Sciences Centre. He has a sample of the Bio Bugs; he said he has something special to show us. I have no people to send, and since I knew you were around . . ."

"And off the case."

Anton paused. "Okay, yes off the case . . . but I thought maybe you'd do me this favor and see what this Doctor has."

Bernadette laughed. "You know Anton—I just love giving you a hard time—of course I'll do it."

Anton said, "Hey thanks, I'm sending a text of the address, and I'll let Doctor Lim know you're coming."

"No sweat. I'll let you know my impressions of the Doctor's findings and call you later today." Bernadette ended the call and punched the address from Anton's text into her Jeep's GPS.

She had no plans for today, other than a run with Sprocket, and hope that her neighbor Harvey would invite her over for a barbeque. They had started a tradition of hanging out together on Sundays some months back. Harvey had knocked on her door; casually saying he had "way too many ribs, beans and potato salad for just himself . . . and if she wasn't doing anything . . ."

Bernadette was glad to join Harvey. The three of them, Harvey, Bernadette and Sprocket, would hang out on Harvey's back porch eating barbeque, and swapping stories. Harvey was the closest thing she had to family in her new city of Red Deer, and it felt good.

Traffic was light on Sunday morning, and Bernadette arrived at the Biological Sciences Building on the University of Calgary campus. It dawned on her as she found parking close by the building that university would not start for another two weeks. She remembered her own university years in Criminal Justice; parking was always a problem . . . but then she'd never owned a car.

A security guard at the front of the building called Doctor Lim, and a tall, thin Asian man in a white lab coat came out of the elevator to meet her, "Detective Callahan," He pumped her hand in efficient quick strokes, "delighted you could come on short notice."

"Happy to be here," Bernadette replied, but she was still puzzled as to what she was here to witness.

Dr. Lim's thin eyebrows knitted into a frown. "You may not be so happy after my demonstration."

Bernadette followed the doctor as he ushered her into his lab on the third floor. The lab was what Bernadette expected, glass tubes running in different directions and numerous machines that hummed and flashed green lights.

The doctor gave her a set of protective eyewear and motioned for her to stand in front of a small plate glass window. Behind it was a stainless-steel pipe. "I received these specimens from Dr. Andrew in Red Deer yesterday. The doctor and I once worked together in the Aberdeen Genetics Diagnostics Laboratory, and he was good enough to inform me of the abnormal biological life forms he discovered."

Bernadette looked hard at Doctor Lim. He had either worked with Doctor Keith Andrew when Lim was very young, or Dr. Lim was much older than he looked. She stood transfixed over the glass looking into an opaque liquid. "What should I be looking at?"

The doctor looked somewhat dismayed. "Oh sorry, I haven't released them yet." He opened a heavy door on one end of the pipe, inserted a piece of iron, and then closed it using a heavy sealed latch mechanism. Bernadette thought a submarine door had less of a closure.

From a vault in the wall, Dr. Lim removed a tiny vial and dropped it into the opening of the pipe. Bernadette watched the vial open, and the iron start to glow. "I saw something similar in Red Deer. Dr. Andrew said the Bio Bugs were aggressive and ate the pipe . . . do you have anything new?" Bernadette looked up at the doctor.

"New?"

"Yes, new. I've already seen them devour metal . . . has anything changed?"

Doctor Lim removed his protective glasses, and wiped them with a cloth, "Yes, I guess I forgot to mention this in my conversation with Agent Anton . . . it's the rate of acceleration . . . look at the pipe again."

Bernadette looked at the metal pipe—it was gone. "Oh my God, it didn't happen that fast in Red Deer on Friday . . . what happened?"

"These biological forms or Bio Bugs as you call them have become more aggressive in the past 24 hours. They've speeded up. I estimate that if one small vial of thirty milliliters was placed inside a pipeline . . . its rate of acceleration would be . . ." The doctor looked up at the ceiling as he did the calculations. "About seventy kilometers per hour."

"That is aggressive. That means if left undiscovered, this small vial could wipe out just under 2000 kilometers of pipeline in 24 hours. This could wipe out many pipeline networks in both Canada and the United States in a very short time." Bernadette said.

"At its present rate," the doctor added, "I think they may speed up even more, and double within the next few days. There seems to be some kind of acceleration agent attached to the organisms."

"Which means?"

"That if these are unleashed into North America, there will not be a drop of oil moving unless it's in a tanker truck or rail car, and the Bio Bugs could learn to have a taste for them as well."

"I don't get it. Someone told me that Bio Bugs were passive things that calmly chewed raw sewage and could turn stuff into methane. What's up with these little guys?" Bernadette peered down through the heavy glass window again. Only a small outline remained.

The doctor took off his protective glasses. "Someone changed their DNA. I've never seen this before, but these microbes have been engineered to become more vicious the longer they are exposed to the elements of iron and oil."

Bernadette pulled her head up from the glass window. She had become entranced looking at the pipe residue. "Did you know about the attack on the young man, Nathan Taylor?" Bernadette took off her own eyewear. "Dr. Andrew claimed the man was attacked through his blood stream due to the high amount of iron in his blood. Will these microbes attack humans as well?"

"Yes . . . I have to say they would. I reviewed Dr. Andrew's study, and the notes he sent on the victim, Nathan Taylor. I believe the microbes will attack any human through a break in the skin, or an entry through the mouth, nose, or ears."

"Why is that?"

"The microbes confuse fats in human blood with oil."

"Fats? What kind of fats?"

Dr. Lim smiled. "The high fats that come from a diet of fatty fast foods. Most of North America has too much fat in their diet, which ends up in their blood."

Bernadette paused. "Yeah, I remember seeing Nathan Taylor's room; it was full of fried chicken and pizza boxes. The kid made himself a fertile ground for a killer micro attack. Who knew?" She thought for a moment of her own love of high fat food and shook her head slightly.

Dr. Lim took off his gloves. "I hope this demonstration was useful to you, detective." He started to walk toward the exit door. Bernadette could see the demonstration, and her visit was over. Dr. Lim was a busy man.

Bernadette said. "Yes, this has been very impressive. I'll report this to Agent Anton De Luca, and I'm sure the Canadian Security and Intelligence Agency will be in touch."

The Doctor paused as they walked out the hallway and to the elevator. "Detective, you must explain to them about the acceleration . . . right now . . . I have no idea how it's happening or how to stop it. I would need a team of scientist in this lab to work on it. I don't have the manpower right now. I don't know if any university does."

Bernadette touched Doctor Lim on the shoulder. "Thank you for your concern, doctor. I'm sure once the proper authorities see your report, they will mobilize the forces to take care of it." Bernadette shook his hand and got in the elevator.

Walking into the bright afternoon sunshine, Bernadette knew the forces that would be mobilized would be the oil companies. Many of them had labs with more funding and more scientists than the universities, but what if they couldn't unlock the aggressive pattern of the Bio Bugs? She knew who probably could . . . it would be Professor Alistair McAllen. She found him once . . . she needed to find him again.

Bernadette tried to call Anton and got transferred to his voice mail. She sent him an email. Her message was simple. From what she had just seen, if the Bio Bugs were unleashed into a major pipeline in America or Canada, they could wipe out an entire pipeline network if left undetected.

Bernadette hesitated at the end of her message. She wasn't sure how to express it without sounding alarmist, but she finally wrote: *You need to locate Professor Alistair McAllen to stop these Bio Bugs or learn how to tame them. Dr. Lim thinks they will also attack humans!"*

Professor Alistair McAllen took a drink of his iced water and told his housekeeper she could leave for the afternoon. He sat in the shade of his back courtyard, the special design of most Mexican and Yucatan houses. The house didn't look like anything special from the front, just a large wooden door opening onto the street.

But the front foyer led into a long hallway and all the rooms led off from a courtyard with a dipping pool and hanging garden. The home once belonged to Spanish nobility. Intricate tile floors and walls inlaid with rare woods spoke of their power and wealth.

McAllen rented the house on a long-term lease from a landlord that accepted double the rent for his privacy with few questions asked. He was able to add his own laboratory with the promise that he wasn't doing anything illegal, just a few "hobby experiments," he'd told the landlord.

He sat in his laboratory now and uploaded the USB stick that Goodman had sent him. Until now, McAllen had only heard rumors of what Goodman and his fellow students were up to. As the design of the microbes appeared on the screen, he leaned back in his chair and muttered, "Oh my god, Goodman, what the hell did you do?"

Zara watched Adlan through the bead curtain that separated the kitchen from the small living room. The heat was stifling in the late day when the concrete buildings of Barcelona gave off their heat like an oven door left open too long.

Adlan talked quietly and softly to four young men in the room. Zara knew his methods. If the young man was Muslim, he told him to wreak his vengeance in the name of Allah. If the young man was Christian, he was to go forth in the name of Christ. But if a young man was godless, if no god called to him because the sheer violence of mankind had left him void of religion—Adlan told him to go forth in the name of vengeance itself.

Adlan only wanted the fighters to attack Russians. The war that Russia had declared over in Chechnya in 2009 was never over to Adlan. As long as one Russian remained on Chechen soil, there was a war to Adlan. Now, he was no longer satisfied with suicide bombings and small attacks on Russian convoys. He wanted to hurt Russia economically. Russia was a powerhouse in oil and gas. If Russia had this power of oil, Europe and his Chechnya would be under its control.

Zara's discovery of the Bio Bugs had given Adlan a new weapon. In the living room, he gave each young man several vials, instructions for their use, touched their foreheads to his, and wished them good fortune.

Chapter Thirteen

Bernadette pulled into her driveway at just past three in the afternoon. A beat up old pickup truck in her driveway announced she had company. She parked beside it, got out her bag and headed for the front door. She knew who would be inside. Grandma Moses had arrived.

Her front door was open; Bernadette knew Grandma Moses would have convinced her neighbor Harvey to open it up. There in the living room, in Bernadette's favorite lounger in front of the television, sat Grandma Moses. The same faded print dress hung over her large frame, white sport socks falling down into old running shoes, and grey hair in two simple braids.

"Hi, Grandma—how are you?"

Grandma Moses looked up from the television show she was watching. "Good Bernie, how are you?"

"I'm good." Bernadette stood there. There was no use in entering into conversation unless Grandma Moses wanted to. She would tell Bernadette whatever she wanted to tell her in due time. To her grandma, there were no pleasantries, no catching up. She existed in right now, in the moment. If you asked her how she was, *"Good,"* would be the answer. If you asked her about her drive down from the reservation, "*Good,*" would be the answer.

Small talk was not a strong suit for Grandma Moses. When she wanted to talk about something important, it would be about your dreams. "How are your dreams?" she would ask. Her soft brown eyes would search Bernadette's face when she was young, as if the merest flicker of an eyebrow would bring something to the surface.

Grandma Moses never followed the Catholic faith like Bernadette's mother or the others on the reservation. She followed the native Dene faith. The spirits of Manitou and the Windigo were real to her.

"I'm going to go for a run with my dog . . . you need anything?" Bernadette asked as she walked to her bedroom to change into her running gear.

Grandma Moses' eyes never left the television set. "No, I'm good." She changed channels from one reality show to the next. On the screen, people were running through an obstacle course while objects were being thrown at them.

Bernadette went next door and knocked on her neighbor Harvey's door. Harvey answered wearing shorts and a t-shirt that said, "***Drill baby, Drill*.**" Someone in the USA had sent it to him as a joke. Harvey took it as an affirmation.

"Hey Bernie, I hope it's okay I let your grandma in. She didn't seem comfortable with me, so I let her into your place."

Bernadette patted Harvey on the arm. "I'm glad you did. She's made herself right at home." Sprocket saw her in her running clothes and was out Harvey's door and at Bernadette's legs in anticipation of the run.

Harvey stood, watching Bernadette and her dog, not quite knowing what to say, unsure of what the arrival of her grandma meant. The old lady was very unusual; she made him feel uncomfortable in that she didn't say much. Harvey could talk to anyone, but the old lady was beyond him.

"I'm doing some brisket on the barbecue . . . if you want to come . . . you know . . . you and your grandma . . . that is if she's up for company?" Harvey finally said.

Bernadette was kneeling down rubbing Sprockets ears. "Hey, that would be great Harvey." She stood up and placed her hand on Harvey's shoulder. "I know my grandma seems a little standoffish and quiet, but she really does appreciate company."

Harvey relaxed and smiled, "How long is she staying?"

Bernadette started her run, Sprocket lopping at her side. "I have no idea," she yelled over her shoulder as she sprinted to the sidewalk and headed down the road.

She smiled to herself; she really didn't know how long Grandma Moses would be here. She would arrive somewhere, stay awhile, and move on. That was just her way. She had no telephone, no Internet, didn't write to people, would just show up and there she would be in a living room somewhere drinking tea, and watching television.

Grandmother Moses raised Bernadette for a few years until she went off to school in Edmonton. Her Grandmother came to her one morning and told her that she saw Bernadette in a dream. She was wearing red, and a flag with a maple leaf flew over her head. She told Bernadette she needed to go to school off the reservation to achieve the dream.

Many years later, when Bernadette was getting her RCMP graduation picture taken, she remembered the words of her grandmother's dream. Bernadette was standing straight, wearing the scarlet tunic of the Royal Canadian Mounted Police, and the red Maple leaf of the Canadian flag was in the background.

Bernadette settled into an easy run. She decided she needed at least an hour, and maybe more. Sprocket galloped beside her, tongue hanging out, looking up at her, and then at the trail ahead. While Bernadette was away, he spent his days with Harvey mostly walking, and running was what Sprocket craved.

Thoughts of the recent case roamed around in Bernadette's head. She was off the case, as usual when something got good, but it couldn't stop her from thinking of it. Sometime tomorrow, she would call Anton, and talk to him about tracking Professor McAllen.

They came to the river trail and fell into another easy pace, sometimes passing other runners, and sometimes being passed. The sun was high, the smell of wildflowers and evergreen made a pungent smell in the hot late afternoon air.

Bernadette got lost in the run, just her breathing, and the pumping of legs and arms, the feeling of one foot leaving the earth and coming down and again. When she was younger, she thought running was like leaping up into the sky with each step—then falling down to earth again.

Two hawks circled high overhead while some magpies squawked and flew from one tree to another, watching and defending their young from the hawks. A squadron of small birds took to the air to chase the hawks away. Bernadette raised her head now and again to watch the aerial display.

She arrived back to her house panting, tired and happy. She gave Sprocket water and drank a big glass herself. Grandma Moses looked up from her chair and switched off the television "They threw me off the reservation," was all she said on her way to the bathroom.

Bernadette let her grandma's words sink in as she showered and changed into jeans and a t-shirt. She knocked on her grandmas door, and told her they were invited next door for a barbeque. Her Grandma came out of the bedroom and smiled. "I like barbeque."

Harvey was his usual talkative self, fussing about with the grill, putting out plates and cutlery on the outside deck table. A few small lanterns hung outside, and the smell of three mosquito coils drifted by, providing a pungent smell to the sweet smell of beef in sauce on the grill.

Harvey had made one of his excellent potato salads, grilled some corn on the cob and his beef brisket was tender with a spicy crust. They ate while watching the stars come out as the sky darkened. Grandma Moses said very little. Sprocket lay at her feet while she looked up at the sky. The moon was only a sliver of light. As a wave of geese flew over, Grandma Moses said, "They need to find their rest."

Harvey lifted his head. "Who does?"

"The geese," Grandma Moses answered. "They were feeding too far out, getting fat on grain; they need to find their pond before last light. To protect themselves from the coyotes and weasels, they will sleep in a pond tonight."

"Oh . . . the geese," was all Harvey could venture. These were the first words he'd heard Grandma Moses speak that evening.

She then rose up, thanked Harvey for the meal, and shuffled back to Bernadette's place. Her worn-out sneakers squeaked her progress as she moved with Sprocket following her, his nose down and an inch from her heels.

When Grandma Moses had closed the front door,

Harvey looked up at Bernadette. "Your Grandma's quite the lady."

Bernadette shook her head. "Yeah, she is quite the lady, and quite strange. I've lived with that all my life. When she wants to talk, she'll talk your ear off, but it will be about the ways of the world or how she sees your progress in it. When she makes small talk that's all it is . . . talk that is really small." Bernadette shook her head again and laughed at her own joke.

Bernadette took a sip of her red wine, "Harvey, there's something I wanted to talk to you about. You were involved in pipelines at one time, weren't you?"

"Yeah, off and on, in between drilling for oil. What do you need to know?"

"I saw something today in a lab; someone invented a virus or Bio Bug that could eat metal. This Professor who showed me the demonstration said these bugs could eat pipelines at a rate of 70 kilometers an hour— "

"Wow, that's fast."

"Well, that's not the worst of it. He said he thought this thing could double its speed in time."

Harvey let out a low whistle and took a long swig of his red wine. "Oh, my god, Bernadette, something like that, let loose on a long length of pipeline, you're talking major destruction."

"Okay, I already got the doomsday scenario from the university Professor, but how could you stop it, like shut a valve down . . . you know . . . like block it maybe?"

"The shutdown valves for pipelines are metal, so if this bug is attacking the outer pipeline, it'll destroy them, too. The only way to stop it would be to find out where it's going, and destroy the pipe in between—kind of like a fire break in a forest fire."

Bernadette drained the last of her wine and stood up. "That's at least some help." She yawned and stretched. "How about if I clean up for you?"

Harvey smiled. "Hey, why don't you go spend some time with your grandma, I'm sleeping in tomorrow."

Bernadette gave Harvey a big hug and went back to her own place. When she arrived, Grandma Moses was sitting back in the lounge chair; the place was in semi darkness, the television off.

"Grandma Moses, did you want to talk about getting thrown off the reservation?" Bernadette ventured as she took a chair across from her.

"No, this is the third time, I always get back on—that's not a problem."

"Oh, right, then everything is okay then?"

Grandma Moses looked at Bernadette, leaned forward and took her hand. "Bernadette, I had a dream that you are going to die."

Bernadette almost jumped back in her chair; she had never seen her grandma so intense. "Die, me . . . when . . . how?

Grandma Moses moved closer off the chair. "I saw a vision of you with a dark, tall man, there was bright sunshine—he is supposed to protect you—he fails."

Bernadette sat staring into her grandma's eyes. "Grandma, I'm in the business of protecting people, and I deal with people who are not very nice. My partner in the detective team is a short, white guy. Maybe you had some bad food the night of your dream . . ."

"Bernadette, my visions are always clear. You need to stay away from this man." Grandma Moses rose slowly from the chair and walked to her room. Sprocket followed her with only a sideways glance at Bernadette.

Bernadette sat back in her chair, regarding her grandmas words, and almost like a poker player went through the odds of her Grandmother being right. Even as a young girl she was careful to follow her instructions, but the dreams weren't always right, not always accurate. She decided she would never take a tall dark partner on the detective team and stay out of bright sunlight when being shot at. With those final thoughts bouncing around her head, she went to bed.

Chapter Fourteen

When Bernadette came out of her bedroom at 6:30 a.m., Grandma Moses was sitting in the chair in front of the television with Sprocket nestled at her feet.

"Coffee?" Bernadette asked as she went into the kitchen. She knew the conversation from last night about dreams of her death would not come up. Grandma Moses mentioned things only once . . . and to the wise . . . that was enough said.

Grandma Moses shut off the television and followed her into the kitchen. "No, I had tea, been up for a while." She sat down at the kitchen table facing Bernadette, "I'm leaving today, going south."

Bernadette turned and looked at her grandmother. She always wondered how old she was. She seemed timeless, just like she dropped onto the earth with those creases on her face, and small lips that rarely smiled. She smiled with her eyes; they twinkled when she was happy.

"How far south?" Bernadette asked.

"Montana."

"We have relatives in Montana?"

Grandma Moses looked out the window; the sun was just starting to rise. A small tree in the backyard filled with birds. "We don't have relatives in Montana. I'm going to the Sundance Ceremony."

Bernadette filled her coffee cup and added her usual mix of cream and sugar. She sat down at the kitchen table and placed her hand on her grandma's wrinkled brown hand. "Grandma, are you going to watch or participate . . . you know one of the ones' dancing and praying?" Bernadette's voice was edged with concern. The participants did not eat or drink for four days.

Grandma Moses put her other hand on top of Bernadette's. "I will be dancing and praying. Don't worry about me, I haven't seen my death yet in my dreams . . . I'll be okay." She got up from the table and Bernadette followed her as she headed for the door. Sprocket followed at her heels.

"Grandma, do you intend to take the dog?" Bernadette asked. She was just a little anxious about her grandma's answer.

Grandma Moses turned back to Bernadette and looked down at Sprocket; she spoke to him in Dene. The dog lowered his head, and with another sideways glance at Bernadette, he took his place by the chair in the living room.

"Thanks Grandma. He's a good running partner."

"I spoke with your dog." Grandma Moses leveled her gaze at Bernadette. "He told me you need to have more sex . . . run much less."

Bernadette watched her grandma go out the door and turned to Sprocket. "So, you ratted on me to grandma."

The dog looked up at her; one eyebrow raised, and then put its head down on the floor in obvious shame.

Grandma Moses backed her old pickup truck out of the driveway. A cloud of black smoke billowed out of the exhaust pipe, the gears clashed, and she was gone. Bernadette watched as the trucks taillights disappeared. She shook her head; the old woman did not have a cell phone, much less a phone in her home. The Internet, Facebook, and Twitter were foreign to her, and yet she move around from place to place with ease.

Bernadette filled a thermos travel mug with coffee and headed for work. She arrived at a little past seven to a wonderful sarcastic reception from the other detectives and RCMP officers asking her how the vacation in Victoria was. Some wanted to know if she had time for any of the tourist sites. One wanted to know if she'd brought back any salmon. She smiled, waved at them, and headed for her desk.

After a meeting with her chief of detectives, and then meeting with the other detectives, she was caught up with recent cases, warrants, and reacquainted with the pile of paperwork on her desk. Sometime around 5 p.m. she took time to look at the number of text messages she had. There were seven from Anton. He had some questions about her meeting with Doctor Lim at the University of Calgary.

Bernadette pushed her paperwork aside, took a sip of her freshly brewed coffee and dialed Anton's number, putting her feet up on her desk.

"Bernadette—finally! Look, I didn't want to bother you at your detachment by phoning you," Anton said when he answered.

Bernadette chuckled, "And seven text messages—this is not bothering to you?" She took a swig of her coffee,

"Anton, I'd like to see what happens when you're really trying to get hold of someone."

Anton paused. "Yeah, okay, seven texts are a little excessive, but this report from this Doctor Lim at the University has a lot of people on edge."

Bernadette flicked a piece of lint off her t-shirt. "How about Patterson, the wonder boy who kicked me off the case—just how edgy is he?"

"There is a saying in Italian for Patterson's situation, *intrapplato nella merda profunda,* which means trapped in deep shit. The FBI are pissed that we let something this big get invented and get into America."

"Wait, don't they have an FBI Agent with the guy who bought it from our Canadians?" Bernadette took her feet off her desk and grabbed a piece of paper to start doodling people and contacts. Her mind worked best in visuals, even if it was visual doodles.

"Yeah, I know, but the FBI thought the pipeline killer thing was a farce until they saw the report from Doctor Lim . . ."

"And now they're scared shitless—oops, I mean witless," Bernadette said.

"You could say that, but the Russians, man, they're the ones who are throwing the most heat."

"What's up with them?"

"Well, for starters, they think Zara Mashhadov should never gotten into our Country, fake identity or not, and they are very upset she landed in Europe with a whole batch of Bio Bugs they know are going to be unleashed on them." Anton paused for a moment, and lowered his voice, "I heard the Russians threaten that Patterson better never set foot on Russian soil as they would love to show him their displeasure."

"Wow," Bernadette said as she doodled. She had scribbled a stick picture of Patterson with a club over his head and big NYET sign. It looked good to her. "So, other than to fill me in, how can I help you?"

Anton paused; his breathing was audible over the phone. "You could help us find Professor McAllen, who all the higher ups think might be able to find the antidote to these Bio Bugs."

Bernadette sat up straight in her chair, "So now McAllen is of interest to you. What changed?"

"Someone in authority in the US and Canadian governments realized that these bugs could cause massive infrastructure damage to pipelines and get this." Anton lowered his voice again. It was obvious to Bernadette there were others nearby. "Someone in a senior government position has floated a theory that these bugs could go viral and attack other metal works—like buildings, railways, ships, who knows? I just got off the phone with Patterson and he was almost foaming at the mouth."

"And they think McAllen could help in this? But do you think he will? Remember he's a wanted man in the USA and Canada. We've put a price on his head, and he doesn't like oil companies. Did anyone think of that? You know those guys in high places who think when we find McAllen that he'll jump to our rescue?"

"They've put complete immunity for McAllen on the table. He produces an antidote, and just like that they'll absolve him and all his friends of all past crimes as well. A complete pardon."

"Wow," Bernadette said. "That's a pretty desperate measure. Are you sure that Martin Popowich doesn't have any idea how to turn the Bio Bugs off? I mean after all, didn't he work on the project with Goodman?"

Anton hesitated for a moment . . . a door slammed behind him as he walked into a secluded office. "Okay, here's the thing. Assad grilled Popowich about the Bio Bug formula, and whether he could turn it off or stop them. Popowich is like a second year Chemistry student—he has no idea. He swears Goodman was the brains."

Bernadette said, "Yeah, but Goodman's brains were last seen splattered by a 10-inch frying pan all over his ex-girlfriend's kitchen, and according to the computer techs the formula has been taken from Goodman's computer—probably by Zara."

"Popowich thinks Goodman was in contact with McAllen. He said that Goodman bragged that only he knew where McAllen was."

Bernadette leaned back in her chair, rested the pad of paper on her lap. "Okay, so the hunt is on, and you're admitting—sorry . . . asking your best female detective RCMP tracker in all of Canada back onto the case?"

Anton paused. "Good god Bernadette, you're making it sound like I've got to do penance and three Hail Mary's to get you back."

Bernadette laughed. "God, I love it when you beg Anton. Okay, I'm yours. I'll go tell my chief I'm working with the slick, tall dark Italian from CSIS." Bernadette said the words tall and dark, and the memory of her grandma's words sent a chill down her spine.

"Hey, Bernadette that's great, I'm glad you're on board in your usual humble style. When can you be in Edmonton to start work?"

Bernadette did not answer. She wished her grandmother had never said anything to her about her dreams. But these were just dreams—she needed to get this crazy stuff out of her head.

"Bernadette, you still there?"

"Yeah, Anton, I'm here. Just writing some things down." Bernadette sat up, ran her fingers through her hair and took a deep breath. "Look, I've got to clear a few things with my chief. I'll get back to you by tomorrow as to when I can come up, okay?"

"No problems, take all the time you need, just get here yesterday . . . you know the drill."

Bernadette hung up the phone, scratched out the words "*Tall, Dark*" that she had written on her pad. She had no idea why she would write that. She breathed deeply, took a big swig of her coffee, and pulled the mountain of paperwork towards her. She needed to get her mind off her grandmother and her dreams.

McAllen sat in the courtyard of his villa in Merida, Mexico, with his laptop perched on the dining table. It was late evening. The courtyard was cool; a small waterfall provided a soothing background noise, and a noisy parrot punctuated the evening stillness with screeches.

McAllen did not like the parrot. His friends, Sebastian, Percy, and Theo, had bought it for him before they left for Ecuador. It was, "Something to remember them by," they said before they piled into a minivan and headed south. He would rather they had given him a turtle or a fish. The parrot screeched again, just to remind him how much he disliked it. McAllen thought the feeling between him, and the parrot was mutual.

For the past few days, McAllen had been trying to unlock the formula that Goodman had used to make the Bio Bugs so aggressive. First, he had to find out where

Goodman got the original Bio Bugs. The one thing that McAllen had loved about Goodman was that he showed his work. He wasn't one to produce a formula without showing how he got there.

McAllen took a pull of the Corona beer by his side, and munched on some fresh taco chips his housekeeper had made. A small drop of pico de gallo made a splat beside his keyboard; he frowned and wiped it away with his hand and sucked on his fingers.

The key he was looking for was deep into several pages of text that Goodman had made. There were also a few scans of articles about the Titanic that McAllen came to. He shook his head and took another pull of his beer while examining the article. It was right there before his eyes. In December of 2010, two researchers from Dalhousie University discovered new metal-eating bacteria from the Titanic that were super aggressive.

The bacteria were dubbed BHI and were claimed to be consuming the Titanic at a rate much faster than expected. They even claimed it was indeed a "bad bacteria."

The other scanned sheet of information was an article with headlines claiming *Metal-Eating Bacteria Corrode Pipes in Oil Industry.* Researchers unraveled how certain types of bacteria were able to use iron in the metabolic process.

McAllen sat back and let his thought processes work over the two pieces of information. Goodman had obviously acquired a sample of the BHI bacteria and enhanced its metabolism. There was already a picture of the pipeline on the web in Red Deer that had been affected by the Bio Bugs. He could see this was not any normal leak. The pipeline had been turned into a Swiss cheese of perforated holes.

The formula was there, the Bio Bug was there, and as

the last light ebbed out of the Yucatan sky, McAllen saw exactly what Goodman had done. The link he had used to turn on the Bio Bugs.

A small note claimed that VMAT2 + BHI = NANITES. This was a footnote on page 10, and then there was something else. McAllen had skimmed over it the first time. There was a video link embedded in the document.

McAllen clicked the video link, and Goodman appeared. He was sitting in front of his laptop, in what looked like the University laboratory.

Goodman leaned into the webcam and began, "Professor Mac, I'm sorry . . . if you received this document, then probably something has gone very wrong." He pulled back from the laptop briefly. "My goal was to present this to you in person. I was proud of my little Bio Bugs . . . the nanites."

McAllen put the video on pause and picked up a pen and paper. He was hoping Goodman might give him some clues on how to develop a countermeasure to the formula. He clicked the foreword button.

"As you may have seen," Goodman said in the video, "the nanites are highly aggressive. I'm kind of proud of that. You see, I had to use some molecular biology and with some help from the biology wing and the developments in MAGE, I was able to isolate the VMAT2 and splice it with the BHI Bio Bugs from the Titanic." Goodman paused and smiled. "I know, pretty awesome, isn't it?"

Goodman put his head down for a minute, and then brought his eyes up to focus on the screen, "The only problem is Professor, I don't know how to turn it off or stop these things. My original test in the lab showed these things keep multiplying and speeding up. The first time we put them in a pipeline in Red Deer, they would have destroyed everything for miles, if the pipeline had not been disconnected." Goodman paused, "And something else you should know is these Bio Bugs become even more aggressive in salt water. You've seen from my notes where I got the bugs from," Goodman shrugged on screen, "Okay, I'm kind of proud of finding these bugs from the Titanic," Goodman frowned, "But when we put them in salt water, they developed into a wave that worked together to source out metal. I can't explain it, but hopefully no one will let these go in the ocean before a way to stop them is found.

The screen went blank for a second, and then came on again. "Professor, I'm sending this formula to you, and perhaps you can find a countermeasure for my invention . . . sorry to be such a screw-up." Goodman reached forward to the webcam on top of the laptop, and the screen went black.

McAllen made his notes. The MAGE that Goodman had mentioned was a term for Multiplex Automated Genome Engineering. With this novel technique, a research team could rapidly refine the design of bacteria by editing multiple genes in parallel instead of targeting one gene at a time.

He reasoned that someone at the university must have helped Goodman to isolate the gene he needed in the BHI bacteria, and helped him splice that with the VMAT2 gene, the God gene as it was called.

The God gene had been discovered some years earlier and was claimed to have the code for production of neurotransmitters that regulate mood in humans. "But what would the gene do in bacteria?" McAllen wondered.

Here were bacteria, brought up from the depths of the ocean that had been feasting on the Titanic for decades, and thought to be aggressive. How would it react with a spliced-on dose of attitude? The forming of waves in salt water to seek out metal was the strangest thing McAllen had ever heard of. This could only mean the bugs had developed into some kind of sentient being. They somehow worked together, like what fish did when schooling for synchronized hunting or protection. He wondered if the bugs had learned this from years of being on the Titanic.

McAllen faced a problem. He had an idea how to turn off the aggressive bug that Goodman had created. But he hated oil companies. He blamed them for the leukemia that killed his children. Living beside a large refinery for years as he did research for oil companies—he should have known better. But the money was good back then; until he watched his children die a slow death. This Bio Bug displayed before him would destroy pipelines, and probably even refineries. This little bug could level the playing field. But it could also create a massive attack on all metal infrastructures in the world.

How large was his hatred? He wondered. How far did it reach? He sat back, finished his beer, and wondered what he would do.

Chapter Fifteen

Sarah Collins closed the door softly to the room on the third floor of the Courtyard Marriott Hotel in Missoula Montana and made her way to the elevator. Hensley was still asleep at seven in the morning. The extra sleeping pill Sarah had crushed up into his milk the night before would give her the time she needed to meet with the FBI agents detailed to shadow her.

The morning breakfast crowd in the lobby was mostly oil workers piling their plates at the buffet. Sarah made eye contact with a man and woman and followed them to a quiet area in the lounge.

The woman was Carla Winston, black, mid-forties, dressed in jeans and t-shirt. The man was Luis Valdes, late twenties, a slender, good-looking Latino with just a bit of swagger that let people know how handsome he thought he was. Sarah never really liked Luis; she always felt he was judging her for having to sleep with Hensley. And he was.

Sarah sipped her coffee as she sat in the lounge chair.

Carla sat beside her, and Luis took up a position beside Carla to be on the lookout in case Hensley should walk in the room. They had newspapers with them, raised up as they spoke as if discussing the day's news that issued forth from USA Today.

Carla looked up from her paper. "How's Hensley holding up?"

Sarah didn't look up from her paper. She took a sip of her coffee. "He has a bit of a fever. That broken tooth of his is nasty, and he's become a real pain in the ass. He doesn't want to travel today. He said last night he wanted to stay another day."

Valdes looked in Sarah's direction. "Maybe Hensley wants a little more Sarah time—wadda ya think? He set his shiny white teeth into a smile, perhaps showing he was only joking. Sarah wanted to launch out of her seat and throw her coffee in his face.

Carla saw Sarah's jaw line ripple with tension. "Valdes, how about if you do recon from that chair over there" She motioned with her paper to a chair twenty feet away. "I'll continue with the briefing from here."

Valdes' smile faded. He took his paper and coffee and moved out of earshot of both Carla and Sarah. Carla turned to face Sarah. "Look, I know Valdes is a bit of an asshole, but he does care for you. He's totally pissed that you have to spend time with Hensley. He's always mouthing off about how stupid the FBI is for putting ladies like you in this position."

Sarah turned her paper and took a quick survey of the room. "Yeah, I know, all the male FBI agents think this is a nasty detail, because none of them have to do it." She leaned over slightly towards Carla. "You know how many times I've wanted to strangle Hensley in his sleep? When that son of a bitch wants to cuddle at night and cup my breasts just like my boyfriend Jonas—you don't think I want to throw an elbow into his face?" A small unwanted tear made its way down her face—she brushed it away.

Carla dropped her paper. She wanted to touch Sarah, grab her, and give her a hug. She couldn't do any of that. Words were all she had. "Look, girl, I know this is the bottom of the pit for shit details, but there was no other way we could get close and follow this guy."

Sarah squared her shoulders and picked up her paper. "Hey, it's okay, I'm over it. Big girls don't cry. Do you have any more Intel on what the agency thinks these Eco Warriors are up to?

"We thought Hensley might tell you. The other members have disappeared. The agents tracking them lost them near Seattle." Carla scanned the room one more time before looking in Sarah's direction. "These guys don't communicate by cell phone or use the net. This is the most low-tech surveillance I've ever been on."

"Yeah, I hear you. Hensley won't let me in on any of his plans. He moves the vials with the Bio Bugs into our room every night and puts them under his bed. I have no idea how he communicates with the others." Sarah took a sip of her coffee. "He did let on that in two days' time they would commit a very large action—something that would get them noticed."

"Does he tell you where you're headed?"

"Nope . . . we get up every day, and I have no idea until the car is heading out of the parking lot. Sometimes we double back—sometimes we stop—he's always watching the traffic behind us as I drive. He's looking for cars or trucks that follow us to see if they're tailing us," Sarah said.

"We've been careful. We change the chase cars every 10 to 15 miles, and then rent new ones in each town. Has he had any suspicions?"

"Not yet—none that he's mentioned, but when we get into the wide open Montana countryside, traffic on the roads is pretty sparse. I expect you'll have a problem."

Carla stopped for a moment. A person who looked like Hensley walked into the room, she watched him meet with some other oil workers. "We already have a drone ordered and there will be Black Hawk helicopters a few miles back—he won't see us."

"I hope not, he's been getting edgy lately."

"What kind of edgy?" Carla looked directly at Sarah. She had to fight the urge not to touch Sarah's arm.

"He goes through my stuff all the time, my toiletry bag, and even my tampons looking for tracking devices. He says the Fed could be planting stuff on us when we are out of our hotel room." Sarah shifted in her chair. "He gives me these full body massages that he says are to relax me, but I can tell the way he touches me—he's looking for the microchip tracking device under my skin."

"Look, you need to be careful. The moment you think your cover is blown; you take this guy down and bring us in. We don't need him trying anything on you."

"As in trying what? The guy is 100 pounds soaking wet. I could throw the little jerk across the room."

Carla paused before she said; "I hope you can do that in your sleep, too."

Sarah bit her lip. "Look, I'm in this for the long haul. We need to follow this guy to the leaders of the movement and get all of them at once, take them out of the equation." She put her paper down and got up to leave. "I'd better be getting back to the room. This thing should be over in a few days."

Carla watched Sarah pick up another coffee and head towards the elevator. Valdes came back and sat beside her. "That is one tough lady." Carla said.

Valdes stared in Sarah's direction. "I'm sorry if I was out of line with her. I have an older sister about her age—I don't like what the Agency is making her do."

"No, none of us rank and file does, but the bosses think this is the big plan—get in close and destroy these guys from the inside."

"Did you tell her what we found out about Hensley?"

Carla stared at Valdes. "No, I didn't tell her."

Valdes leaned towards Carla, his voice down to a whisper. "You don't think she should know we found Hensley's DNA on a dead female FBI agent—the one who was trying to infiltrate his group six months ago?"

Carla looked away from Valdes. "This thing is over in two days. If I tell her about the previous agent, she's liable to kill Hensley the next time he tries to touch her. She's tough, but she's also volatile right now. I'll need to handle her carefully."

Sarah balanced her coffee as she slid the key card into the door of the room. The lights were still low. She assumed Hensley was still sleeping. She closed the door softly behind her and walked quietly into the room. She didn't notice Hensley wasn't in bed.

Hensley came at her from the bathroom as she walked past. He threw his arm around her, and put her into a chokehold. "Bitch—where the hell you been all this time—who the hell you been talking to?" He was breathing heavy. His arm was shaking.

She dropped her coffee and instinctively grabbed his arm with both of hers. She had to keep her airway clear—stop herself from choking and passing out. "I was down getting a coffee . . . I wanted to let you sleep."

His breath was hot, his voice a strange whisper. "I woke up the moment you left—it takes 45 minutes to get a coffee?" He tried to squeeze harder, but Sarah pulled his arm forward, denying him the leverage around her throat.

"The place was packed with oilmen and tourists; I found a place in the lounge and read the newspaper." Everything in her screamed to stay calm, she'd been placed in a chokehold numerous time in training. Her instinct was to throw her left leg behind his, pound him with her right elbow and throw him to the floor. A quick punch to the solar plexus or throat would end this in a second. It would also reveal her cover.

Hensley tried to squeeze harder. "I should end you right here bitch, just leave you right here . . ."

"Who's going to drive the car? You need me for that." Sarah blurted out the words. She had to reason with him. He was groggy half the time with the painkillers he was on and couldn't drive. She hoped he saw the logic. In one more second, she would have to get out of this chokehold.

Hensley weakened his hold, "Aw shit—Becky, I'm sorry." He softened his arms, held her in a hug. His hot breath nuzzled into her neck.

She wanted to throw him more than ever. A quick flip followed by a life-ending punch to his throat. Fighting the urge harder than ever she said, "Honey—it's okay. You're just stressed from the pain . . ." She patted his arm and kissed it softly as he let go.

Sarah supported Hensley as she took him back to the bed, put him under the covers and cuddled up behind him. In a few minutes he was snoring. She wondered how long she would be able to keep this up before she snapped.

Chapter Sixteen

It took a full day of pushing paper and helping the other detectives write up warrants before Bernadette was free to leave for Edmonton. She had to go over to Harvey and let him know she was leaving for a few days and take him Sprocket to look after.

Harvey never minded looking after Bernadette's dog, her place, her lawn, and probably would have looked after her life if she let him. The last item, Bernadette found tempting, but that was not going to happen.

Harvey greeted Sprocket as the dog came through his door, and they played together as if long last pals had been reunited. Bernadette had heard a rumor that Harvey took Sprocket on strolls past the hangouts of ladies, the Tim Horton's, the local beauty shops. Walking slowly by with Sprocket, Harvey used the good-looking and friendly German Shepard as his conversation starter.

There were always rumors in a small city like Red Deer, but Harvey had no end of lady friends, and Sprocket, of course, was not saying anything. Bernadette had given Sprocket one last hug, then a big one for Harvey and hit the road late Tuesday afternoon. Her usual small bag was in the back of the jeep with five days of clothes and her workout gear.

She met up with Anton late Tuesday night, caught up on their investigation of what was now called the Pipeline Terrorists, checked into a hotel near the Canadian Security and Intelligence Service and didn't sleep well that night.

Bernadette had never been inside the CSIS building. This was Canada's version of the CIA. They oversaw Canada's security, the gathering of intelligence for worldwide threats. They had analysts for business crime, cybercrime, and any other crime they could dream up. She, on the other hand, responded to the usual violence of a personal nature.

The building she was about to visit the next morning was all about people or groups of people in nations that wanted to do violence to Canada. She tossed and turned until 4 in the morning, hit the Gym at 4:30, and was ready for Anton when he showed up at the hotel at 7 a.m.

The CSIS building was nondescript; most people in Edmonton would not know it existed. There is no address for it on the CSIS website. You work there or get invited there only if you have clearance.

Bernadette's clearance got her into the outer offices where she found a sea of mostly young energetic faces. The scene before her looked like a professional business office. Everyone was in some kind of business attire; clusters of people examined data on laptops and poured over white boards filled with local and worldwide threats.

Anton guided her down a series of hallways and to a boardroom. She felt out of her depth here. A sense of panic gripped her. Here were the brightest young men and women brought together to analyze crime threats using technology, and she worked on instinct and intuition. She had worn her best jeans and freshly pressed t-shirt—she stood out like a shoplifter at Wal-Mart. She swallowed hard as they entered the Board Room.

Bernadette sat in a boardroom with Anton De Luca and three other CSIS agents waiting for the arrival of Security Chief Patterson. There was no hiding Patterson's dislike of Bernadette, which she found a relief. She could be with straight him. As long as she was not insubordinate, she would be fine. CSIS was once an offshoot of the RCMP, and even though some of them dressed casually, there was still a sense of order that belied a military organization. They were Canada's defense against terrorism, and they took it seriously.

Patterson breezed in, made cursory hellos to everyone that seemed to include Bernadette and began, "Here is where we are. The FBI lost the other group of these Ghost Shirt Eco Warriors, and they only have visual on Talbert Hensley, who is in the company of a female FBI Agent in deep cover." An aide to handed him a sheet of paper.

"We have a report that these Eco Warriors or Terrorist is funded by an Aaron Barteau, formerly of the very wealthy Barteau Chemical family. His father died and left him billions. Somehow, he developed a conscience, and instead of funding clean water or clean air projects—which we of course would heartily endorse . . ." Patterson looked around the room for effect. ". . . He has put money into these crazed Eco Terrorists to rain havoc on industries in North America."

An aide punched some keys on a laptop, and a picture of Aaron Barteau appeared on a television panel in the front of the conference room. Anton leaned forward, "Do we have anything that ties this Barteau to our group?"

Patterson shook his head. "The FBI has a lot of hearsay. There were some meetings between some suspects, some people they think are members and this Hensley guy, was staying at a hotel close to Barteau. We think they had a meeting, planned this purchase, and planned their point of attack from his place in Maine." Patterson looked over the paper in his hand. "Unfortunately, Barteau was only recently a suspect, so they have no recorded surveillance of the meeting."

Bernadette hated to state the obvious, but it was there. "So, basically, all we have is the FBI following this guy, and hoping he meets with some contacts they can arrest that will lead them to Barteau, and bust this group?"

Patterson looked across the table at Bernadette. His eyes squinted with the obvious tension he felt in answering her question. "Yes . . . yes . . . that is exactly what we have . . . at this moment." His mouth moved as if he wanted to say more. Anything more to improve their situation, but there was nothing—he dropped his head back to his paper. As if some new hidden message would appear there.

A young aide piped up. "Well, we do have the search for Professor McAllen to deal with."

Patterson threw the aide a nasty look. Anton shifted uncomfortably in sympathy for the young man's lack of tact.

Patterson looked up; the item was on the table. It needed to be discussed, but it was painful to him. He had already thrown Bernadette off the case because he thought McAllen was not a factor in this case—and now he was a vital part of it.

Patterson cleared his throat, "Ah, yes, Professor Alistair McAllen." The aide punched keys on the laptop and the professor appeared on the screen. The professor looked scholarly, a small smile graced his lips as he stood with a group in cap and gowns at a university function.

Bernadette swiveled to look at the picture. "Don't you have anything more current on him, something in the past year before he fled Canada?"

"We don't know if he fled Canada," Patterson interjected.

Bernadette swiveled back to face Patterson. "I can assure you that McAllen is no longer in Canada."

Patterson leaned forward in his chair; his words came out slowly. "And, just how, Detective Bernadette Callahan, can you assure us that McAllen is no longer in Canada?" He added a slight smirk.

"He sent me a postcard of himself and his friends on a beach. The postcard had a Mexican stamp on it. I turned it over to CSIS over a year ago. It seems no action was taken on it," Bernadette said. "I think he was just playing games after he escaped capture last year."

Patterson blurted out the words. "Postcard . . . he sent you a postcard? Well then, I guess we start combing all the beaches of Mexico, as I understand everyone here could use a holiday, I presume we start as soon as possible," Patterson said. He looked around the table to bring all the others into this obvious amusement.

"You don't have to waste your time on that—I know where he is." Bernadette stared down the end of the board table. This felt like poker to her; she was waiting for Patterson to call her hand.

Patterson shook his head in disbelief, smiled at the others seated at the table. Most of them smiled back except for Anton. "You know where he is? Well then detective, perhaps you would share this amazing intelligence with us."

"He is somewhere on the Yucatan peninsula," Bernadette said. She leaned back in her chair, faced Patterson directly and laid her cards on the table. "The picture on the postcard was white sand beaches, something you see in that area."

"And white sand beaches in Puerto Vallarta, or Huatulco did not rate in your assessment?" Patterson widened his eyes at Bernadette as if he was speaking to a three-year-old.

Bernadette smiled, "Well, you're right they would have . . . until I saw the sign under a large magnifying glass in the background." She leaned back in her chair; satisfied she had annoyed Patterson enough. "The sign was pointing to Tulum. That is, as I am sure you all know an ancient Mayan site."

Patterson leveled his gaze at Bernadette, his shoulders hunched up, his displeasure obvious. "And when were you going to share this information—I assume you've known this for some time? McAllen has been a fugitive and wanted by this agency since last year."

"Actually, Sir, I only discovered it this very morning; I had given the photo to agent De Luca here a day after I received it which was over a year ago, but never had examined it closely. Agent De Luca lent me one of your high-powered magnifying glasses and there it was."

Patterson pursed his lips, "Okay, granted you have a postcard of McAllen from Mexico. We can start our search there to find out where he is now. . ."

"He's still there," Bernadette interrupted.

"Why do you think that? This man is a wanted felon for attempting to sabotage North American oil. Why do you think he would send you a postcard from Mexico and then stay there? This man is supposed to be a learned professor —why would he think we're that stupid?"

Bernadette paused, tapped the pen on her notepad, "Because smart people think everyone else is dumb. McAllen is hiding in plain sight. He thinks we think he's moved on, and he hasn't—he's still there."

Patterson placed his hands down on the table, preparing to make a statement when Anton cut in. "Sir, I have a report that Paul Goodman made two trips to Cancun in the past six months. He could have used the supposed vacations to meet with McAllen."

Bernadette quickly added, "I think McAllen would be in a place that he could meet with some of his former students from the University of Victoria. He was close with his old Vietnam War buddies; he lived close to them for years. He is a creature of habit. He needs to be close to people he knows."

Patterson looked around the table. "And how exactly do you expect to locate our fugitive? I imagine the Mexican Police Force will not have the manpower to give you. Sure, they'll put up a poster or two on the net . . . but I doubt they'll pursue it seriously."

Bernadette was doodling on her pad and looked up. "I think we can find McAllen from Goodman's past contacts. I have a feeling that Goodman was able to contact McAllen on a regular basis. McAllen was his teacher, his mentor . . ."

"You think you're going to find email for phone records, between McAllen and Goodman? We've had a team combing through Goodman's laptop and cell phone, they reported no contacts to any addresses in Mexico.

"No I don't. I doubt if the two were that stupid. I think we'll find old-fashioned mail drops. Snail mail is still the hardest thing to track if not sent by courier. I think Goodman was posting letters and sending information to

McAllen from a contact in Canada or the USA to Mexico," Bernadette said.

"And how exactly did you ascertain that?" Patterson asked.

"It's what I'd do if I wanted to stay totally off the grid, off the electronic surveillance that the FBI, CSIS and numerous other agencies employ. Good old-fashioned snail mail isn't monitored unless you're in prison or a suspected terrorist. Goodman was neither," Bernadette said.

Patterson stood and straightened his tie. "Agent De Luca, Detective Callahan, I really hope you're right about this. Oil pipelines throughout the world are about to be attacked by a vicious Bio Bug, and unless you find this man, there is no way to turn these things off." He walked out of the room, his young aide following close behind him.

Anton sat quietly as the other CSIS agents left the room. He looked over at Bernadette. "Well, I do hope you're right about this—as I really do enjoy my job, and I'd be terrible as a priest, if you get my meaning."

Bernadette let out a nervous laugh. "Relax Anton, look, at the worst you get a little beach time, a little tequila, and I take all the heat. And yes, you'd still be a cute priest."

Anton dipped his head slightly. "Oh my God, Bernadette, right now I'm trying to think of a good Italian saying for where you've put us." He raised his head and smiled, "but nothing comes to mind."

Bernadette gave Anton a rap on the shoulder. "Finally, I've made my Italian stallion speechless."

Anton shook his head and motioned for Bernadette to follow him. They made their way to the commissary, picked up a couple of sandwiches and cokes and found a picnic table on the lawn.

"You really think you have this McAllen pegged—that

he's where you think he is—still in Mexico's Yucatan?" Anton asked after a few bites of his sandwich.

Bernadette finished chewing on her sandwich and swigged her coke. "There's something about this guy, something I saw in him. I just think that's his M.O."

Anton shielded his eyes from the bright afternoon sun. "I hope you're right for the sake of oil, and our sake. Patterson will hit the roof if we've led everyone on a dead end."

"Well, I don't give a damn about Patterson. Sorry to be rude, but that son of a bitch thinks I'm about as good as Tonto to his Lone Ranger . . ."

"—Whoa, Bernadette." Anton put up his hand.

"What do you mean whoa? You think the guy's just as much of a jerk as I do."

"Yes, but he's an effective jerk. He gets things done for the agency, especially in dealing with the politicians. He's got to keep some guy in Ottawa happy, who's got to keep someone in Washington happy. And so it goes. He's got the FBI and Interpol on his ass every time he screws up."

Bernadette looked away, rolled up her sandwich wrapper and tossed it with a wide arc into the trash bin. "I didn't know you were so cozy with Patterson."

"No, it's just I see how I have to work with him to get my job done. Yeah, his instincts can be off. They can be off by a long shot, but he gets the overall picture—he's trying to protect the world from the bad guys."

Anton stopped his soliloquy as a young agent stepped up to their table. "We've got a situation developing Agent De Luca." He handed Anton his cell phone.

Anton scrolled down the screen and looked up at Bernadette. "Damn it, they lost them. We have a Russian Federal Security Services person we're in contact with.

They've been on the trail of two Chechen Terrorists they believe are in possession of the Bio Bugs."

"Where'd they lose them?"

"A city called Samara in Russia. Unfortunately, it's a major oil pipeline transportation hub. There's lots of rugged terrain there, and the pipelines are above ground—they could strike anywhere."

Chapter Seventeen

Beslan and Elbek watched the Russian oil workers walk from the main control room of the pipeline pumping station. They'd lain there for hours. Mosquitoes feasted on their exposed skin, and ants crawled over them. The forest where they lay smelled of sweet pine and dense earth. Down below them the Volga River—the pride of Russia in song and story—rolled slowly by.

It had taken Beslan and Elbek a week to get to this location. Their meeting with Adlan in Barcelona, and then obtaining the Bio Bugs from him seemed in the distant past. From Barcelona they'd taken the ten-hour train trip to Paris. Train travel had less security, fewer passport checks.

They travelled as Spanish Nationals, as far as Berlin, but they had to be careful. If their passports were scrutinized and their faces put through facial recognition software it would turn up the truth. They were both Chechen, wanted by Moscow for what Russia considered terrorism, and Chechens considered defense of their homeland.

From Paris they took a train to Berlin. They shredded

their Spanish passports, produced their fake Russian ones, and took the train to Moscow. Their connections in Moscow were tense. Both men felt eyes looking at them. The train conductor spoke roughly to them as they boarded the train to Samara City; their passports were thrown back at them. The man muttered under his breath to their faces, a nasty Russian word that meant "filthy Arabs."

Both men were used to such abuse. They were both dark-skinned and black-haired with sharp angular faces that stood out from the typical white Russian. They let the conductor make his comment, and then muttered under their breaths how he was a "filthy Russian."

With little sleep and in need of baths and decent food, they arrived in Samara City. A man met them at the train station and took them to his house. He was a Chechen like them, but light-skinned, tall, and blonde. He called himself Sergey. He fit in with the Russians. He supplied weapons, a GPS and maps of the pumping stations they wanted to target.

As they left that morning for their target, Sergey said, "You know the Americans who threw the tea into the harbor in Boston before their revolution would now be considered terrorists."

Beslan had smiled at Sergey. "Yes, my friend, but the winners write the history books; the losers descend beneath the waves of infamy."

As the light faded in the sky, they inched their way forward. The pipeline was elevated, a large swath of overgrown grass provided easy cover. The pumping station had no fence, no armed guard, only a sign that proclaimed in several languages that this was a restricted area.

Beslan stopped, looked back at Elbek and smiled, his one gold tooth flashed. His eyes, now almost closed from mosquito bites, brimmed with excitement. "Elbek, this will be easy, you see how lazy these Russians are. We will be in and out in no time."

Elbek raised his head, "Belsan, you were always the optimist. Once we get in and make our deposit of these bugs in their pipeline, you don't think they'll have the whole Russian army after us?"

Beslan laughed softly, "My friend, it will be like old times back in Chechnya, the Russians stomping around in the woods looking for us, and you and I picking them off from up in the trees."

Elbek wiped the sweat dripping into his eyes from his face. "Yes, my dear friend, you are a dreamer. Let's get this one done, and if we live, we hit the next one 150 kilometers to the west, God willing."

Beslan winked and adjusted his R4 assault rifle. "Are you kidding? Of course we will live. We will go back to our village, and I will marry your sister, have many children, and you, you tightfisted bastard, will be forced to provide many presents to all the children I produce from my excellent loins."

Elbek dropped his face into his hands. "You are more than a dreamer . . . you're a fool . . . don't you think my lovely sister could find someone better than you? I think a short man with half a penis would be better." He slapped his friend's foot, and then held it for a second in a mock embrace.

Beslan made only a soft grunt in reply. He adjusted his rifle and moved his grenades from his belly to around his back. They inched slowly past the perimeter of the pumping station, and into the yard. Four young Russian workers walked from the main pumping station and control room toward the sleeping quarters.

They froze. The laughter and shouts of bravado from the young Russians echoed around them. They could hear their conversation. They were arguing over the Russian Premier Soccer league. One of them proclaimed in a loud voice how the team Spartak Moscow would wipe the field this year, and the others shouted back more loudly how the local team of Krylia Sovetov Samara would have their banner year.

Their conversation fell away as they entered their quarters and went inside. Beslan motioned with his hand to move, and they crawled once more. In a few more minutes they were within 50 meters of the main control room. No cover, bare ground. They needed to run hard. They did.

Panting, they flung themselves against the doorway, opened the door, and dropped on all fours into the low light of the control room. Either no one heard them, or the controllers were asleep. With the amount of vodka, the Russians consumed on a daily basis, it was not a stretch of the imagination to think that.

Using hand signals for communication, they crouched low and moved slow. The control room was hot. Machinery pumped the oil down the pipeline. A steady hum permeated the room. A smell of oil burned the back of their throats. They slowed their breathing as they moved forward.

A small door at the end of the corridor announced control room in Russian. This would be the place to inject their Bio Bugs . . . Elbek pointed his hand to his lips, signaling silence to Beslan, as he opened the door.

One lone operator sat at the controls. He was on his cell phone, his fingers busy answering a text message. The control room glowed in a sea of soft lights. Most muted, some blinked . . . showing the pressure of the oil flowing from Russia to Europe.

They crept slowly, first Elbek, then Beslan towards the operator. Elbek held a wire cord in one hand. He intended to choke the operator to death and take over the controls, and then open the main pumps to inject the Bio Bugs.

They crouched and inched closer. Beslan's foot hit a small bucket. The bucket clanged over the metal flooring. The operator turned, saw the two Chechens with guns and murder in their eyes, and fled.

It happened inside of a second. Elbek turned to Beslan, "You stupid bastard, could you have been clumsier?"

Beslan rose on his knees, "Look, I was following your path . . . you idiot."

Elbek put his hand to his chest and lowered his voice. "Okay, they know we're here, let's get the bugs injected and see if we can get out of here fast."

"Okay, I agree, let's focus on our mission," Beslan said.

Elbek took over the controls, opened the main valves and turned to Beslan. "Okay, all the valves are open." They walked into the main pumping station. It was deserted. If the workers were smart they would be calling for the Russian military. The army station was some 15 kilometers away. They had time to inject the Bio Bugs and get away.

Beslan took the pouch with the vials, poured all of them into the opening of the pipe and smiled at Elbek. "You see, now we will do the rest of the job, return to our village, and you will give your sister away to me in marriage."

Elbek was about to respond when he heard trucks screeching to a halt from outside. Peering out the window, he saw four Russian Tiger trucks come to a halt. The Tiger trucks, that looked like an American Humvee, with a large caliber machine gun on top, spewed a crack team of Russian military from their doors.

Beslan placed his hand on Elbek's neck and brought his

forehead to his. "You know I've loved you like a brother, and I would love nothing more than to spoil the little brats you'd give my wonderful sister, but I think this is not in our stars."

Elbek pressed his head against Beslan's. "God willing, we will meet in paradise."

They embraced, and then Beslan took out his cell phone and typed a text to Adlan in Barcelona. He needed to know they had only managed to sabotage one pumping station. 10 more vials were in the woods were they had crawled from. The Bio Bugs would soon die without being released to attack iron and oil. Beslan felt a sense of loss for having left them there.

The Russians were shouting for them to give themselves up. The soldiers advanced slowly, checking their strength, to see what they would do.

Beslan took Elbek by the shoulders. "There is no use to fight. If we do, we may be injured and taken. We must go with our purpose in hand, we did what we came to do, now we will leave here as martyrs."

Elbek nodded his head and smiled. "Yes, my friend, you are right. You are always right."

They pulled all the pins on their grenades and embraced. As the Russians came through the doors with their guns blazing, they were torn to pieces by the explosions.

Adlan sat on the tiny balcony of the apartment in Barcelona. The balcony was barely big enough to hold a small chair. He balanced his tea on his knee and thumbed through his cell phone reviewing his text messages. When he came to one from Beslan, he sighed deeply, and looked upward. A small tear made its way down his cheek. He did not try to brush it away.

Zara appeared at the balcony window. "How is it with Beslan and Elbek, do you have news?" The answer was obvious from Adlan's face. She felt a need to comfort him, and placed a hand on his shoulder.

Adlan stared up into the Barcelona night, "They injected one pumping station . . . they have taken their own lives to avoid capture."

Zara squeezed his shoulder, "And the other two?"

Adlan looked up at Zara, his eyes brimmed with tears. "They are safely on board their target."

"Safely on board . . . they are safely on board what?"

Adlan looked back into the sky. "You will see, the world will see . . . very soon."

Anzor and Kerim stood on the deck of the Russian oil supertanker, Asheron. The tanker steamed slowly through the Bosporus Straight, the lights of Istanbul winked on as night descended. They were the last two crewmen to sign on. Their documents as Able Seaman were in order. That they did not speak much Russian was of little concern to ship management. Their duties would be general maintenance and cleaning, with some standing watch.

Anzor and Kerim's journey to Russia had been easy. Neither of them was on the radar for Interpol or the Russian Intelligence and Security force. They were new recruits. Travelling on fake Russian passports, they'd flown to Paris from Barcelona after their meeting with Adlan. They took a connecting flight to Sevestapol the home of the pipeline terminal and port for Super Tankers in the Black Sea.

Their biggest concern was getting on a crew of a super-tanker, but within three days, they were successful. Anzor told Kerim that Allah smiled on their mission. Kerim wasn't so sure. The younger brother, he'd been forced into this mission by his parents—he thought Allah would have had different ideas.

The Asheron needed extra crew for the 40-day trip through the Mediterranean, the Suez, and down Pirate Alley along the treacherous coast of Somali, but it was hard to find willing crewmen. Ships increased pay rates, but thoughts of being captured by Somali pirates and spending days off the coast of Somali waiting for ransom or for commandos to storm the ship for their release were not appealing.

Anzor put his arm around Kerim's shoulder. "Fortune smiles on us my brother, and getting hired on this ship shows us we are blessed in our venture."

Kerim shrugged his shoulders and only a slight smile forced its way to his lips. "Anzor, you know I love you, and have always followed you in your vengeance against the Russians, but are we on the right path?"

Anzor said, "Any strike against the Russians is a correct one."

Kerim looked at Anzor. He was much smaller than his brother, a slight wisp compared to his tall and thick sibling. "I do not know. This vessel carries three million barrels of oil; Adlan wants us to set the Bio Bugs in the middle of the Greek Islands. It sounds like he wants to attack the cruise ship and tourist industry rather than the Russians."

"Look, this is a Russian oil tanker; it will come apart at sea. You and I will watch in wonder from the life boats, and see the world condemn the Russians." Anzor placed his mouth close to Kerim's ear although there was no one close to them on the massive tanker. "But I know the real reason."

"And that is?" Kerim said.

"The Turks will finally close the Bosporus to the Russian Tankers. This will mean they must build expensive pipelines, and every time they do we will destroy them. We will empty the coffers of these Russian when they can't ship their precious oil."

Kerim didn't answer. He watched the ocean foam below the tanker, and the lights of Istanbul fade in the background. A light ocean breeze picked up as the ship turned its bow into the Sea of Marmara, on its way into the Aegean Sea and the Mediterranean. The air was fresh and clean. Kerim breathed in deeply and wished he were somewhere else. He loved nature, clean water, flying birds. The contents of the hold were brimming with death for the sea and all sea creatures. He wondered if he had the stomach to go through with the mission.

Chapter Eighteen

From the level of activity in the building, it was evident that something major had developed as Bernadette and Anton walked in. Agents huddled around laptops in offices and pointed at data, waving their hands, as if they were manufacturing new facts in thin air.

Anton looked at Bernadette. "Looks like something's happened. Get a coffee, and I'll meet you in my office."

Bernadette smiled. "So, I'm cleared for intelligence service, but not that cleared."

Anton said, "Let's say, if I have you wandering around the building and Patterson sees you, he's liable to remember why he doesn't like you—again."

Bernadette patted Anton's shoulder. "Not a problem, you have real gourmet coffee here. It makes the RCMP stuff look like sludge. I'll be in your office kicking back until you return the Intel. I think I might get to like this assignment."

Anton shook his head and walked away. "Yes, I'm just here to look after your every need."

Bernadette found the agency coffee room and put in a coffee capsule of Columbian Supreme and added the half and half coffee cream from the fridge and her usual large dose of sugar. She was just muttering to herself how she could get used to this when Anton walked back in the room.

"Hey, you've got to come with me."

"I thought I was going to be in the way."

Anton just shook his head. "Look, just follow me. You've got to see this latest satellite feed of the Russian pipeline from the CIA."

Bernadette followed Anton down the hall to the main situation room. An array of large screen monitors displayed various geography from around the world. The center screen held a latitude and longitude for Russia. A long length of pipeline was disappearing before their eyes.

A group of agents milled around the screen, pointing out the progression of the destruction on the line. An agent sitting at a desk with a laptop was punching up other sites and satellite photos. Patterson stood there, arms crossed, giving commands for different satellite views.

Anton and Bernadette stood at the back of the room; Anton leaned over and said, "This is the CIA Satellite over Samara, the area where they lost the terrorists."

Bernadette didn't look at Anton; her eyes were transfixed on the screen. The pipeline was vanishing—a wake of black oil left in its path. A small army of trucks was racing alongside it. "Is this real time?"

"Yes, it is," Anton said. He looked down at this cell phone and started to read a text. "The Russians says a main pumping station got hit by terrorists a half hour ago. They blew themselves up and took some soldiers with them. They assume the Bio Bugs stolen from the University of Victoria are responsible for this destruction."

"Can you send the Russians a message, and tell them the only way to stop the pipeline destruction is to break it, like a fire break in a forest fire?" Bernadette asked, looking at Anton.

"How do you know this?"

"Just send them the message. I'll tell you later." Bernadette looked back at the screen. Two trucks stopped beside the pipeline. Small figures ran frantically around the trucks. They looked like they were trying to close valves.

Anton tapped furiously on his cell and hit send. "Now you want to tell me why you think this will work?"

Bernadette looked up at Anton, and with all the seriousness she could muster, said, "My next door neighbor is a retired oil worker. He said the only way to stop the bugs would be to break the pipeline. You can't do it with valves because all the closures in the pipeline are metal and they'll eat right through them."

Anton ran his hand though his hair. He gazed at his cell phone. "The Russians got the text, and my contact hopes you're right."

They looked back at the satellite image again. Two more trucks had stopped beside the pipeline. This time the images showed the trucks start to fade away. Only tires remained. Human figures ran away from the carnage. Bernadette stared hard at the image. What was happening to the trucks . . . was this a bad satellite feed?

The satellite followed the pipeline over mountains and through forests, and across streams; it was still being destroyed before their eyes. Someone in the crowd of agents called out, "We estimate the destruction at eighty kilometers an hour, and it is increasing speed by three kilometers every two minutes."

"My God, how is it possible to be gaining speed?" Anton asked.

"The professor said at the University he thought the bugs would do this. He said they were learning as they were released into the oil," Bernadette said.

The next image the satellite showed was a long valley, the pipeline dropped down sharply toward a large river. Black smoke could be seen just before the river. Two large bulldozers pushed hard at the trestles of the pipeline. The satellite zoomed in on them as they rammed into the trestle, then backed up, and rammed hard again.

The trestle swayed, and then collapsed, taking the pipeline along as it collapsed into the river below. The pipe was broken, spewing its oil down the sides of the bank and spilling into the rushing water. Inky black foam appeared in the river. The bulldozer operators stopped their machines and watched the destruction of the pipeline coming toward them.

The destruction stopped at the broken pipe. The pipeline on the other side of the river did not disappear. A cheer went up in the situation room from all the agents. Anton turned to Bernadette. "I'll have the Russians send a thank you note to your friend, perhaps some Vodka and caviar?"

Bernadette put her hand up. "Save it. My neighbor, Harvey Mawer, is second generation German-Canadian. His grandfather was a German soldier who perished in a Russian prisoner of war camp—and he hates caviar—calls it fish bait."

Anton was about to say something when the voice of Chief Patterson was heard throughout the room. "Attention everyone. The show is over, all those working this case specially follow me, the rest of you, get back to your other cases and duties."

Anton, Bernadette, and four other agents followed the Chief down the hallway. They entered a small meeting room and took their seats. Patterson took his place at the head of the table and looked at the agents on his left. "Well, we've just seen a demonstration of how destructive these Bio Bugs can be and how they can be stopped. Are there any reports from our scientists about how these things can be destroyed?"

The agent with the identification badge, Clayton Jessup, fumbled with his cell phone and scrolled through his notes. "I've been in contact with two universities and three major oil companies. They all say this biological organism is beyond anything they have ever seen. One oil company claims they could have an answer inside of three months, but the universities say it would take them longer."

Patterson turned to another female agent who was sporting the name Brittany Krieger on her ID badge. "Where does that put us?"

Agent Krieger tapped on her computer. "Sir, if the Bio Bugs were reproduced and exposed to major pipelines—and with the rate of acceleration we've just seen . . ." She paused as if she couldn't believe the answer appearing on her screen, "It would mean some fifty to seventy percent of North America's and Europe's pipelines destroyed inside three months."

Patterson looked around the table. "I think we now know our objective—it would be to find this Professor Alistair McAllen, and hopefully, if you can track this man as quickly as you say you can Detective Callahan, we may find a way to stop these things sooner." Patterson's gaze rested on Bernadette.

She felt his gaze, and the eyes of all those around table,

burning a hole into her. She doubted if she had ever felt more outside of her own comfort zone, and more vulnerable. She had to succeed. She'd need something more than her intuition; she would need hard work, and a damn good dose of luck.

Chapter Nineteen

FBI Agents Carla Winston and Luis Valdes watched undercover agent Sarah Collins pull out of the parking lot of the Marriott Courtyard Hotel in Missoula and head down the highway. Talbert Hensley was slumped down in the passenger seat. It was 7:30 a.m., much earlier than they had ever hit the road, and a whole day ahead of when Sarah had said they would depart.

Carla instructed two agents in a green pickup truck to begin the first shift on following them. She took a sip of her coffee and said, "Well, let's see where they're headed today."

Luis Valdes pulled their car out of the parking lot and waited a good five minutes before joining traffic. The radio link in his ear was giving him instructions from the chase vehicle, "They say they've taken the 200. Got to be headed for Great Falls."

"Yes, they are. I'll alert our Air Force drone to take over and tell the chase car to hang back some five miles. That's a quiet road, and Hensley will spot us if we follow too close," Winston said.

"Copy that," Valdes said. He set his jaw in a hard line, his fingers clenching the wheel.

"Something bugging you, Valdes?"

"Yeah, I want this mission to end with me putting Hensley's face into the ground, and the capture of the all the other shitheads he's working with."

Winston stared at Valdes for a moment. "This guy has really got to you, hasn't he?"

Valdes turned towards Winston. "Look, like I said before, I'm all American, all FBI all the time, but putting a female agent in jeopardy like we are . . . well it just doesn't feel right."

"Damn it, Agent Luis Valdes, you all of sudden sprouted some man genes—God almighty, I almost like you." Winston turned back toward the road and sipped her coffee.

"I don't know what you call it, but I know what I feel . . ." Valdes put his hand to his earphone. "The forward tail thinks they've been spotted . . . they're pulling off the road."

"Shit, what kind of rookie agents have I got here that they can't do an easy tail in the back of goddamn Montana?" Winston finished her coffee and threw the empty cup into the back seat.

Sarah Collins pulled the car over. Hensley was getting agitated. "See, I told you, four cars back—green pickup. I made that asshole right out of the parking lot. See, that son of bitch, you see him . . . son of bitch . . . fucking Feds' all over the fucking place." He bounced in his seat as he crouched down looking into the side mirror.

Sarah turned her head and looked back down the road. "Hensley, that pickup truck just turned off down there.

That's no tail, that's a freaking coincidence of some Montana farmers or oil workers going to work. It is the goddamn morning. And why the hell did we have to get up and go right away this morning? I thought you wanted to stay another day. We even paid for the night."

Hensley kept his head down, watching the side mirror. "Look, we got things to do today, got to put some miles on . . . now get back on the road."

Sarah watched Hensley's hand twitching. The heavy painkillers she had him on for his broken tooth and bruised jaw were probably producing some side effects. She wondered if she should up his dosage, but she needed him lucid for the directions to the other parties of his mission. Hopefully at the end of this day, there would be a capture of his compatriots, and she would be free of this.

Winston and Valdes hung back a good ten miles. Valdes was getting directions from the recon drone over head. By the time they reached Great Falls, there were two other FBI cars with them, and two others were joining them once they came into the city.

In Great Falls, the drone operator informed them the car carrying Sarah and Hensley had stopped in front of an electronics store on Highway 87. After the pair left the store, two agents rushed in to find out what they'd been doing there.

"Hensley bought a cell phone," Valdes reported to Winston.

"A cell phone? Why the hell after all this time would he buy a cell phone? If he'd had a cell phone all this time, we wouldn't need to be putting an agent in harm's way to track his sorry ass." Winston sat back in the passenger seat shaking her head.

The next stop was a small pawnshop. But Hensley didn't

go in. The drone observed him buying an object from a man beside a van. The image of the object the drone operator reported was a handgun—large caliber."

Winston almost vaulted out of her seat. "Now that little shit has got a piece. Well, damn it, doesn't that just sweeten this mission something awful?" She looked at Valdes. "You know if you want to shoot this son of bitch when we capture his friends, you be my guest . . . okay scratch that . . . just kidding."

Valdes hands tightened on the wheel. "Heard you the first time."

Sarah made a right turn out of the pawnshop parking lot and headed the car onto Highway 87. Hensley sat beside her, placing the hollow point shells in the 357 Handgun he purchased in the parking lot. He now motioned with the gun, as if it was a pointer. Sarah could see the safety wasn't on. For the first time in many months, she began to worry about her safety.

Winston was on her cell phone to FBI command. "Look, the guy's got a gun; we are in a different situation all together. I want that Blackhawk and Army commando team scrambled ASAP. We've already figured were he's going . . . yes that's right, 87 leads to the 2, and that leads to a whole bunch of pipelines and pumping stations. You tell those boys to be in the sky and be ready . . . because we are going to take down Hensley and his friends. And I don't want my agent hurt . . . you got that?"

Winston dropped her phone to her lap. "My God, there was nothing in the psychological profile of this guy that showed him to be this out of character."

"You mean like his DNA all over a dead female Agent? I think someone missed the character workup on this guy . . . big time," Valdes said.

Hensley was starting to nod off. His right hand clutched the large caliber gun, and his left held the cell phone. Sarah kept the car at a steady 70 miles an hour on the two-lane secondary highway, avoiding any bumps in case the jolt would make the gun go off. Hensley's finger was on the trigger, and Sarah glanced to see if his finger was twitching.

A half hour later, Hensley jolted awake. He aimed the gun at Sarah, and looked behind him, staring down the highway. "You see that green pickup that was following us?"

She glanced into the rearview mirror, "Hensley, I told you, that pickup turned off a side road. There's nothing behind us but a bus that has been trying to pass me for the past twenty minutes."

"Where are we?"

"We just turned onto Highway 2, and just outside of Havre. Which way do I turn?"

"Turn right, and stop in Havre, I gotta take a piss." Hensley slumped back down into his seat. He pulled up his cell phone and started texting.

The next thirty minutes went by slowly for Sarah. They stopped at a gas station in Havre, but Hensley told Sarah to stay in the car. She watched the bus pass them. A little girl waved at her from the window. After their road stop, Hensley was on his cell phone constantly texting back and forth between someone, somewhere. The gun lay in his lap, still pointed in her direction.

Just past Glasgow, Hensley told her to take a left on a small road called the 24. The signpost said Baylor and the Canadian Border.

The narrow road headed north, past wide-open prairie, and a few signs that said "No Hunting" that were riddled with bullet holes. A hawk flew overhead while a lone cloud floated in the Montana sky.

"Pull over," Hensley said. His gun was pointed at her. He stared at her. His eyes were wide, as if he'd woken up to something. This time there was no need to interpret his actions. "Get out of the car." His voice was even, no trace of his former drug addled shakiness.

"What is it . . . . what's the matter sweetie?" Sarah ventured in a soothing voice. She thought he was having another episode, just like back in the hotel, when he grabbed her. Perhaps it was the drugs she was giving him.

"Out of the car god damn it—now!" His eyes were narrow, his face set in a mask of pure hate.

Sarah got out of the car. She did a quick look behind her. There was not another car in sight. The Drone would be overhead, but it was an observation Drone. She had been briefed that it was designed for Border Patrol duty, no missiles, no firepower of any kind. There was just her and this drug-addled kid with a large caliber weapon.

"Okay, Hensley . . . look we need to talk this through . . . you're a little on edge . . . we have to meet your friends, put these Bio Bugs into a pipeline, and get moving . . ."

Hensley looked at her, he said nothing. He was looking at his cell phone, reading a text. He lifted his head, looked her up and down. "No, there has been a change of plan . . . Sarah Collins."

Sarah felt a jolt down her spine. *How did he know her real name?*

Sarah moved slowly towards Hensley, hoping to reason with him, and get the gun. "I don't know what you're on about, my name is Rebecca Jones . . . you know who I am, I'm your Becky . . ."

Hensley fired the 357 at her feet. The shot echoed over the flat landscape. "Don't lie to me, bitch. My people tell me you're FBI, sent to hang with me, and see if I'll lead you to them." He walked closer, his arm with the cell phone extended. "Now . . . I got a little surprise for your people . . . call them."

Sarah wanted to say *call who,* but she knew it was useless; her cover was blown. She had a number, a main number for a patch through to Carla Winston, and she dialed it. Winston came on the phone, tentative, as she didn't recognize the number, "Agent Winston, our suspect wants a meeting."

"We're on it." Winston said and hung up.

Ten minutes later Winston and Valdes pulled up in their car. A black suburban and green pickup truck was behind them. Three more cars appeared from the other direction, and two Blackhawk helicopters appeared out of the low horizon.

Sarah turned to Hensley. "Is this the attention you wanted, because you got it."

Hensley grabbed Sarah, and spun her around. "Tell your boss to approach, and slow, no gun in her hand."

Sarah gave the instruction into the phone, and Winston walked slowly toward them, her gun was left with Valdes, her hands raised in the air. "Now, this situation can end very quickly, Mr. Hensley, with you in our custody, and those little Bio Bugs in your trunk safely put away, or with a whole bunch of gunfire, and you leaving here in a body bag."

"Hey, I got your agent, and a gun pointed at her head. You're going to tell one of those helicopters to take me, my little vials, and this bitch out of here—you got that?"

Winston stopped some five feet from Sarah and Hensley. "No, that's not going to happen. The FBI doesn't do travel arrangements for terrorist and felons. We have only one flight plan filed for you today, and that is to a jail cell. Now, what exactly would you like to do?"

Hensley grabbed Sarah's hair tighter and placed his own face closer to her. "First tell your helicopters to back off, I don't want those snipers up there with a clear shot."

"Okay, I can do that, now we're making a little progress." Winston spoke into her phone and both choppers veered and fell back. One went left and landed in the field, the other right and hovered over the highway two miles away. Winston could hear in her earpiece that the sniper had set up in the field as soon as the helicopter set down. His spotter was beside him. Hensley head was right beside Sarah's. Winston cursed under her breath as the spotter called out, "No shot."

Hensley reached his hand with the cell phone toward Winston. "My people want to talk to you."

Sarah could feel Hensley shaking as Winston came forward to take the cell phone. The phone rang. The screen went to video. Winston held the phone out in front of her. "Whom am I talking with?"

Three men in ski masks appeared on the screen on the phone. "You're speaking with Commander Numero Uno, and his minions, Dos and Tres. We are here to inform you that you have been the victims of our carefully planned subterfuge for the past three months."

"Uh-huh," Winston said. "Well, I'm always up for some good stories, so tell me what you boys have been up to."

Numero Uno could hardly contain himself. His smile evident under the ski mask, "You've been chasing Talbert Hensley all over the lower 48 with what you think is a cache of Bio Bugs, when in fact . . ." He paused for effect and looked back at his compatriots . . . we stole those bugs from Hensley at the ferry. Hensley is a decoy."

"That's right, you shithead FBI agents, I've been leading your dumb asses all over the USA, and my guys have been heading for the real target," Hensley said. He was holding onto Sarah even tighter. "And guess what? I got me some good FBI ass the whole time . . . isn't that right, agent Collins?"

Sarah's face turned red. An angry red. There was no humiliation, only a sense that she would deal with this piece of shit holding the gun to her head.

Winston shook her head. Her earphone would be feeding this information from the terrorists directly back to command central. All the FBI brass would be finding out in seconds how screwed up this mission had become.

"And now, since you guys are the masterminds of all times, where exactly are you?" Winston asked the question just for the hell of it, she didn't expect an answer.

"Alaska." Numero Uno panned the camera back, showing a long pipeline snaking down the mountains. The pipeline showed a large hole, where they'd made an opening at the top. The two other men were taking the vials out of their bags and pouring their contents into the pipe.

He panned the camera back to himself. "In mere seconds Alaska's lifeline to Prince William Sound will be gone. These bugs will eat their way right to the terminal, and maybe even take out an oil tanker. And my compatriots and I will disappear into the Alaska wilderness."

Winston could hear the earpiece crackling, "*We have the coordinates, we have birds in the air. ETA in two minutes.*"

Winston played for time, "Now, how can we be sure you've the right Bio Bugs, and something we didn't just plant for Hensley to buy up in Canada. You know we've got our eyes and ears everywhere. We've been watching those kids up in Canada for some time. We had them infiltrated by the RCMP some time ago." Winston was stalling, needed them to stay on the phone as the Air Force was screaming in from Elmendorf Air Force Base near Anchorage. The jets were honing in their phone's GPS signal.

"Ha, we know that's bullshit . . . and matter of fact . . . look at the pipeline, it's starting to disappear right before our eyes. We're streaming this live to YouTube to show the world what our organization can do." The camera phone panned down the valley, as the pipeline was rapidly coming apart, oil gushing out as its conduit was disappearing.

Winston heard the jets over the phone even before the terrorist did, she only heard a, *"What the fuck?"* followed by large caliber machine gun fire and explosions. The Air Force had learned from the Russian experience. They had been told to blow up any pipeline infected with the bugs far enough down the line to stop them. The terrorists were fair game. Dead was fine, they didn't have to worry about tracking them in the wilderness.

Winston handed the phone back to Hensley, "Well, your friends have been terminated compliments of the US Air Force. They found out how fast we can track the coordinates on a phone call. You have the choice of meeting their fate, or coming quietly to live a long life as a guest of the Federal Government."

Sarah felt Hensley shake even harder. He started swearing at Winston when Sarah took her chance. He had relaxed his grip on her to take back the phone, and it was all she needed. She grabbed his gun arm with one hand and pointed it upwards. The gun went off.

Before Hensley could pull the trigger again, she pounded his ribs with her elbow. The sound of a large volume of air expelled forcefully from his lungs was satisfying. She whipped around and threw a knee into his groin. Hensley was down, but he held onto the gun.

He was about to raise it when a shot rang out. His head

bounced back into the earth. Standing beside Sarah with his gun smoking was Valdes. He raised his gun and put another round through Hensley's heart.

Winston placed her hand on Valdes' gun hand. "Okay, he's dead enough already. I got to file reports for all the ammo you put in that guy."

Valdes looked at Sarah. "Yeah, you're right. I guess he's dead enough."

Sarah watched as Hensley's body was zipped into a body bag. No county Medical Examiner was called. This was federal business. His body would be transported by helicopter to the Air Force Base, and the FBI would take care of the paper work.

Winston came over and stood beside her, "You alright?"

"I'm trying to register a feeling . . . nothing's coming to me," Sarah said. She turned toward Winston. "I've been on this case with this guy for three months, sleeping with him, making like I was in love with him, to get to find out about his friends . . . and I find out this was a decoy."

"Hey, Sarah . . ." Winston placed a hand on Sarah's shoulder. "This undercover stuff is not cut and dried. Look, we did get them, but not in the way we thought we would." Winston moved a little closer to Sarah. "Take some time off, maybe even take a vacation, and once we find another den of bad guys, I'll get you back out here."

Sarah pushed herself away from the car, and faced Winston, "No, there won't be a next time. Some people are cut out for this undercover stuff, but not me. I'm going back to Baltimore, there's a job waiting for me with the Baltimore Police Force."

"A uniform, you want to be back in uniform after being with the FBI?"

"Yeah, damn right I do." Sarah took a square stance in front of Winston. "You know, in a police uniform, I know who I am, and who the bad guys are, at least I think I do." Sarah took her car keys out and started walking to her car.

"What do I tell Section Chief Briscoe at Headquarters?" Winston yelled after her.

Sarah stopped, put on her sunglasses and smiled. "Tell him, he can sleep with the enemy for his country, because this girl is done."

Sarah got in the car and headed down the highway. The GPS in the car told her she had 31 hours of driving to get back home; she planned to have many telephone conversations with her boyfriend, Jonas, on the way. Perhaps he'd accept her marriage proposal by the time she hit the outskirts of Baltimore.

Chapter Twenty

"You were right," Anton said looking up from his laptop in his office.

"I never get tired of hearing that—but right about what?" Bernadette asked. She was sitting across from Anton savoring her cup of gourmet coffee from the CSIS coffee room. Her latest coffee was a Peruvian. She had tried Costa Rican and Columbian, and once she tasted all of South America, she was thinking of trying the Ethiopian.

"About the diversion at the ferry terminal with Talbert Hensley and the FBI Agent," Anton scrolled down the report on his laptop. "Looks like the Ghost Shirt Eco Warriors took the real vials from Hensley's car and attacked a pipeline in Alaska."

Bernadette put her coffee down and sat up in her chair, "How much damage did they do?"

"Not too much. The USA was on high alert because no one knew where the other Ghost Shirt Warriors were. Their F-16's made a large enough gap in the pipeline with one of their missiles that the Bio Bugs were stopped."

"And the Eco Warrior guys that planted the Bugs, where are they? Did they get them?" Bernadette asked leaning forward to look at his screen.

Anton looked at the report. "Oh, they got them, heavy machine gun rounds from an F-16 can end anyone's day. They decided they were a threat, took them out and that was that."

"No, I wouldn't say that it's over . . ."

"Why not?"

Bernadette sat back in her chair, took a sip of her coffee. "Because, the formula is out there, and until we find out how to turn it off or reduce the effects of the Bio Bugs, this thing could return to North America, only with someone more skilled at delivering the threat."

"You mean not broadcasting the attack on YouTube?" Anton said.

"Yeah, that would be a start, but we don't want the terrorists to know that," Bernadette chuckled. "Thank God some of the people we deal with are not that bright."

"So, where too now?"

"I'd say we head back to Victoria," Bernadette said holding up her hand, "Now, I know you're going to say that the Victoria police force and your CSIS agents went through everything that Goodman had and didn't find anything."

"No, I wasn't going to say they didn't find anything—I was going to say they found nothing as in *meno di niente* which is less than nothing, or *assolutamente niente,* which is . . ."

"Okay, I think I get the gist of that," Bernadette said with a frown. "Enough already with the Italian lessons."

Anton smiled. "So, what are your thoughts?"

"Simple, you and I are flying back to Victoria, and

giving Goodman's place another once-over, and this time we do a little creative thinking."

Anton turned from his computer. "You think my people don't think creatively?

"Oops . . ." Bernadette said. "Looks like I just stepped on some pretty big concepts of investigation from the Canadian Security and Intelligence Service." She sat straight up in her chair and looked at Anton. "What I'm saying is every investigator looks for something that someone may be hiding. What if that person knew that one-day we, or someone like us, would come looking for his connections to McAllen? What do you think he would do?"

"Hide them deeper?" Anton shrugged.

"Nope, hide them in plain sight. What you and I need to do is go to Victoria and look for what is obvious. And somewhere there, we'll find Goodman's link with Professor Alistair McAllen."

Anton got up and stretched and grabbed his jacket off the chair. "Well, why not? There's nothing here but a bunch of bosses who would like us to be at meetings or fill out reports—let's make tracks."

Bernadette and Anton made the 5 p.m. direct flight to Victoria with only minutes to spare. Anton always kept a travel bag in his car, and they picked up Bernadette's on the way. They settled back in their seats for the one-hour flight.

Bernadette noticed that Anton was getting extra attention from the good-looking airline attendant. "Is there any lady who is not susceptible to that charming smile of yours?"

"Yes, indeed there is," Anton said, his black eyebrows knitted into a serious frown. "My mother."

"Ah, the Italian mother, the careful guide and eternal

observer of the Italian son," Bernadette said with an equally serious look.

Anton couldn't hide his smirk, "What? You, Detective Bernadette Callahan, have some experience with Italian men and their mothers?"

Bernadette shook her head, "No, mine is worse—a Greek man and his mother."

Anton patted Bernadette's arm. "Oh my God, my heart goes out to you. An Italian mother wants her son to marry a virgin that will be a good cook, but not as good as her of course, and who will be a good mother, not as good as her of course, and will look after her son, but . . ."

"But not as good as the mother of course," Bernadette interjected.

Anton smiled, "No, a daughter-in-law will never look after the son like the mother—it's Italian tradition. Now as far as Greeks go, my understanding is you're a *Xenos*, or stranger from the start and it doesn't matter if you were a princess, you'd never be accepted."

"Ah, you've met my boyfriend's mother."

Anton laughed. "No, a lot of mothers like her. I grew up in an Italian neighborhood in Toronto and hung out with a bunch of Greek kids going to university." Anton turned and looked at Bernadette. "I don't mean to pry, but how is this going, this Greek guy and you. Is it serious?

Bernadette nudged Anton's shoulder. "Let's just say, it's one of those on again off again relationships, that's cooled by the steely glare of the mother."

Anton smiled and picked up his computer to look at recent reports he had downloaded before takeoff. The pretty airline attendant came by again to ask Anton if he needed anything—for the third time.

Bernadette sat back in her seat and pondered what she

wanted to do about the good-looking Constable Chris on Galiano Island. There was no use in telling Anton the details. They were weekend lovers. A weekend at Banff Springs, a weekend in Victoria, and then there was the weekend in Toronto.

The mother had smiled, served all manner of foods, and sprinkled the conversation with how many of the pretty young women (she meant much younger than Bernadette) were coming around to see if Christos, his mother would never call him Chris, was coming home soon.

Bernadette had been cold before. She had nearly frozen on a lake one time chasing an escaping suspect on a snow machine. Her toes, fingers, and face nearly frostbitten. But that episode with Chris's Greek mother in the kitchen in Toronto was the coldest she'd ever been. She felt intense cold just thinking about it.

They arrived in Victoria to an airport awash in tourists. Tourist buses were either boarding or disembarking passengers. Suitcases were piled high on the pavement, with tour guides holding signs aloft announcing their charter or tour. Anton and Bernadette threaded their way past the confusion and picked up a rental car.

It took a full hour in late day traffic to get to Paul Goodman's apartment. Matt Letourneau, the detective they'd met a few days before, was at the apartment to greet them. Bernadette saw as he walked up that the blue jeans were the same. So were the faded sports coat and the striped shirt. The tie was different; it had less mustard sauce on it than the last one.

Anton shook Letourneau's hand. "Hey detective, thanks for meeting us here, we know it's late . . ."

"By my standards it's early. Remember, we detectives have no lives—we leave that for our ex-wives. We live our lives vicariously through them—on Facebook," Letourneau said while smiling and shaking Anton's hand. "Now, how can I help you?"

Bernadette shook Letourneau's hand; she instantly liked him. "We need to take another look at Goodman's apartment, and we think he may have left an address or a clue to some other persons of interest in this case."

Letourneau took out a key for the door. "Well, you can look all over the place, but most everything was taken to the crime lab, books, notebooks, and then your lady CSIS agent —ah, I think her name was Samantha—she signed off on everything." He shook his head as he turned the key in the door. "Sorry you had to come all this way—had I known in advance, I would have told you to save the trip."

The detective swung open the door to the small apartment and switched on the light. A barren space with a kitchen table, two chairs, and a pullout sofa greeted them. The glow from a streetlight outside made the room look even more desolate. Three tall bookshelves were empty. A shelf where the television once stood had a lone TV cable outlet dangling as if looking for a connection.

"See, I told you. We stripped this down to the bare walls. They went through the garbage, the recycle, even checked the unused toilet paper, and they came up a big zero," Letourneau said.

They stood back in the hallway. Bernadette stared at the peeling wallpaper and smelled the mustiness of the place for the first time. Then a door opened from the apartment across the hall. A little lady stepped out with her dog. Bernadette didn't know who looked smaller, the lady or the dog.

The lady wore bright yellow slacks, a brilliant white blouse, and a matching yellow jacket with a jaunty yellow hat, something all the rage, called a fascinator. It was almost a pillbox pasted to her head with small sequins attached to it. The dog, a small white Scottish terrier, wore a similar jacket, and the exact same hat. Bernadette had never seen a dog dressed up to match its owner. She thought the ensemble might have looked better in a circus act.

The lady looked up as she closed her door. "Who are you looking for?" She regarded the three of them with suspicion, looking them up and down as if she was seeing a police lineup. "There's no use knocking on the poor young man's door—he's dead you know." She squared her shoulders as if the information needed a formal delivery.

"Yes, we know. We're police ma'am," Anton said. He produced his CSIS badge. "This is Detective Letourneau of the Victoria Police and Detective Callahan of the RCMP."

The old lady eyed the badge, and almost spat out her words. "I couldn't get even one policeman to come by when I was broken into a week ago—now here you're all standing around a man's apartment when the man's dead. A wonderful lot of help you police are at catching criminals. Back in my day . . ."

"I'm sure the police will be by your place to take fingerprints and process your place for insurance purposes," Bernadette interrupted. "I know that at this time they are stretched quite thin with the investigation of this poor young man's murder."

The old women paused in her tirade, "Yes, yes, quite right, the poor young man . . . after all no one really took anything . . . only something belonging to Paul."

Bernadette asked, "Do you mean as in Paul Goodman, the man who was murdered?"

"Why yes, that is exactly it. Paul gave me a hardcover book, and a notebook." She leaned forward and said in a whisper, "He said he needed it kept safe; it had important information. I was to give it to no one. I think he was worried about that little Russian girlfriend of his, met her once, never liked her, looked too fancy for me . . ."

"When did this break-in happen?" Anton asked.

"Well, last week, just before Paul was killed, but the thief was smart, jimmied the door all quiet like so as if I wouldn't know—but I knew." She squared her shoulders even more. "You know how I knew?" She threw a bright smile into the question, as if asking a class.

"No idea," Detective Letourneau volunteered.

"Ha, I put a little thread on my door jamb every time I went out, just like I read in them spy novels, and one day I come back, and sure enough the thread is gone, and so is Paul's notebook . . . but they didn't get his book . . . they had no idea."

"And you say they left the book behind?" Bernadette said.

"Yes they did, ha, there was no way they knew about that . . . Paul was clever," the lady said.

"Did you happen to read what was in the notebook?" Anton asked.

The lady put her head down and shrugged her shoulders, "Well, I know I wasn't supposed to look, but I did." Her eyes lit up, "In case it was something to do with national security, just like in the spy books."

Bernadette said, "I am sure what you did was fine, and did you see anything of importance?"

"Well, a lot of funny formulas, and the address of a man, with a nickname, like Mac or something like that," the lady answered.

"The address—do you remember it?" Bernadette blurted out.

The lady shrugged her shoulders, "Sorry, just looked at it for a moment. Some Mexican name is all I recall . . . never seen the name before."

"And you still have Paul's book?" Bernadette asked.

"Ah, the book, yes I do." She reached into her pocket, fished out a large jangle of keys that instantly had the small white Terrier jumping at her feet. The dog was confused. He had to pee, and the opening of the door meant that was being delayed. The little dog stamped his feet and whined to show his frustration. "Now, don't you fuss, Dixie, you'll get your tinkle time right after I help out these people," the lady said.

A moment later she appeared with the book. The book was dark maroon with faded gold writing. The cover read ISSAC ASIMOV. Inside the cover, the title was *The Foundation Trilogy*. There was *The Foundation*, *Foundation and Empire*, and *The Second Foundation.* She handed it to Bernadette. "Any idea about who this writer is?" she asked.

Anton took the book from Bernadette, and ran his hands over the outer bindings, "One of the greatest science fiction writers of all time. It seems like Goodman was a fan."

Anton opened the book and fanned through the pages. There was nothing there, no notes, and nothing fell out. Bernadette took the book from him. "You need to look for what isn't there," she said with a smile.

Bernadette opened the book wide and shook it. A small piece of paper fell out of the spine. It wafted to the hallway floor like a singular butterfly just set free from its cocoon. "Yeah, now that is what I'm talking about it."

Anton picked it up, "Um huh, we got an address in Santa Fe for a Mr. Emilio Sanchez. Thank you, ma'am . . . sorry, I didn't get your name."

The lady smiled, "Mrs. Emma Thornberry-Masters. My late husband was an operative with M-I5 in England before he retired, and we moved here." She pulled her shoulders up, her full height now approaching Bernadette's shoulders. "That's why I knew to help Paul—that Russian girl, Smirnoff she said her name was . . . I knew she was a phony the moment I saw her. Never trusted the Russians." Emma Thornberry-Masters knitted her thin brows to show her disapproval.

"Thank you very much for this," Bernadette said taking the book. "All the law enforcement agencies are in your debt for your service."

Mrs. Thornberry-Masters smiled brightly, looking down at her little white terrier. "Hear that Dixie? We've been a help to Canada, isn't that wonderful?" Dixie jumped on his hind legs, pawing the air. He yelped, probably to get the attention of his mistress—that he really needed to pee, and the carpet was seconds away from getting it if they didn't get moving.

The lady locked her door, and with her little white Scottish terrier prancing at her side in its matching yellow ensemble, they headed off into the late Victoria City evening.

"That was a stroke of luck, running into that lady," Detective Letourneau said while watching the little lady disappear out the door.

Bernadette turned to the detective. "You know I find if you work hard enough, you'll get in luck's way." She looked at the address Anton held in his hand. "So, who do we call first, CSIS or the FBI?"

"I'll call Patterson first, tell him what we have. He's got an FBI contact in the Southern USA, and a short while from now, if Mr. Sanchez is home, he's about to get a very rude awakening from a bunch of FBI Agents.

"That's good news; hopefully we'll be able to locate Professor McAllen before Zara does," Bernadette said.

Anton looked up from dialing his phone. "You think Zara Mashhadov broke into the old lady's apartment and stole Paul's notebook?"

"I'd count on it. I think she got Paul Goodman talking about Professor Alistair McAllen, and probably how brilliant he was, and he wouldn't tell her where he was hiding. She met our lady from next door, realized Paul and her were friends, and realized Paul may have been hiding something from her with the old lady," Bernadette said.

Anton shook his head, "My God, your mind works in more angles than an Italian soap opera—how do you think like that?

Bernadette smiled, "Because, I'm devious, trust no one, and—I'm a woman. Now let's get going—Zara has a three to four day head start on us, and when she runs out of Bio Bugs, she'll be looking for the formula."

"But she stole the formula from Goodman's computer," Anton said.

"Do you think that Goodman would have left the entire formula on his computer, unprotected by a password? A password that probably only McAllen has?" Bernadette asked.

They walked out of the apartment building, Anton looked at his watch, "Looks like we missed the last flight back to Edmonton, but hey, I know the concierge at the Fairmont Empress Hotel. I can probably get us rooms, and there's a great Italian seafood restaurant in the inner harbor, I'll call and get us a table."

Bernadette smiled at Anton as they walked to their car, "Of course you do, Anton, of course you do."

Mrs. Thornberry-Masters watched Bernadette and Anton say goodbye to Detective Letourneau and get into their cars and leave. Dixie was busy hoisting a leg and jetting a furious stream at the lamppost. His eyes closed in the apparent relief he was feeling.

"Weren't they nice detectives, Dixie? And quite understanding of our predicament with being robbed of Paul's notebook—my heavens Dixie—I just remembered something . . ." She pulled a cell phone out of her yellow purse.

She placed Dixie's leash over her arm, and with a furrowed brow locked in concentration, she punched the keys on her screen. "Now do you remember the code, Dixie?" She smiled down at her little dog that was busy shaking his leg and smelling around for other dogs that may have left their mark there as well.

As if the answer came to her from above, Mrs. Thornberry-Masters began typing again, "Ah yes, that's it, got it." She typed the last few letters into the cell phone and hit send. "Dixie, it was only 2 weeks ago that Paul had me set up this thing called a Twitter account. You know he didn't trust that Russian, don't you know . . . and neither did I."

Sometime just before midnight, McAllen received a message on Twitter. It was from Dixie. Accompanied by a picture of Dixie dressed in a Scots Tartan and sporting a Tam were the words, "Dixie says, the address of the second foundation has been found."

McAllen shut down his laptop, and prepared to leave his place in Merida, Mexico. The code had been set up with

Goodman some time ago. It was Goodman's idea of using Isaac Asimov and his Foundation Trilogy as the code. The Foundation book was the one that was kept in secret. It had the address of their mail drop. It would be only a matter of time before Sanchez was leaned on and McAllen's location found.

McAllen would take his laptop and a few clothes and be gone by early morning, long before anyone in his neighborhood was up, long before his housekeeper arrived. He already had his second place planned. He'd taken Goodman there once. He hoped Goodman didn't write it down anywhere—he had to chance it.

"Do you think they'll let us go to Mexico to chase McAllen?" Bernadette asked. They were back in Edmonton. Waiting outside the office of Chief Patterson.

The address they'd found in the book for Sanchez in Santa Fe turned up a very scared Mexican American who was forwarding mail from Goodman to his Aunt in Merida, Mexico. He said he only knew Goodman and was doing him a favor. But the hunt for McAllen now led to Mexico, as far as Anton and Bernadette were concerned.

The door to Patterson's office opened, and Anton was motioned inside. He gave Bernadette a wink and disappeared into the office.

Five minutes later Anton appeared with a broad smile, "Okay Bernadette, here's the deal, yes we get to go to Mexico, as observers and consultants." Anton frowned slightly as if to put his point across, "This means we do not get in the way of the actual investigation or capture. Do we understand that?"

Bernadette leaped out of her chair, "Absolutely. Now, look I need to make a quick drive to Red Deer to repack my suitcase."

"But we leave tomorrow morning."

Bernadette glanced at her watch, "Look, it's three o'clock now, it takes just over an hour and half to my place, I throw out the jeans from my bag, throw in my Khakis and a few things, and I'm back by this evening. No problem."

Anton sighed in resignation, "Okay, okay, but if you're not at the airport at 0700 hours tomorrow morning, I'm going solo—you got that?"

"Roger that," Bernadette said over her shoulder as she walked out of the building.

Traffic wasn't too bad leaving the city. It was just before five when Bernadette pulled into her driveway. She went next door to find Harvey. He wasn't home yet. There was no sign of her dog Sprocket, so she assumed they'd gone on a walk somewhere.

She grabbed her bag out of her Jeep, and had it emptied and replaced with her Mexico travel clothes in four minutes. She was always good repacking for travel. When your wardrobe consisted of jeans and t-shirts or Khakis and t-shirts the mix was easy.

Bernadette stood over her suitcase wondering if she'd pack a pair of shorts when her cell phone rang. The call display showed Mary Cardinal, her aunt back on her reservation in Northern Alberta.

Did she have time to answer this call? Should she? What if her Aunt Mary was sick? Guilt and her love for Aunt Mary made her answer the phone.

"Hey Aunt Mary, how are you?" Bernadette said as she winced with her guilt, and closed her suitcase. She decided against the shorts.

"It's me Louis," came the reply on the phone after a pause.

"Louis . . . what's up, where's your mom, is she okay." It was her cousin Louis that she despised.

There was a long pause on the phone. "Look my mom is fine, I just needed to talk to you, and I knew you'd never take my call if you knew it was me."

"You're absolutely right Louis, and I'm hitting the end button right now . . ."

"Wait—I need your help."

"Okay, Louis, get this straight, if you're in trouble with the law you need to remember that I am associated with the law. All I can do is tell you to march yourself to the nearest RCMP detachment and turn yourself in. I will then call your mom, my very lovely Aunt Mary and tell her that her dumbass son turned out to be as stupid as I said he was."

"No, you don't get it, I'm not in any trouble, but I want to get my hands on some of those Bio Bugs—I heard about it in the news—that you were on the case. Me and the brothers on the reservation, we could use them to stop the pipeline they want to put through here, and even help out other native bands. Don't you understand, with the Bio Bugs, we'd have the power to take control of our own destiny?"

Bernadette put her hand to her forehead, "Oh my god Louis, you are dumber than I thought you could be. You are speaking to an officer of the Royal Canadian Mounted Police about committing an intended crime. It is only because I think your mother is wonderful that I'm not going to call the local RCMP detachment and have you arrested . . ."

"You need to decide whose side you're on. You know,

come over to the side of your native roots," Louis said. His voice was now loud and edged with anger.

"Don't talk about my native roots Louis. Don't you remember calling me a half breed in the school yard, and what else did you call me—oh yeah—a baked potato, white on the inside and brown on the outside. You claimed I'd never be a true native, never be one of you, well guess what, you're right. I'm not on the side of white or native, I'm on the side of justice. You got a problem with pipelines crossing your lands, get a lawyer, and don't ever let me hear you're looking for a weapon of destruction, because I'll come up there and kick you in the balls so hard your eyes will pop out your head—just like I did in the school yard years ago."

Bernadette didn't wait for Louis's reply; she shut the phone off, grabbed her bag and headed for the door. She'd send Harvey a text to let him know she'd be back in a few days.

She opened the door, and Chris was standing in the doorway.

Chapter Twenty-One

Zara stood in the small kitchen, eyeing what there was for food in a tiny refrigerator and the three shelves that were the pantry. The refrigerator held some yogurt and cheese of questionable expiry dates, and the pantry had a large packet of tea. Adlan and his four Chechen fighters had lived on two things—tea and takeout.

The empty Kabob boxes were piled high outside the kitchen door, to make claim to the cuisine that had been consumed in Zara's absence. Now as she stood making a list, she decided she would make Adlan some of his favorites. She would start with a good, hearty borscht soup. Although it was hot outside, she would make it and they would have it cold. She would add a dollop of cold sour cream. Then she would make a Shashlik Tarka, a meat pie with lamb. Khinkali, his favourite dumplings, as well as some Golubtsy, a stuffed cabbage that was her specialty, would accompany this.

She would purchase a bottle of good Spanish wine,

possibly a spicy Rioja, and perhaps even a small bottle of Arak. Adlan used to love to sip Arak, liquor that tasted of anise. He would drop in ice and some water, and they would sit and talk for hours of what their homeland was like before the war with Russia.

Adlan was in the other room. He sat hunched over a desk gazing at his computer, and locked into a discussion on his cell phone with the two remaining Chechen fighters. They were somewhere at sea and Adlan was tracking their progress, looking at the best place to make the attack on the oil tanker, and questioning them about where they would place the vials.

A scientist named Ramzan, and an engineer named Kheda, both Chechens, were on the other line; they were conferencing about the best place to attack. Kheda told Adlan he didn't think the Bio Bugs would penetrate the second hull of the tanker. Ramzan thought they would. From what Ramzan had heard of the attack on the Russian pipeline, the Bio Bugs would not stop at one hull; they would go further and consume the next one. Ramzan postulated that the bugs might keep going, even in a saline environment.

Ramzan's voice was faltering as he spoke, as if unsure of what he was reading. "The notes that your person brought back from Canada state that these organisms come from the depths of the ocean. There is a chance they may eat everything in their path . . ." He paused. You could hear him take a deep breath, "But I'm only speculating . . ."

"So you're saying, Ramzan," Adlan cut in, "that when my people release these bugs, they may continue going—eating everything that has metal in the sea?"

"Yes, that is a possibility, only a theory, and of course,

we would have to test it to ensure that our premise is correct," Ramzan said.

Adlan pounded his fist on the table. "I have no time for your theories—we will find out everything we need to once the bugs are released into the ship—you can watch CNN, and you can validate your premise."

"Anzor and Kerim, you hear me?" Adlan shouted into the phone.

A weak voice replied, "Yes." It wasn't clear if it was Anzor or Kerim. Zara thought it would be Anzor.

"Stick with the plan. I want the shipping channel I've chosen for release of the vials. Make sure you release where you can do maximum damage," Adlan shouted into the phone.

"Yes," came the reply.

Zara stood at the kitchen door listening to Adlan. He snapped his phone shut and threw it onto the floor. It bounced along the carpet and ended up by a chair. He put his head in his hands and breathed deeply. Zara knew there was no use in approaching him now.

She walked quietly out of the apartment. The Boqueria Market on Barcelona's Ramblas street would have everything she needed for the feast she would make for Adlan tonight. She grabbed her three shopping bags and checked herself in the hall mirror.

Zara wore a brown Abaya and a black hijab headscarf that covered her hair. She added a pair of dark imitation Dolce and Gabbana sunglasses to hide her eyes. An Arab woman in the Ravel neighborhood was not uncommon—she would blend in perfectly.

It was already 9 a.m. and she needed to get going. The streets would be scorching with the temperatures reaching

37 Celsius by midday. She descended the stairs, smelling the morning coffee and fresh bread from other apartments. A mixture of voices, some Pakistani, some African, blended into a steady stream of background noise—and then she stopped—there was someone speaking a language that always struck fear in her. It was Russian.

She was at the bottom of the stair, her hands on the door to exit. She froze. Two men walked by in the street. They were speaking Russian to one another. They were dressed in dark pants, white shirts, dark jackets, and black shoes. There was an air of determination about them. Zara felt dryness in her throat. Her breathing became shallow.

Her first thought was, *Russian tourists, they are everywhere now—how can I be so paranoid?* She tried to let these thoughts soothe her paranoia, a technique she used so she would not panic. She would wait, watch the two go down the street, and then resume her journey to the market.

Zara took a deep breath, let it ease out and was about to push further out of the large apartment door when she caught sight of two more men. They met the other men on a corner. There was something about them. They were athletic-looking, *and also wore jackets. Who wears a jacket in the heat of Barcelona in August?* She thought.

The answer came to Zara like a bolt of electricity running through her body. These men were SVR, the Russian Foreign Intelligence Service. Everything about them screamed it to her. She watched through the crack in the door. They were motioning with their hands, looking at their phones. Their jackets would conceal weapons: guns, handcuffs, and Tasers.

One of the men looked back down the street toward Zara. She backed away into the shadow of the doorway.

She didn't close the door, for fear they would see it. Her heart pounded; she was sweating in her abaya. A long moment passed before she felt safe to look out again.

They had gone. The street was empty. A few children played down the street, and an old woman dressed in a hijab and abaya walked slowly with her daughter as they carried packages back from the market.

Zara composed herself and headed back up the stairs. Adlan needed to know the Russians were in the neighborhood, and they could only be looking for her. She had left a trail to Barcelona from Canada. She was in danger and so was Adlan.

Bernadette couldn't speak at first. Seeing Chris there, he'd been the object of her avoidance for four weeks. Here he was in the flesh—remarkably good-looking flesh, but with it came the guilt of her non-commitment.

"I see you're heading somewhere," Chris said softly, eying Bernadette's suitcase.

Bernadette put the suitcase down, "Ah . . . yeah . . . a major case in Mexico, we got a lead on McAllen . . . and well you know, just got to follow the leads . . ." She let her words trail off.

"Are you on the case with Anton?"

"Anton?" Bernadette looked at Chris, his eyes had this accusing look, and the name Anton, had the sound of an accusation in them.

"Yes, Anton, I'm wondering if perhaps . . . you know . . . if you and him were now an item because . . ."

"Oh no," Bernadette blurted out, her brain putting together Chris's train of thought, "No, Anton and I, no we're not in any way romantically linked, oh no, not even in the slightest," She suppressed a slight giggle at the thought.

"Then why haven't I heard from you in over four weeks?"

Bernadette looked at her watch, it was 6pm, and she had to be at the airport in less than twelve hours. Chris needed an explanation. She pulled him inside the door and closed the door behind him. She had some explaining to do.

Viktor Lutrova looked at his latest text message. There was no sign of Zara Mashhadov. There were now five teams of Russian Foreign Intelligence Service in Barcelona, and another three teams were on their way.

They had arrived by commercial flights from Amsterdam, Paris, and Frankfurt. No Russian agent would land direct from Russia. They wanted their presence to be unknown. A house had been rented on the outside of Barcelona. The house was chosen because it was not close to other houses and had a basement. An interrogator was waiting there. He was waiting for the capture of Zara Mashhadov. He would extract the location of Adlan Kataev from Zara. The interrogator was proficient at this job, and only needed Zara to begin his duties.

Viktor glanced at his cell phone; another sweep of the Raval, Barcelona's seediest area had revealed nothing. He was sweating. The heat of the stone buildings produced an oven-like affect for those foolish enough to be outside in it. Barcelona's populace went to the market early, then stayed indoors until after a late lunch that was followed by a nap and would only come outside in the evening for dinners that began at 10 p. m. and ended at midnight.

Agent Bronislav appeared at Viktor's side, "I think we need to dress up our female agents."

Viktor dropped his phone to his side. "Dress them as what—Flamenco dancers?"

Bronislav was taken aback by Viktor's comment. "No, I think we should get Arab dress for them. They can wander the streets and not draw attention—like our men are doing."

Viktor dropped his head slightly. "Yes, you're right. We stand out like idiots walking around in our European clothing in an Arab neighborhood. Zara has spotted us by now, and will be hiding deep in her hole like a rabbit."

Bronislav shook his head. "Don't worry, it's early yet. We have more agents coming, and Zara is going nowhere. And if she's with that bastard Kataev, they can rot together until we catch them."

Viktor smiled. "Bronislav, what would I do without your optimism?"

Bronislav laughed as he walked away. "You would be a traffic cop in Moscow."

Viktor watched Bronislav walk down the filthy street. Bronislav was Viktor's second-in-command. He was mid-thirties, tall, and carried himself with an air that told you he felt good about himself. All the other agents liked him. He always made sure he was at your back.

Viktor was late forties, short for a Russian, with dark features and dark brooding eyes. His mother claimed there was some Manchurian influence in his father's family, an influence that gave him a broad nose, broad face and thick features. His father never confirmed the genealogy as he was out of Viktor's life soon after he was born.

Viktor Lutrova was the senior field officer with the SRV. He had spent several years in Chechnya hunting the

Chechen terrorists, and his latest mission was to hunt the Chechens abroad. The Russian Foreign Intelligence service had long ago taken on the methods of the Israelis and the Mossad. You hunt them wherever they are—before they are able to attack your homeland.

Viktor was moved back to Russia in 2010, just after the bombing of the Metro station in Moscow by two Chechen women. Defending Russia against Chechen terrorism was made more complicated by the corruption of the Russian border patrol. A 5,000 Ruble note stuffed into a fake passport was all that most people needed to get across the Russian border.

Viktor made several attempts to discuss the lack of Russian border security with his superiors, and how it made his job harder when the border was so porous. After each attack on Russia, borders were closed, a few officials were fired, and then everything went back to the way it was, with the exception that it now took a 10,000 ruble note to get past some of the more discerning Russian border guards.

Viktor's cell phone rang. The caller was one of his agents covering the Boqueria Market off the Ramblas. "What have you got?" was Viktor's greeting.

The caller was Lena Batkin, a new hire right out of Moscow University, and other than her ability to speak Arabic fluently, Viktor was not sure if she was much use. She hadn't developed any instincts yet. "We haven't seen anything all morning. Now that it's late morning, we're getting all the tourists coming by."

"And she could blend in with the tourists—couldn't she?"

Lena paused on the phone. "Yes, she could do that."

"Good, then stay there, and keep watching the market to see if she shows up." Viktor punched his keypad to close his phone. He shook his head at the rookies that he was getting lately. His division should be staffed with the brightest and the best, and he was getting daughters of police chiefs who had done a favor for someone in the service, or had paid a bribe.

His cell phone rang again. This time it was Bronislav. "I think we have something."

Viktor shielded his eyes from the high sun, "Where are you?"

"I'm just down the street, by the local market—we've been showing Zara's picture, telling the Arabs in the neighborhood that Zara was a kidnap victim and we're offering a 5,000 Euro reward for information on her whereabouts."

"Good thinking. I hope you have a spare 5,000 Euros," Viktor replied.

Bronislav chuckled into the phone. "I think I have some counterfeit stuff on hand . . . so do you want to hear what I've got?"

"Sure, I'm always amazed at what information someone will come up with for 5,000 Euros. I'd tell you I'm a direct relation to Stalin," Viktor said.

"Okay, this shopkeeper here says a woman matching Zara's facial feature was in his shop just yesterday. The shopkeeper's wife said that the woman spoke Arabic but with a dialect she'd never heard before," Bronislav said.

"Well, if someone had never heard Chechen Arabic, then yes, it would sound strange. Did they say where they think she lives?" Viktor asked.

"Yes, the shopkeeper's wife watched her walk down the street, and enter the building you're standing in front of."

"Call all the other agents. Get a car and tell our interrogator we will have a nice warm body for him very soon." Viktor punched his phone closed and looked up at the building he was standing in front of. They would wait until night, and enter the building quietly. Using listening devices and tiny cable cameras they would find out where Zara was. Viktor felt the triumph of her capture very near—he hadn't been this happy and excited in months.

Chapter Twenty-Two

The oil super tanker plowed deeper into the Aegean Sea on its journey to the Mediterranean. Its blunt edged prow threw a thick sea spray over its array of pipes and valves that served to offload the mass of oil in its hold.

On the bridge deck, one crewman sat in the command chair. There was no wheel, but a lever on each side of the chair that sent instant commands to the mass of diesel engines below. An officer of the watch sat in the chair beside him, watching the horizon and the monitors displayed on the console in front of him.

Behind the crewman and the officer were another series of computer stations with rows of monitors. One officer watched a series of monitors that showed the immediate area around the tanker. Another monitor showed all vessels within 100 nautical miles.

The tanker was three football fields long and one wide. It took a full 15 minutes and eight kilometers to come to a stop and needed a full two kilometers to make a turn. A ship like this needed other ships to keep out of its way. The officer on the radar made sure of that.

The tanker held three million barrels of oil. With a double hull and a state-of-the-art leak detection system, it was deemed to be one of the safest tankers afloat. But if they had a fire or collision, they were sitting on a disaster at sea.

Another crewman watched a series of monitors that showed a bank of green lights. In both Russian and English, the warning stated:

FIRE CONTROL PANEL: ANY FIRE ALARM SHOULD BE TREATED LIKE A GENERAL ALARM.

Anzor and Kerim were at the center of the ship, kneeling, and chipping away rust from the deck. From the bridge, they looked like mere ants on an expanse of metal. Anzor sweated in his coveralls. He was a large man and sweated easily. He stood up, arched his back, and looked down at Kerim. "I think I know how we will attack this monster."

Kerim did not look up from his work. "And how do you think we will do that?" He enjoyed the work he was doing. He hoped Anzor would fail, and they would sail for the full month on this magnificent ship.

Anzor wiped his face with a rag from his back pocket. "I met a man from Kurdistan last night named Goran. He is the one who oversees the main pump room. He will show me how to put our little bugs of mischief into all the compartments of this mighty ship and pull her apart." He threw his other hand into the air, to punctuate his statement.

Kerim looked up at Anzor, squinting in the sun. "And how will you make this Kurdistan man help you sink this vessel? Kurds do not hate Russians; they hate Turks and

Iraqis. I remember my school teacher telling me the Russians were aligned with the Kurds."

"Yes, yes, that is all true, but Goran thinks I want to become a lifetime sailor on tankers just like him. I told him, I no longer want to be a lowly maintenance worker." Anzor puffed out his chest. "Yes, I am quite the storyteller. I told him of my struggle to feed my wife and five children, my old mother who needs an eye operation, and several other tales of woe."

Kerim sat back on his heels and pointed with his chipping tool at Anzor. "So, you have told this man a pack of lies to curry his favor—if he only knew you were a single man who couldn't commit to a decent woman, he would spit on your shadow."

"Ha, this is very true, but what can I do? I am a marvel when telling tales . . ."

"What do you think this is, a luxury cruise? That we pay you to gab all day while we sail amongst the sights?" The words of their foreman brought them back to reality. Neither of them had seen him approach. Kerim and Anzor bent down with their chipping tools and waited for him to depart.

They chipped away in silence, until their foreman was gone. "We will be close to Mykonos and Naxos in three days. It will be imperative that we release our bugs into this ship then," Anzor said. His head was bent down over his work. A bead of sweat edged its way from his eyebrow to his nose.

"Why do we do it there?"

"Maximum bloody damage," Anzor said. "The shipping lanes are tight there. The coast of Mykonos will feel the blight of this monster's hold, and people will rise up in hatred of the Russians." Anzor bent down to his work, and they spoke no more of the plan for the rest of the day.

Kerim watched Anzor ingratiate himself with the Kurd called Goran. At each mealtime Anzor was at this side. Anzor would fetch Goran more tea or an extra sweet from the canteen. He sat in rapt awe as he asked Goran to tell him more about his home life, his past voyages, and the many values of being a merchant marine sailor.

By the third day, Goran was offering to give Anzor a lesson in his pump room as Anzor told Goran this was the job he wanted to do, and wanted to see if he was capable of it. As they walked out of the dining room, Anzor took Kerim aside.

Anzor looked both ways up the gangway to ensure no one would hear them. "Look, tomorrow night Goran will take me to the pump room to give me a lesson in its operation and you will arrive soon after with our little vials."

"But how will we put the vials into the pump room mechanism with Goran still there?" Kerim looked around as he spoke softly.

"Easy, we will kill him."

"Kill him . . . why do we need to do that?" Kerim whispered. A tightening in his throat cut off his voice. Kerim was committed to the cause, but had never killed a man, and did not know if he had the will to do so.

Anzor shook his head in disapproval. "My little brother, if we let him live, and if he survives the sinking of this ship —what do you think happens to us?"

Kerim bowed his head. The answer was obvious. He was no suicide bomber or willing to kill himself to sink this ship. The death of Goran was now an obvious choice. Something that just had to be done. "I guess you're right."

"That is the spirit. Now I will give you a wrench and when Goran and I are talking, you hit him a mighty blow to the head."

"You want *me* to kill him!" Kerim blurted out the words out. He clasped his hand to his mouth and looked around. No one came out of the dining room. No one had heard them.

Anzor pulled Kerim close. "Look, I will keep him busy talking, and you come up from behind him. Very simple. One blow and he's done."

That night Kerim did not sleep. He tossed from one side of his small bunk to the next. Beside him in the small, darkened room that they shared, Anzor snored softly. He knew that killing someone had always been a possibility the moment they agreed to this mission. He thought it would be a bomb—triggered from a remote area—and that many Russians would die.

Now, an unsuspecting man from a small village in Kurdistan must die, and by Kerim's hand. In the darkened room, Kerim took his hand from underneath his blanket and put it close to his face. A small light shone through the portal. He could see his long slender fingers and small hands.

He had wanted to be a teacher, perhaps of history, or geography. As a young boy, he buried his face in books while his big brother Anzor stormed around their village getting into trouble. His mother told Kerim he should be more like his brother, a man who would make something of himself.

Kerim remembered his studies of Greek ships powered by rowers, their holds filled with olive oil and wine as they wallowed in the sun on the way to ports such as Acre in ancient Phoenicia, or Jaffa in the Kingdom of Israel and Alexandria in Egypt.

He sighed, listened to the soft snores of his big brother, and wondered if, on that day in his village when his brother told him to follow him to jihad, if he should have said no and left for England. He had been accepted at a teachers' college there. The headmaster of his village knew someone who got him in. In three years, he could have been teaching in Saudi Arabia, or the United Arab Emirates.

A beam of moonlight displayed his hand before his eyes. A hand that should have pointed out places on a map to students was going to take a man's life. Kerim's stomach churned, and a dry retching feeling rose in his throat.

The morning broke in bright sunshine. The day shift met in the mess hall and consumed breakfast with a large measure of tea and coffee, then moved onto their chores. Kerim and Anzor resumed their duties on the deck, chipping away at the rust, and then applying paint.

Anzor explained the plan to Kerim in exact sequence. The pump room was the heart of the super tanker. The room connected all twelve of the individual compartments containing the oil. Emptying their vials in there and turning on the pumps would immediately inject the bugs into all the compartments. They would then proceed to the deck, wait for the ship to come apart and board the lifeboats with the other crew members.

After Anzor had finished Kerim swallowed hard, "Is it still necessary to kill Goran?"

Anzor stared at Kerim and gripped his shoulder, squeezing hard. "My little brother, our friend Adlan asked me if you had the courage for this mission, and I said yes. Our mother asked me if you had the strength to be a true fighter, and I said yes. Now, I will only tell you one last time, tonight you will summon your courage to strike this man down. That is the last word on this matter." He knelt back on the deck and resumed his work.

They did not speak again until just before 10 p. m. Anzor came to their cabin and handed Kerim a pipe wrench. "Conceal this in your coveralls. I am meeting Goran in the pump room in 20 minutes." Anzor turned and left.

Kerim stood in his cabin. His hand felt the cold steel of the pipe wrench. A cold clamminess grew in his hand, and he felt a tremor in his wrist. He dropped the pipe wrench then picked it up again, sitting on the bed to calm his nerves.

He stared down at his watch. The time advanced. He willed it to stop. Each time the second hand swept around the face another minute brought him closer to his date with death. But it would be the death of an innocent man—by his own hand.

At 10:45, there was no more waiting. He could stall no longer. He tried to stroll leisurely down the gangways, smiling at the few other crewmen he met. The pipe wrench felt like a massive weight dragging at the inside pocket in his coveralls. He concealed it with his hand and willed himself to move forward. His feet felt like lead, he walked stiffly, and was sure everyone noticed.

He avoided the elevator and took the stairs down, hoping he wouldn't meet anyone on his way down. He was in luck. The stairway was empty. His boots clanged as he walked on the metal stairway. They made a thunderous noise in his ears.

He reached the pump room deck and walked slowly to it. The pump room was easily accessible; no security was present. The room was used for offloading or loading crude. Other than Goran, few crewmen ever came here.

Kerim pushed the heavy door to the room open. Anzor and Goran were at the controls of the room, deep in conversation. Kerim removed the pipe wrench from his pocket and crept forward. He could see Goran's shiny, hairless head. A silver earring hung from one ear.

As he approached, he could see the detail of Goran's head. It was smooth. A head shaved perfectly with a cream applied that made it shine in the overhead lights. Kerim imagined his wrench striking that perfectly smooth head, the head gushing blood, and Goran falling to the floor, eyes wild with shock—his lifeblood flowing from him.

He stopped for a moment. Goran reached back with his hand. He scratched his head. *Did he anticipate the blow that was about to be struck?* Kerim wondered. Kerim inched forward again, holding his breath.

Two feet from Goran's back, he stopped. He could feel the warmth of Goran before him. See the drops of perspiration forming on his neck making their way down into his t-shirt.

He raised his wrench and struck.

As Kerim came down with his wrench, Goran came up with his hand to scratch his head again. The wrench hit Goran's hand and bounced out of Kerim's hand. Goran turned to see Kerim standing there.

"What the hell?" Goran yelled, his eyes wide with fear. He could see the intent of murder in Kerim's anguished face.

Anzor jumped Goran and pulled him to the floor. Goran twirled as he fell, and seized Anzor by the throat. They rolled over the steel floor as Kerim moved out of their way. Kerim was frozen, transfixed, watching his brother grappling with the man.

Anzor pulled his hands from Goran's back and grabbed his throat. Two men, locked on each other's throats, grunting, thrashing with their feet to gain a foothold and add more strength to their death grips.

Anzor saw the wrench beside Goran's head; he released one hand, grabbed the wrench and struck him. The crunch of metal on bone echoed in the room.

Goran screamed in agony. He reached for the wrench. Anzor struck again. He struck Goran in the forehead. Goran went limp. A pool of blood formed at his head.

Anzor knelt beside Goran. His coveralls were covered in blood. He struck two more blows at Goran. There was no sound from Goran. Steel met bone. The sound echoed around the room.

Kerim tapped Anzor on the shoulder. "I believe he is dead, my brother."

Anzor stood. He wiped sweat and Goran's blood from his face. "Yes, I believe he is. You have the vials?" he asked, wheezing with exhaustion.

Kerim produced the vials from his other pocket and gave them to Anzor. He could not look Anzor in the eyes. He knew he was a failure once again. Anzor took the vials and emptied them into an opening in the pump room manifold.

In the past three days, Goran had explained to Anzor just how the pump room connected each of the holding tanks on the ship. He dumped the vials in and hit the switch that connected all the holding tanks. The large motor hummed.

Anzor smiled at Kerim. "This motor is used to balance the oil in the tanks; today we use it to distribute our Bio Bugs to destroy this ship."

Kerim watched Anzor's face. It showed only the delight of the mission. There was a large gash on Anzor's arm. A wound from his struggle with Goran, it dripped blood onto the machinery. Kerim reached to tend to it, and Anzor brushed his hand away. There was an unmistakable look of disappointment he couldn't miss.

"How long until the bugs take effect?" Kerim asked.

"I'm not sure. We will go back to our room, wash up, and wait. Hopefully there will be an abandon ship call a few hours from now, perhaps by morning . . ."

Anzor stopped as he felt the ship lurch to one side. Usually, the super tanker rolled to one side then the other. This was unmistakable, the roll was deep—too deep. "I think they have already begun to attack the ship—we must hurry."

The officer of the watch on the navigation deck felt the lurch of the ship. The officer had been in collisions at sea before. But this didn't feel like that. He ran to the control panel. The crewman was standing wild eyed before the panel. The panel was a mass of red lights. Bulkheads were caving in—the sea was rushing in. The officer of the watch hit the abandon ship alarm, then grabbed the radiophone to issue a May Day call.

Anzor and Kerim ran from the pump room. The elevator was already out of commission. They could hear men running up the stairs. They joined them. The claxon was sounding and the abandon ship message was being repeated in Russian, Arabic and English.

They made it up four flights of stairs before Anzor stopped, wheezing. His bulk worked against him on the climb. "Look, Kerim . . . we can walk up . . . this ship will not break apart so fast."

He stopped as he heard water rushing from below. They looked down the stairs to see water mixed with oil coming fast.

"We must run, my brother. We need to get our life vests and get to a boat. You can rest there." Kerim grabbed

Anzor, and then pushed him from behind as they made the last four decks.

The scene on the ship's deck was surreal. The ship was listing badly; men were rushing to the lifeboats. They grabbed life vests from a cabinet and lurched towards the stern. There were lifeboats on either side.

"Quickly Anzor," Kerim yelled above the sound of the claxon and address system. "We must make it to our lifeboat station."

Anzor moved slow. He was wheezing from the run up the stairs, and not used to having his younger brother give him orders. "They will wait for us—they will bloody well wait for us."

As Anzor was not moving fast enough, Kerim decided they were closer to the port side lifeboat. He pushed Anzor in that direction. A bright moon shone over the ship that was now laboring heavily in the seas. The bow of the ship was submerged. They staggered down the slanting deck to the lifeboats. As they got to the port side, they saw that boat was already gone.

They needed to get starboard. That lifeboat was their designation. The crew wouldn't leave without them. At least they hoped. They staggered upward; the slant of the ship was rising, and they grabbed the railings to move forward.

They reached the lifeboat. It was still there. Several crewmembers milled around it; the Bosun was yelling instructions in Russian. As Kerim reached the lifeboat with the panting Anzor he could see the problem. The lifeboat was stuck with the pitch of the ship. He remembered seeing this on the Costa Concordia. He never thought he would be trapped by the same problem.

Kerim looked at Anzor, "Anzor, it is no use; we must jump into the sea."

Anzor's eyes went wide. "Into the sea—I cannot swim, I will drown."

"No, no my brother, you will be fine. We will go back to the port side. It is almost even with the sea. We will float away, light our life vest beacons, and be picked up." Kerim waved his hand to the sea around them. "You see, there are many ships lights around us—we will be picked up in no time."

Anzor was like a large bull being led by the little Kerim. He resisted the entire return journey down the slanting deck. He was coming up with even more reasons why they should try to free the other lifeboat when the super tanker gave another sudden lurch.

Kerim pushed Anzor before him, and in seconds they were swimming in the warm sea. Kerim grabbed the back of Anzor's life vest, and swam with him in tow. Kerim had always been a good swimmer.

The moonlight revealed the super tanker, its lights still shining, with large holes in its sides. Kerim called back to Anzor. "You see the bugs have done the work faster than we thought. Are you not happy with your work?"

Anzor turned his head, but did not reply. He was keeping his gashed arm above the seawater. His large body was now covered in oil that glistened in the moonlight, his belly rose up above the water, and he was powerless in the water as Kerim pulled him along.

A small wooden fishing boat came chugging into view. A group of Greek sailors called out to them. Kerim waved his hand. "You see Anzor, like I said. We are saved."

Bernadette had intended to tell Chris about her strange childhood, her lack of trust in the sanctity of marriage, and long term relationships—instead, she gave Chris a hug first, and he hugged back. She kissed him. He kissed her back.

Inside of three minutes they were headed for her bedroom, yanking at each other's clothes and leaving a trail of pants, shirts and underwear until they reached the bedroom and commenced frantic lovemaking.

Much later they lay entwined on the bed. Chris traced his hand down her shoulder and along her back. She rolled over and looked at her watch, it was nine o'clock. "I've got to get going," she said as she got out of bed to get her clothes.

"What time's your flight?"

"7 am, but I must check in at 5:30am for the flight to Houston that connects to Mexico. I was supposed to be staying at a hotel near the airport tonight."

"Leave early in the morning," Chris said as he rolled out of bed, and stood naked in front of Bernadette.

"Oh my god, you're hard as rock."

"Yes, as a member of the Canada's national police force, I stand on guard for thee!" Chris laughed as he moved closer.

In minutes they were back in bed together. Bernadette realized Chris did have a good idea. She had eight and half-hours before she checked into her flight.

Chapter Twenty-Three

Captain Lars Johannes was called to the bridge of the cruise ship *Empress of Europe* at 2325 hours. He was just about to fall asleep in his quarters after a long day of navigating the Greek Isles. Their previous port was Santorini, and berthing the massive cruise ship into the Caldera with its treacherous rock outcrops was never an easy task. And all the while, he had to keep smiling as the captain of one of the world's largest cruise ships.

The ship was 1,181 feet long, 208 feet wide and over 225,000 tons, with a full capacity of over 6,300 passengers. This warm August night, while sailing at 22 knots to make their next port in Dubrovnik, the ship was at capacity.

Arriving at the massive bridge, set in darkness with blue lights for reading instruments, the captain found the officer of the bridge. "What's the situation?"

The officer pointed to the sweeping radar in front of them. "We've received a report from the Greek Coast Guard that an oil supertanker is in distress and sinking 25 nautical miles off our starboard." The officer was young, in his late twenties, and a Norwegian from close to the captain's hometown.

"Very well, make our speed to 25 knots, and inform the crew on lifeboat decks three to make ready for rescue when we reach the destination. Call our ship's doctor and have him muster all medical personnel to be on deck three for any casualties."

"Aye, aye Sir." The officer picked up his phone and began calling orders in a quiet and calm voice.

Captain Johannes watched his young officer in action and felt a pride in watching what his mentoring had done with the young man in three short years. He would be a fine captain one day. He looked over the calm seas, the bright moon that illuminated the sky and wondered what could have befallen this supertanker. He then realized something he needed to do. He had to call the head office in Miami.

Any time his cruise ship veered off course, company policy stated that the department of operations must be informed. As this ship was the largest and most prestigious of the fleet, that meant that the Vice President of Operations, Niels Bleeker, must be contacted. Bleeker was Dutch, recruited from a large Dutch cruise company three months earlier, and Captain Johannes hated speaking with him.

There was something in Bleeker's voice that grated on Johannes. There was the implied tone that Bleeker's previous Dutch cruise company did everything so much better than the company that Johannes sailed for. Johannes privately mused that Bleeker must have been scorned by a good-looking Norwegian woman to hate the Norwegians so much. It was something he would never voice.

Johannes made the call to Miami Operations. But he did so after drinking a cup of tea on the bridge, and getting a full briefing about weather conditions, all other vessels in the area, and what other ships were coming to the aide of the stricken tanker. It took a full 45 minutes for him to do this. By the time he picked up the satellite phone to make the call, they could see the lights of the supertanker on the moonlit horizon.

When Johannes reached Bleeker he could tell he was not in a happy mood. It was 6 a.m. Miami time, and a Saturday morning. He gave Bleeker a quick summary of the situation and the readiness of his ship's crew to aid the stricken vessel.

Bleeker inhaled sharply before his reply. "Why is our star cruise ship, with over 6,000 paying passengers aboard, going to the aid of an oil tanker, which will be wallowing in a sea of thick crude oil? Not only will it take a day in port to get the oil stains off the *Empress of Europe's* beautiful white hull, but the stench of oil will also make our passengers sick."

He inhaled again as he launched into his tirade, "If you venture into that morass of thick stench—which I forbid you to do—I would have over 1,000 emails from passengers in three hours complaining of nausea and missed port tours."

Johannes cut in, "But the law of the sea states . . ."

"Damn it, Johannes, I know the law of the sea. It states that all those that are able should give aid. You are going to call the Greek Coast Guard, tell them you've developed engine trouble, and steam away at 10 knots, then in one hour from now, you'll fix your engine trouble and make your next port of call, and 6,000 plus paying passengers will happily be taking tours that they've paid us good money for."

"But we are the closest to give them aid," Johannes cut in. He was a seventh-generation Norwegian seafarer. Any mariner in trouble was his concern. This had been taught to him by his grandfather in Stavanger and handed down from one mariner to another."

"How close are other ships?"

Johannes scanned his radar screen. "There are other ships at 10 and 15 nautical miles. We are only 3 nautical miles away. We could easily pick them up and hand them over . . ."

"Damn your thick Norwegian skin, Johannes, I've told you what you need to do. Turn your ship due north toward your next port, and tell the Greek Coast Guard you have engine trouble. You carry out this order, or you will be relieved of duties at your next port." Bleeker slammed the phone down.

Captain Johannes stood at the bridge, the phone clenched in his fist, his knuckles turning white as the blood drained from his hand. The grip on the phone was the one he imagined around Bleeker's throat. He slammed the phone down. "Damn."

His first officer visibly jumped beside him. The captain was never one for outbursts, not even in their most dangerous times of sailing. The crew watched the captain as he gave instructions to the first officer; they could see something was wrong.

"Slow speed to 10 knots, and turn back to our previous heading," Johannes said in an almost whisper to the first officer.

"Aye, aye Captain," the first officer repeated, then he gave the same instruction to the helm. The entire bridge crew knew what had happened. The head office in Miami had overruled their captain, the one they all admired and would do anything for. They were not going to the aid of fellow sailors; they were making like they were disabled and heading for their original port.

The captain stormed off the bridge, the bridge crew could feel the heat of their captain's anger as he walked by. It blended with the heat of the shame they felt for the actions of their ship.

Captain Kostas Yannatos on the Greek Coast Guard ship of the Hellenic Navy received the news from the Cruise ship *Empress of Europe.* He did not challenge the vessel's information about being damaged. To Captain Yannatos, a deeply religious man, everyone's actions were between themselves and their God.

Captain Yannatos told his helmsman to increase the speed of their 190-foot boat to its maximum 33 knots and informed the other ships in the area to make haste, as the cruise ship would no longer be the first on the scene. He put down his phone and made the sign of the cross over his chest, hoping they would be in time to save the sailors from the sinking tanker.

Chapter Twenty-Four

Adlan watched the BBC Europe News. News of the sinking supertanker in the Mediterranean was now breaking across the screen, with pictures of a map where the sinking was taking place.

News reporters, barely sounding awake, were weighing in from Athens, Haifa, and Istanbul. They were trying to talk coherently about a tragedy at sea involving an oil tanker. They were piecing the story together from Coast Guard reports. There would be no light for another five hours. No news helicopter would fly until dawn.

The ship's owners, located in Sevastopol, Russia, did not want to comment. They were digesting the news themselves. There were three million barrels of their precious oil, to their knowledge, gushing out into the sea. They hadn't even thought of the ecological damage. They just saw money leaking out of the hull of their tanker. Thirty-three million US dollars of crude oil was leaking into the Atlantic. They were liable for the huge cleanup bill. Several in the board-room reached for a Vodka bottle.

The Greek Prime Minister made a statement regarding the potential destruction to the Greek fishing fleet and the tourist industry. Adlan could see the underlying tension on the Prime Ministers face. As if the Greek economic crisis had not been enough, the strikes, the loss of tourism—now this—millions of barrels of crude oil washing up on the picturesque Greek Beaches from Santorini to Rhodes. The losses would be catastrophic, and Adlan rubbed his hands in glee.

Zara stood in the kitchen and watched Adlan. They were holed up in this apartment until someone came for them. The clock was ticking. Either the Russian Security forces would find them, or the men Adlan had called to rescue them would get to them first.

Adlan's cell phone rang. He put it to his ear, with a quick, "Yes. Speak." He listened intently, nodded a few times, shook his head a few times, and then hung his head in his hands as he put the phone down.

"My scientist friend tells me that he cannot break the password for the formula you brought from Canada." Adlan waved his hand at the television. "This was the last of the bugs in the hold of the supertanker. We just made a statement to Russia, by destroying pipelines and one of their great ships, and I have no more of this marvelous weapon."

Adlan turned and gazed at Zara, "Unless you know who your dead Canadian friend gave the password to, then our campaign is finished before it gets fully started." He waved back at the television. "So many more pipelines . . . more ships . . . I could get a hundred men lined up to do this destruction . . ."

"But isn't it in the book I brought?" She thought of the book she had stolen from Goodman's elderly neighbor. She thought she had closed all the loopholes and brought everything to Adlan.

"No, it was only a notebook of chemical formulas, very basic musings according to my scientist friend. He even tried using some of the names of the chemical elements to unlock the formula, but nothing worked . . . perhaps someone else has this password?" Adlan searched Zara's face for an answer. She could see he was desperate to get his hands on more of this new weapon.

Zara's face lit up. "Yes, yes, his professor friend, he talked about him with great reverence, and there was an address in the back of the book—in Mexico."

Adlan stood up, and stretched. His shirt was covered in sweat. "Then that is where we are going."

"Are you not satisfied with the destruction done already?" Zara asked.

"Ha, not even close. I will not be satisfied until the last pipeline in Russia stops delivering oil and every Russian tanker is sunk into the ocean. The Russian banks will dry up—their military will be broke, and they will leave my Chechnya in peace." Adlan sat down again and watched the TV.

Zara placed her hands on her hips. "And how will we get to Mexico? I told you the Russians are in the street looking for us."

Adlan didn't turn, he only raised his hand as he said, "They've chased me for years. I've felt their breath on my neck every time they're close—we will be fine."

A knock came at the door. Zara walked slowly to answer it. She held her breath as she opened the door. She expected to see Russian Security Forces. Instead, a man stood in the dimly lit hallway, wearing a bright green jacket and pants, with large bands of sliver stripes around the arms, torso and legs of his outfit. *Barcelona Sanitation Corporation* was written in Spanish on a badge of the jacket.

The man nodded to Zara, introduced himself as Cayo, and walked into the apartment with a large bundle under his arm. The bundle produced two outfits in sizes to fit Zara and Adlan, as well as work boots and gloves.

Adlan smiled at Zara. "You see Zara—transportation has arrived." He put on his uniform, donned the boots, and Zara did the same. Zara tied a bandana over her hair and wore a set of protective glasses. Adlan put on a baseball hat. Their disguises were complete.

They walked quickly down the stairs, Zara aware of the clump-clump that the work boots made. Her heart beating so fast she could hardly breathe. She expected a Russian agent to jump out of every apartment door they passed.

In the darkened street outside, a Barcelona Sanitation truck was idling. A stream of diesel from the twin exhaust pipes mixed with the humid air and stench from the street. Zara's stomach did a double take from the anxiety and the smell.

Cayo instructed Zara and Adlan to follow him as they picked up trash along the streets and dumped it into the back of the truck. They hung on the back of the large truck, its air brakes sounded, and they lurched forward. In front of every apartment building, they stopped and picked up trash.

Their garbage truck passed by a group of men getting out of two cars and rushing into a building directly across from where Zara and Adlan were staying. They had the look, the determined fierceness in their eyes of Russian Security Forces as they sprinted toward the apartment door. The same door Zara would always go into when coming home, then go out the back and walk two blocks to their apartment. Adlan had always drilled into her to never go directly into a hiding place. His teaching had saved their lives.

As they bounced along in the back of the garbage truck they passed Spanish Police checkpoints, the Guardia Urbana of Barcelona, and the Mossos d' Esquadra of Catalonia. Zara knew if the latter were at the checkpoints that they were the force looking out for terrorist. They were looking for them. She took a deep breath, steadied herself, and picked up more trash. The stench of the trash engulfed her in the humid Barcelona night. She kept her head down as they drove by the checkpoints.

After two agonizing hours, the garbage truck left the Ravel area they had been hiding in and bounced down a main street, then onto a dimly lit side street. Cayo motioned for them to follow him. In a small doorway they shed their uniforms and said their goodbyes to Cayo. As the garbage truck pulled away, a white delivery van pulled up.

Zara remembered little of the next several hours inside the van. The van smelled of Spanish sausage and ham. The pungent ripeness of Chorizo sausage was in her hair by the time they got out of the van outside a small village. The village signs were in French.

There was a shower in the small house, a change of clothes, and Adlan gave Zara her new passport. She was a Canadian again, a former Czech, named Leona Novak and Adlan was Alex, her husband. They lived in Toronto and were travelling from Marseille to Atlanta and then to Cancun.

Adlan gave Zara the backstory for their cover. Something he always did. They would have to go through US Customs to go to Cancun, Mexico, and a Canadian passport was their best bet for travel. Adlan said, "Zara, the

Mossad of Israel's Secret Service, the CIA, and even Al Qaeda use the Canadian passport for travel, should we not follow their example and use the best?"

They left Marseille at 6 a.m. the next morning, caught the connecting flight in Atlanta with no questions from US customs authorities and landed in Cancun after a 20-hour flight. Zara only breathed a slight sigh of relief as they travelled toward the town where they thought Professor McAllen might be hiding.

She knew when they found McAllen if he did not give them the password they needed to open up the Bio Bug formula that Adlan would torture him until he did. Adlan knew how to torture; he had learned from what the Russians had done to him. And they had done everything possible. His body showed the scars.

Bernadette woke up at three am. Chris was still sleeping; he lay like a Greek god, with muscles that look like they'd been chiseled out of marble. She grabbed a small blanket from the bed, and wrapped herself and went into the kitchen. A full moon was shining in the window.

A slight doubt settled over her. In between all the love-making they'd talked about their future. Maybe they'd both just quit the force, and take other jobs, and maybe move to Vancouver or to Calgary where they could work for private security companies in the oil industry, and make real money, and have real vacations.

She poured herself a glass of water and powered on her phone. She hadn't checked texts or emails for hours. In just four hours from now she was supposed to be boarding a plane to join the hunt for McAllen. The unexpected arrival of Chris had put this large question mark on her future, what was she to do next?

A stream of messages and texts flowed across her phone. They were all from Anton. Where was she? He'd called her hotel, the one she was supposed to have checked into near the airport. Was she planning to make the flight?

Bernadette closed her eyes tight, and then opened them wide. "Yes," she texted back to Anton, "I'm on my way."

She didn't bother going back into the bedroom to get dressed. She grabbed some clothes from her suitcase, put them on and headed out the door.

She left a note for Chris.

Sorry, duty calls. Perhaps love will find a way, I'll see you when I get back.
And yes, I do love you.
Bernadette.

She backed out of her driveway at 3:30 am. She would make that flight, she might have to put the siren on, and clear the way on her radio with any other officers on the road, but she would make that flight.

Chapter Twenty-Five

The super tanker bled oil. The Bio Bugs ate through the double walled hull, and thousands of holes developed that gushed the black oil into the sea. The ship took on water and started to sink quickly. A sickly wrenching sound was heard by the sailors in the lifeboats as the tanker started to descend beneath the waves.

A small freighter approached what was left of the tanker. Only the stern section and top wheelhouse remained. The Bio Bugs attacked it from the outside. The freighter was sinking in a matter of minutes and issuing a Mayday distress call. The Greek coast guard that came to the aid of the freighter found their ship started to sink as well.

The Greek coast guard Captain sensed there was a strange force in the water and informed all other ships to stay clear of the area. He got his men into lifeboats and watched as his beloved ship sank below the waves, disappearing at an alarming rate. He called the Greek Navy and told them to send helicopters to the area; there was something ominous in the water. He thought perhaps the Russian supertanker had released it.

The Greek Coast Guard Captain watched a wave leave what was left of his ship, and head for the only set of blinking lights on the moonlit horizon. It was the cruise ship. He called the Coast Guard dispatch on his cell phone. He told them to let the cruise ship know they were in trouble if they continued at their current speed. He hoped the captain of the cruise ship would understand his message. Captain Johannes of the cruise ship Empress of Europe received the message from the Greek Coast Guard, "There's some kind of wave heading for us sir, and we're to make all possible speed to leave the area." His first officer reported.

Johannes went onto the flying bridge and picked up a set of high-powered binoculars. The sea was smooth as glass. A bright moon shone in cloudless skies. He thought maybe it was a rogue wave. But even if it was, his ship could withstand almost any wave.

"Do you see anything?" Johannes asked.

"Yes, I see it," the first officer replied. "I see a wave of thirty meters high and about one hundred meters wide. I estimate it is traveling at 18 knots. At our present speed this wave will reach us in 20 minutes.

"Very well," Johannes replied. He thought of his options. If he put his engines at full thrust the Greek Coast Guard would know he was lying about his engine trouble. And throwing full power to engines took time. A massive cruise ship like his wasn't a speedboat.

Johannes turned to his first officer, "Monitor the wave, I'm sure this is a wave from the sinking of the tanker."

The first officer gave a crisp "Aye, aye Captain," in reply, and the captain made his way back to his cabin.

The captain was just getting into bed when the bridge called to tell him the ship had suffered a hull breach. Before the captain could get his clothes on, the ship was listing badly. By the time he reached the deck the abandon ship announcement was given. He never reached the bridge to consult with his crew; a massive lurching of the ship threw him overboard.

Kerim watched the black wave attack the freighter, the Coast Guard vessel, and then head toward the large profile of the cruise liner on the horizon. He saw the how fast the Bio Bugs attacked and disintegrated each of the vessels. Kerim thought, *"What madness have we unleashed from these vials?"* This was supposed to be an attack on one Russian oil tanker. It was now an attack on any metal vessel in the area.

The small Greek fishing boat was made of wood. Kerim, a scientist at heart, figured the propeller was made of brass, and that was the reason that the boat was still chugging along, its prow pushing the waves at a laboring 8 knots. The captain and two crew of the fishing vessel had decided they had rescued Kerim and Anzor from the tanker; and that was their contribution to the rescue effort. The scene of sinking ships around them was frightening. They were now plowing their way away from this strange wreckage of ships as fast as their boat could chug.

Anzor lay on the deck, his large stomach heaving as he tried to catch his breath. His arm was bleeding. A steady stream of bright red blood gushed forth and mixed with the black oil on the deck. Kerim realized he had to staunch the blood flow. He grabbed a rag from a coil of fishing lines and attempted to tie a tourniquet above the wound. As he did so, the oil-soaked rag brushed the wound.

Anzor looked up at Kerim, "Thank you my brother, you saved my life. I realize you have some shortcoming as a true warrior, but you are brave and . . ."

Kerim looked down at Anzor. Anzor's eyes went wide, his mouth opened in anguish. "What is it?"

Anzor shuddered, "Kerim, I feel like I am burning inside . . . I . . ." His body went limp and started to shrink in size.

The Greek sailors cried out in fear. They could see Anzor drying like a black olive in the late sun. His eyes became sullen; his large stomach flattened and fell below his rib cage in seconds.

"Anzor, Anzor, what has happened to you?" Kerim asked, slapping his brother's cheeks. He could see it was no use. Anzor was dead. The once mighty, bellicose, and sometimes brutal Anzor lay on the deck, half his former size. Something had got inside him from the sea and killed him from inside.

Kerim heard the Greek Captain of the fishing boat yell something to the deckhands. A moment later, Anzor was taken from Kerim's lap and thrown overboard. Kerim did not protest, he understood the fear, the strange events the Greeks had just witnessed. They stood on the deck and made the sign of the cross as Anzor's body sunk beneath the black waves.

Chapter Twenty-Six

Viktor Lutrova sat hunched in the back of the Mercedes SUV. He held a cell phone to his ear; his other hand massaged the back of his neck.

His eyebrows were furrowed, his lips tight. He nodded only once or twice or said, "Yes," in Russian to the caller on the phone.

Bronislav leaned against the back of the SUV smoking a cigarette, a cloud of smoke mixed with his breath in the early morning air. Elena Batkia strolled by the window of a French bakery. The *Boulanger* was not open yet. They wouldn't open for another hour. Smells of baguette and croissant assailed their nostrils and made their stomachs grumble with hunger.

They were in a small French village just outside Marseille. A tip from an informer had led them here. The informer sold passports and stolen credit cards. He then sold information about his buyers, for the right price, if the buyers were of value.

Adlan and Zara's faces were not only in circulation

among the Russian Security Forces and Interpol; they were circulating in the underworld of criminals who wanted to make money off them. Money, big money was being offered for their whereabouts.

Bronislav met the informant, an Algerian with eyes that darted about constantly when he talked. Bronislav reasoned the eye movements were because the Algerian was playing so many sides; he could never be sure who would be coming after him.

With the exchange of ten thousand Euros, they had received the new Canadian passport names of Adlan and Zara. Elena ran a flight check for Marseille, the closest airport, by tapping into the Interpol database and found the destination of the "Canadian" travelers.

Viktor was giving the information to his direct boss in Moscow, with the Russian Security Force. From what Branislav could make of the phone call, the information was not being received well by Moscow.

Viktor got out of the SUV and slammed the door. His scowl was still in place. Branislav handed him a cigarette. Viktor shoved the cigarette in his mouth, lit it and inhaled deeply.

"What's up?" Branislav asked.

Viktor looked at Branislav and exhaled a stream of tobacco smoke above his head. The cloud floated into the morning air, thick and blue. "Our bosses in Moscow are pissed." He shoved one hand in his pocket and took another deep drag of his cigarette. The tip of the cigarette burned an angry red. "They found out from recent texts sent from the terrorist that attacked the pipeline and the oil tanker that it was Adlan they were communicating with."

"It's just as you thought, Viktor. You said that Adlan was behind the pipeline attacks."

Viktor shook his head and expelled another stream of blue smoke into the air. "Yes, but being right doesn't matter to Moscow. They want results. They wanted the capture of Adlan, and his little tart Zara. We've failed to capture him in Barcelona, now they want us to follow him."

"They want us to chase him to Mexico?" Branislav looked at his watch. "They are about to land there."

"Yes, that's exactly it. Do we have any agents in Cancun?"

Branislav chuckled. "Hell no, we probably have a bunch of drunk Russians there on holiday. There might be a vacationing agent amongst them—you want I should check?"

Viktor put up his hand. "No, no, we just need a tail put on them until we get there. We need a fixer."

Ramón Martin was a Russian fixer, a former lawyer who was now a go between for the Russian Embassy in Mexico City and anything that needed doing in Cancun—for Russians.

Cancun was a new destination point for Russians. Hot weather, great beaches, good food, and booze—lots of booze put Cancun on the map for Russian tourists. Ramón could not get over how Russians got into trouble when they drank. The Mexicans drank, they partied, they felt sleepy, and they went home to bed.

Not the Russians. There seemed to be centuries of pent-up angst left over from their journey from the Tsar to Communism, and their present strange blend of Capitalism with Mafia connections that even they didn't understand. When they drank, a gene they called, "Mother Russia," seemed to come out. The Russians drank, then sang, and then drank some more. There never seemed to be an end point—until they passed out. And unfortunately, that could take a long time for a Russian. Their ability to consume alcohol was legendary on the beaches of Cancun.

Ramón had a steady run from one hotel to another on the hotel strip, and then to the drunk tanks on both the beach and in the city. He made payoffs; he handed out cell phones, and consoled morose, hung-over Russians. It was his job to "fix things."

When he got the call from a Russian Security Agent from France telling him to put a tail on two Chechens, he realized he was out of his league. He'd never followed anyone. Not even his cheating wife. A divorce was too costly, and her lover gave her great presents. And she left him alone.

So, Ramón was in a quandary. He had no experience with following people and being discreet, and the few people he could think of to help him in such a matter were out of town.

He decided on a GPS tracking device. His friend, Cesar, owned an electronics shop. Cesar had tried to sell Ramón such a device, "just so he could see where his cheating wife was going." And of course, Ramón did not want to know. But such a device would work well for his mission with the Russians.

Ramón picked up the mini GPS tracker, paid the exorbitant fee charged by his friend Cesar, because according to Cesar, "it was the last one in town." After paying the five hundred US dollars, he also paid an extra one hundred to active the device and another hundred for one month of usage and monitoring, which was the minimum.

Ramón hoped he could recoup all of his cost from the Russians when he met them at the airport. As he rushed out the door he only faintly heard the last instructions from his friend Cesar, "Ramón, remember its battery life is 10 days, and it uplinks one hour per day."

He made it to the Cancun airport just in time to meet the flight the suspects were on. He stood in the waiting area, trying to be as inconspicuous as possible, but having never acted like that before, he had no idea what inconspicuous should look like. So he stood behind a pillar with the picture of Zara and Adlan. A small Mexican boy eyed him suspiciously over his taco.

Ramón finally saw Adlan and Zara come through Customs, and walk towards the rental car outlets. They carried one small bag between them. Zara looked beautiful, dark hair, dark eyes, and perfect skin. Adlan looked the perfect picture of a Mafia hit man. Ramón disliked him the moment he saw him. Adlan had sullen eyes, hunched shoulders, with a walk that seemed to exude menace. Something about him sent a chill into Ramón. He had second thoughts about getting close to these two.

They rented a car from Hertz and walked toward the exit. The usual hucksters selling trinkets, and discounts vouchers shied away from Adlan. His scowl warned them off.

Walking into the warm Cancun night, Ramón saw a problem. He needed to attach his small magnetic device to the rear of their car. Ramón was not a big man, but he was not small either, and he was far from agile. He couldn't imagine himself getting close enough and not being seen.

A young boy was hanging around. One of the many that scrounged for tips by carrying luggage for tourists and getting food orders for cab drivers. Ramón called him over, and gave him the device. "Look, see those two getting into that car? I'll give you one hundred pesos if you attach this small device to the undercarriage of their car without being seen."

The boy looked up at Ramón. "You are serious, Señor? How badly do you need this thing put under the car?"

Ramón got the message, "One hundred and fifty pesos."

"Three hundred pesos and it is done." The boy looked away in feigned disinterest.

Ramón knew the boy had outwitted him. "Very well. Do it for three hundred pesos. Vamoose!"

The boy grabbed the device, which Ramón had already switched on, and bolted in the direction of the car. He ran crouched low behind the row of rental cars, and was behind the car of Zara and Adlan just as they put the car into reverse.

Ramón held his breath. He was afraid the boy would get run over. The boy attached the device and rolled under another car to hide from view as they drove away.

After the car drove away, the boy came back to Ramón, smiling and brushing himself off. Ramón took out his wallet, and counted out 300 pesos. The boy put up his hand, "No Señor there is another two hundred pesos required."

"And why is that?" Ramón asked, upset by such an outrageous request.

"The extra two hundred pesos means I am quiet, and do not tell the rental company what I have just done."

Ramón shook his head. He pulled out the other two hundred pesos, and handed them to the boy. He was impressed by his negotiating skills. The kid might make a good lawyer one day.

Viktor needed to get his team to Cancun, Mexico fast. A commercial flight wouldn't do it. A flight from Marseille to Cancun was 17 hours minimum, and it didn't leave until the next day. They also needed to arrive armed for their search for Adlan and Zara, which they could never put in their luggage, and took time to procure in Mexico.

Viktor made some calls back to his boss in Moscow. Strings were pulled, and within one hour they pulled up to a private hanger beside the busy Marseille commercial airport. A gleaming white Gulfstream 450 stood ready to take them on board.

Viktor got out of the SUV with Branislav, Elana, and Lev. Viktor did not want Lev, as he was an alcoholic. Not a recovering alcoholic, but a going down the road to destruction type, who was more drunk than sober.

But Lev was close by, he could drive, operate a radio and a gun—when sober. As for Elena, Viktor didn't want her along either. He didn't know if she was someone's niece of some high-ranking officer in Moscow, or someone had made a payoff for her appointment. It didn't matter. He would do what he was told, and he was told to take her along.

Branislav carried a duffle bag of weapons. Three Heckler and Koch MP7A1 submachine guns with additional rounds and several stun grenades. He didn't pack one for Elena, as he didn't like the way she handled even a handgun. Her awkwardness and clumsiness with firearms was apparent. He didn't like the idea of being shot in the back by accident. He told her she would get a stun gun and a collapsible baton. She'd scowled at him when told the news, but he didn't care.

Within minutes of boarding the plane they were rolling on the runway. The pilots were paid well for this flight. No cabin stewards were required. Viktor would have them do a weapons check, and get some much-needed sleep. Their flight would be just under 10 hours.

The large plush chairs and couches of the plane were inviting. They took their places on the plane and relaxed into the comfort of the chairs on takeoff. Lev and Elena were asleep in minutes, with Branislav soon after.

Viktor sat in his chair by the window, watching the Mediterranean Sea below. An armada of cruise ships, freighters, fishing vessels and naval war ships from every country were steaming toward the Strait of Gibraltar and toward what they hoped was the safety of the Atlantic Ocean.

Whatever Adlan had unleashed in the Russian super-tanker had most of the world running scared. Viktor wished he had more men for this mission, at least not a green graduate and a drunk. He wished he had more firepower. Timing was crucial. He did not have the luxury to put together a crack team. He was slightly annoyed by his predicament.

He sighed and closed the window blind and settled down to sleep. The last thing he viewed before he drifted off to sleep was a text from a Russian colonel; he was supposed to get the formula for the Bio Bugs, as well as capture Adlan. The Russian Military wanted to see if it might be a new weapon. As sleep overtook his tired body, Viktor thought, *"Just what Russia needs—another new weapon."*

Chapter Twenty-Seven

Bernadette hit the accelerator on her Jeep and only eased off when the speedometer read 140km. She had 126 km to the International Airport outside of Edmonton. It was just past four am as she left the Red Deer city limits. She put on the red flashing light but not her siren. She couldn't take the noise this early in the morning.

The full moon made the double lane highway shine with an ethereal glow. This ribbon of black asphalt leading her to the airport, while her tires hummed and the wind raced by, and her mind tried to make sense of what she'd just done, and what she'd just left behind.

She tried not to make sense of it, of what her heart was trying to manifest. She had to think of the case now. There was nothing else to do. Lack of sleep, and way too much sexual stimulation put her brain on a thin edge where reason could no longer tread.

A bad patch of highway with construction slowed her down to a crawl. Her heart raced as she watched the clock on the dash advance while the distance moved at a snail's pace.

She pulled into the airport at 6:15. She was cutting it way to close to get through US customs clearance. She dropped her car at the valet parking on the departure level, threw them the keys, and pulled her bag out of the Jeep.

She made it through the US Customs pre-clearance by flashing her RCMP detective's badge and a smile along with her passport to get past the minimum required time for customs and security clearance. They were calling her name when she got into the departure area.

Anton stood there, with a large coffee and a look of disbelief, "I thought you were going to bail on me. Do I want to know what happened?"

Bernadette took the coffee out of Anton's hands, "No some things are better left without the story. You can bring me up to speed with what's going on with our world's terrorist and the Bio Bugs on the plane."

After takeoff Anton handed Bernadette his computer and she reviewed the latest developments that were just beginning in the Mediterranean Sea, "Is it as bad as the news reports, I mean do I take 30 to 40 percent off for reporter embellishments? Bernadette asked after looking at the reports.

Anton took the computer and put it away, "No, I think the reporters are being optimistic. They think this tragedy is in one region of the world. Our intelligence believes this is repeatable in every body of water in the world."

"Which means we best find McAllen and hope he has an antidote or a really good way to make the Bio Bugs want to eat something else besides all the worlds metal, and some human bystanders." Bernadette said.

"Unfortunately, that's about the size of it."

They both ate some bad airline food, a breakfast sandwich made sometime in the past 72 hours and reheated to a tepid temperature that just melted the cheese, and then they slept. Bernadette's mind bounced over dreams of Chris and McAllen, and at some point, both of them assumed the visage of villains and then lovers. She woke in a sweat before landing in Houston.

In the one-hour change of planes she looked at a text from Chris. He wondered why she hadn't woken him before leaving. She wondered that herself.

She boarded the plane to Merida Mexico without answering Chris, she'd tell him later, much later, when she figured out the answer.

Two FBI Agents who were assigned as their liaisons in the hunt for Professor McAllen met them at the airport. They introduced themselves as Special Agent Carla Winston and Agent Luis Valdes.

Valdes looked wary, almost suspicious of Bernadette and Anton. From the moment they were introduced, he was stiff and aloof. They followed them to a rental car, stowed their suitcases in the trunk and got into the back seat. The late-night heat cloaked Bernadette's skin like a wet glove and made her realize how tired and in need of a shower she was. She probably looked like she felt, which could not be good. Anton looked like he'd stepped out of a GQ magazine, and she quietly despised him for it.

Valdes got in the driver's seat and adjusted his rearview mirror, his eyes meeting Bernadette's in the mirror. "So, here we have the pride of the Royal Canadian Mounted Police Detective squad. Why didn't you bring your Husky dogs—are they still back in their igloo?"

Bernadette smiled back at him, meeting his gaze in the mirror. "No, we only bring out the dogs for the important stuff, like when we need to sniff out extra special dumbasses. You know . . . now that I'm here . . . I should have brought them."

Winston whipped her head to look at Valdes "That's enough of your Mexican machismo crap Valdes; these people are here on special assignment. This detective is the reason we have a break in our case and any idea about where this Professor is, and any chance of eliminating this Bio Bug threat."

Winston turned in her seat to face Bernadette "You'll have to excuse my agent; sometimes his balls are much bigger than his brains, and unfortunately he thinks with the former."

Valdes averted his eyes back to the busy Merida City Street, his shoulders a little more rounded as he made himself a bit smaller.

Bernadette laughed. "Agent Winston we've both been in the force in our countries for a while, so I totally understand. Now that we've been introduced, how are things going on the case?"

"Not too well," Winston said. "The address you got for us in Merida led to a local lady who we think is this McAllen's housekeeper, but we're not totally sure of that as she's gone to see a sick cousin in Cancun, and her neighbors don't know the address of the cousin or . . ."

"Or aren't about to tell a bunch of FBI suits and Mexican federal's what they know," Bernadette cut in.

"My, my . . . they said at the department you were a quick study . . . yeah, I think you got it. A bunch of agents and some Mexican Federal Police are sitting on the place and waiting for her to return."

"I hope this housekeeper doesn't have a phone where she is in Cancun, or our suspect could be going even deeper in his hidey hole." Anton said.

Winston sighed. "I hate to admit it, but with over 100 FBI Agents in this town at present, roaring around town with over 200 Mexican Federals', I doubt our calling card has gone unnoticed."

"Wow," Bernadette said, "that's a whole lot of manpower to throw at this. And you're right. If our suspect is barely awake, I'm sure he'll figure out there's some major firepower in town looking for him."

"Oh yeah, and the Mexicans like to roam around in those open-air trucks with their M16s showing. Yep, a real circus if you ask me." Winston said.

"Why so much overkill?"

Winston sighed, "Part of it is our own screw up. My unit was the one involved in the false diversion of the Bio Bugs from Canada to Montana. I can't tell you how well that played all the way up to the State Department. My Chief got his ass chewed about two sizes wider, so now, we're here in force with strict instructions."

"To not screw up." Bernadette said.

Winston nodded her head. "Yeah, you got it; obviously you understand police department politics."

They pulled up in front of the Best Western Mayan Hotel. "Sorry about the accommodations, this is the best we could do on short notice. The Hyatt was booked with some Morticians' Convention from Guadalajara. Who knew this was such a busy place?" Winston said.

They pulled their suitcases out of the trunk and Valdes, now somewhat subdued, told Winston he'd park the car, and see them later. Winston spoke to him in whispered tones; he nodded his head and drove off.

Winston said, "Anton, you go ahead and check in. You'll be sharing a room with my partner, Valdes. Yeah, don't worry," she said on seeing Anton's worried look. "He'll be fine. He has this asshole complex he can't quite manage when he first meets people, kind of like Tourettes Syndrome, but he's manageable with my boot in his ass. Now run along and enjoy. You young boys will have lots to talk about."

Bernadette was about to follow Anton into the hotel, and she felt Winston's hand on her arm, a request to talk. She stopped and looked the short lady in the eyes.

Winston looked up at Bernadette. "Now, detective, I have a strict directive from your boss to my boss . . . now how did he put it? Yes, the technical term was he didn't want you fucking up while you're down here." She put her hand up, as Bernadette was about to say something. "Now let me finish, and you can get all up in my grill, but here's the deal. I've spent almost 20 years in the FBI and I've seen every alpha male and kick-ass female who's shot up the ranks and wants to flash their brilliant intuition like a shining meteor to the detriment of those of us in the rank and file."

She squeezed Bernadette's arm just a bit tighter. For a little lady she had strength. "Now I'm not saying you're one of those people who want to show the rest of us up. No, you don't seem like the type, but I'm here to tell you I'm your handler—yes—that's right—handler." She leveled her brown eyes at Bernadette's liquid green. "That means while you're down here, when you have ideas, you bounce them off me. You have concerns . . . likewise. You get no gun, and a short leash . . . is that understood?"

Bernadette stuttered out, "Yeah . . . I get that . . . but I . . ."

Winston let go of her arm, "Hey, you and I are going to get along fine, and by the way I got you your own room, just kind of worked out that way. Let's get you checked in."

Bernadette checked into her room, unpacked and took a long shower, letting cool water run over her to try to wash off the long hours of airplane travel. There was always something about the long hours in a plane that reminded her of visiting prisoners in a jail cell. They had nowhere to go until their sentence was up. And to her, this assignment was like being cooped up on a plane. You were there, with nowhere to go until the thing landed . . . stuck in space.

She turned on her phone and checked her messages. There was another text from Chris. He said he had a message from his detachment that he was needed—duty calls . . . and he added a happy face with a wink. He added . . . stay safe . . . I love you.

She texted back *stay safe.* Her finger hovered over the I button. It should have been an immediate reaction to say I Love You back. She hit send and went to bed.

Sleep took a long time coming. The thoughts of Chris, the thoughts of the case, the hunt for McAllen, and her grandmother's chilling warning of Bernadette's death in bright sunlight. All of this made for a multiple bout of tossing and turning before sleep finally came.

She woke at 6:30 a.m., dressed and found Anton in the lobby. "How are your bunking arrangements going with our angry Mexican American?" she asked as they found a table for breakfast in the hotel restaurant.

Anton laughed as he stirred his coffee. "You know, I think we'll get along just fine. We had a few beers last night, and a few laughs."

"Really? I thought that guy was a serious piece of work

with no sense of humor. How did you get him to lighten up?"

Anton leaned forward over the table and lowered his voice. "I told him that we Canadians are very similar to Mexican Americans. You know how they call them *wetbacks*, because they cross the Rio Grande River? Well, I told him Americans call us *frost backs*, and he laughed so hard beer came out his nose."

Bernadette laughed. "My God Anton, I thought you could just charm women, but you probably should enter politics when you get back home. Huh, who would have thought of frost backs?"

"Hey, on another note, I got us our own car, because my new friend Luis Valdes thinks we should have our own wheels to roam Merida, and he pulled a favor with the FBI guy in charge of rentals, and voilà!" Anton pulled a set of car keys out of his pocket.

"How's that going to sit with Agent Winston? I got a chapter and verse on how we are supposed to be on tight leash and not screw up late last night."

"Things change quickly down here. Agent Winston just got assigned to assist some other higher-up agent and we got set free. Speaking of that, here's Winston now." Anton motioned with his head at Winston approaching their table.

"Good morning, Agent Winston, perhaps you'll join us for coffee . . ."

"No time for that, I'm here to tell you the housekeeper's arrived back home, and we're interviewing her now. Be ready to roll." Winston hesitated for a moment and bent over towards Bernadette. "Look, just because I've been reassigned, doesn't mean you get free rein to do whatever you want—you copy that?"

"Copy that," Bernadette said. She gulped her coffee and headed for the lobby with Anton.

Bernadette and Anton followed several FBI agents out to a fleet of rental cars. They found their car and joined the fleet of FBI speeding through the rain-drenched streets of downtown Merida. They reached the address of the aunt in 20 minutes. The scene at the aunt's place was a Spanish-speaking FBI agent grilling a terrified old lady. The old lady was wild-eyed and wailing. She had no idea that the kind, elderly gentlemen she did housekeeping for was a wanted felon. She gave them the address, and crossed herself several times as the legion of FBI agents left her home for their vehicles.

Now a larger cavalcade of cars careened around narrow Mexican streets. Bernadette sat in the passenger seat of a rented Chevrolet Malibu and wondered what it would be like to actually meet the Professor. The man who had eluded her a year before and made a mockery out of the RCMP and combined Canadian armed forces. She relished the chance to see cuffs on him. It would feel good. It would feel like closure.

She decided she would put the cuffs on him, and then tell him he'd been pardoned, and given a walk on all his past and present crimes. She knew she'd feel better that way —if only for a few seconds.

The place they arrived at was a solitary large blue door on a narrow street just past the center of Merida's Historic district. Two FBI agents armed with door rammers took care of the door, and a tight cord of agents covered in body armor made their way into the villa with guns bristling.

Bernadette walked into the villa followed by Anton. They found the FBI giving the "all clear." There was no sign of the professor. A desk where his laptop had lain showed a slight cover of dust, a wallboard where notes had been tacked was stripped, showing all the signs of a hasty exit.

An exhausted FBI agent dressed in black coveralls and bulletproof vest came over to Bernadette and Anton. "Looks like someone tipped off our man. Maybe got wind the RCMP was on his tail." He smiled towards Bernadette.

The lead FBI agent turned to several other agents and started giving orders to check every rental unit in Merida. He wanted a photo of McAllen circulated to every rental agent in Merida, and every hotel canvassed. He yelled, "We're going to track this man down."

Bernadette took Anton aside. "You know that isn't going to work."

"Why is that?" Anton asked.

"Well for one thing, McAllen is ex-military. I doubt if he'll be hiding out in this same neighborhood, especially if he knew we were coming. Either someone close to his housekeeper tipped him off, or someone from the university who knew we are getting close to his Mexican hiding place."

"So, you think he's left the country, split for Belize, Costa Rica, or somewhere else in Latin or South America?" Anton asked as he watched the FBI take apart the place looking for clues.

"No, he's in another small town close by, probably a little fishing village," Bernadette said.

Anton shook his head. "How can you be so sure of that?"

Bernadette motioned for Anton to follow her outside. When they were out of sight of the FBI, she showed him a post card. It was a photo taken of McAllen's friends, Sebastian, Percy and Theo with Grace and Margaret in the background. They had fishing rods and fish. The caption read,

Hey Mac, we'll get some of these out at Cris when we return next month. The postcard was dated July 23rd, and the postage stamp was from Costa Rica.

Anton flipped the postcard over. "Where did you get this?"

"It was on the floor as we walked in; McAllen must have dropped it on his way out. All these guys stepped over it storming in. I can't help it if these guys can't bend down to pick up easy evidence," Bernadette smiled as she stuffed the postcard into her pants pocket.

Anton motioned for Bernadette to come outside, "Look, great . . . you got another postcard. You can add that to your collection.

"Just a minute, I'm going to type in Cris, Yucatan, Mexico, on my cell . . . and . . . I got nothing." Bernadette looked up at Anton with a frown.

"What if it's code for something?"

"Yeah, of course, these guys were ex-military. There's no way they'd use the exact name of a place. I'll bring up Google Maps—he's got to be somewhere close by if his buddies were coming back."

"Look at small villages on the coast and see if anything might have a name starting with C."

Bernadette's finger flew over her phone. "I got nothing on villages with a C. Wait . . . what if it's the second name, and they shortened it?" Bernadette looked up, her face beaming. "San Crisanto is a little fishing village on the coast. And it's a short drive from here."

Anton shook his head. "You think they'd use the Cris for San Crisanto? My God, Bernadette, how do you get that kind of thought train? Why couldn't Cris be some guy or girl's name?

Bernadette's' brows furrowed. "Look Anton, when you

spell the name Chris for a man or women, you use an H. This has only the C R I and S. And they say, they'll get some of these fish out at Cris; they don't use the possessive form, which would indicate a person. You see that, it's code. Hey, and at this point . . . it's all I got . . . I say we go with it."

Anton sighed, "Okay, I'll inform our Agent Winston we have a lead . . . a strange lead, but a lead anyways, and see what she wants to do with it."

Bernadette grabbed Anton's arm, "Are you kidding? Look, first they'll think we're crazy, and if they go along with it they'll bring in a team of FBI and all these Mexican Federals with M16's which will get McAllen killed. I want him alive."

"So, you suggest we just go off on our own in search of McAllen without informing the FBI?" Anton asked the question to be sure of the depth of the trouble he was about to get himself into.

Bernadette patted Anton on the shoulder. "Look, the lead FBI agent gave instructions to the others to comb the area for McAllen . . . we are just combing in another direction . . . and we'll call them when we find him . . ." Bernadette stopped in mid-sentence. She watched a blue Chevrolet drive by slowly with two occupants.

There was something about the woman in the passenger seat that looked familiar. The woman's eyes shot straight ahead as the car passed. The driver was looking straight ahead as well. To Bernadette that was odd behavior. Most people would be curious as to all the cars parked at funny angles on the street, and a bunch of men and women running around in black coveralls and jackets that said FBI on them.

Anton watched the car as it drove down the street. "What is it?"

Bernadette shook her head. "You know it's weird, but I've seen that woman before, the one that just drove by—she looked similar to Zara Mashhadov."

"Are you sure?"

"No, her hair was completely different . . . I'm probably seeing things. She was last reported to be in Barcelona."

Zara turned to Adlan. "Do you think anyone recognized us?"

"How could they? They don't know we're in the country. They think you're hiding in Spain, and half of Europe thinks I'm in Russia. No one knows us here."

"But that woman, I'm sure she was police. I saw her look at me, and she stared at me, like she was trying to put a name to my face."

"Ha . . . Zara, it is because you are pretty, and she is probably a lesbian. Don't worry, you'll see, no one knows we are here."

Zara sat back in the car seat and adjusted the car's front vent to blow cool air on her face. The exchange of looks from the woman on the street suddenly made her very hot. Also, it was the first time in a very long time that Adlan had called her pretty.

She pulled out the notebook she had stolen from Paul Goodman's neighbor and looked at the page. The address they just passed was compromised, and obviously the professor was not there. Otherwise, they would have seen him being dragged out of the house. That was the reason they had made the slow drive by, just to be sure.

"We will have to try the other address; it shows it is a small village on the coast . . . I think some 70 kilometers away." Zara pointed to a map as Adlan navigated the narrow streets.

"Good, we will head there in the morning. We both need some rest. A tired warrior is not a good warrior." Adlan smiled at Zara as he narrowly missed a Mexican coming out of a house with his wife.

Ramón the Russian fixer shuffled back and forth wringing his hands, watching the gleaming white private jet pull into the hanger. He had pulled many strings, paid many bribes to get this jet to arrive at this hanger.

Again he was out of his league. The Mexican Customs Agents at the Private Executive Terminal in Cancun knew what he wanted. He wanted no checks of luggage or passport checks of the passengers, and no checks of passengers on the return trip. They simply smiled and said, "It could be arranged." The arrangement was twenty thousand US Dollars.

The Chevy Suburban the Russian wanted to rent came all the way from Tulum. There was an additional cost of five hundred dollars, plus fifteen hundred dollars for the week minimum. Ramón was out of pocket some twenty-three thousand dollars what with the GPS locator he'd placed on the rental car of the Chechen's. He was hoping the arriving Russians had a quantity of cash on hand. He'd take US dollars or Euros, and hoped they didn't carry rubles.

Rubles he could exchange at only a few moneychangers in Cancun, and they would be sure to beat the hell out him on the exchange. He always got taken by at least 20 percent on rubles by those low-life bastards.

The door of the plane opened and out stepped a short heavyset man with a scowl. He looked around, sniffed the air, and ventured down the tarmac towards Ramón. After him came a tall man who looked like a weightlifter with biceps bulging out of his jacket and a barrel chest. He carried a large duffle bag that looked heavy even for him. A young pretty girl exited last with a briefcase. She had a slight smile and looked out of place with the other two.

Ramón came forward to introduce himself to the first man getting off the plane, "I am Ramón. I am your contact here in Mexico," he said in halting Russian.

The short dark man came forward. He produced a fist of thick round fingers in a strong handshake. "I am Viktor . . . the tracking device we asked you to place is on their car? I understand from your text message that you did not have the manpower to have them followed."

"Yes, yes, I have it here." Ramón produced a USB stick. "You will find the activation codes and the program on this . . . it is all as you requested." He took a moment, breathed in deeply to hide his nerves. "I have had many expenses for your requests, and perhaps we could arrange your payment."

Viktor handed the USB stick to the young lady walking behind him, "Payment? You will get payment when we find out if this tracking device works, and we have found who we are looking for. We should be done with this mission in 24 hours. Meet us at the airport, and we will double what you paid in expenses."

The man carrying the duffel bag came up to Ramón." You have the vehicle we ordered?'

"Yes, I was able to get the latest Chevy Suburban," Ramón said.

The man's face brightened. "In black?" he asked.

"Ah, no, there was only white available," Ramón, offered. He could see the man's disappointment.

Viktor said something to the man in Russian, and then turned to Ramón. "It's okay . . . my friend likes the black ones because he sees them driven by the American CIA. Not to worry. White will be fine." Viktor patted Ramón on the shoulder.

"Now, I have one more thing for you to help us with." Viktor said, jerking his thumb back in the direction of the plane, "Our friend got a bit air sick . . . doesn't like planes . . . perhaps you could help him off the plane.

"Of course, certainly," Ramón said. He hurried past the two men and the woman to the plane. Two pilots were hauling a man down the stairway. They stood him up, and for a second he seemed erect, then he crumpled to his knees and landed on his face. The pilots shook their heads in disgust and walked away.

Ramón knelt beside the man. The smell of alcohol rose off him in the hot sun. Ramón gagged and coughed. His eyes watered. "Ay, dios mio!" Ramón muttered to himself. "This man smells like he's been marinated in alcohol."

With a mighty heave, Ramón got the man to his feet. Somehow his legs held. With the man leaning on him and breathing a breath so foul that Ramón was sure it could shrivel a Tarantula, they made their way to the hanger.

The young Russian lady held the back door open and pulled the seat forward. With the help of Viktor, they shoved the drunken man into the third row seat. He hovered there for a moment, and then slid to the floor.

"He hates flying!" Viktor said as he got into the truck.

He rolled down the window, and gave Ramón a "Thank you," in Russian, and the truck took off out of the hanger.

Ramón watched the four Russians disappear down the street. He was hoping he'd see them again in 24 hours. He had just been promised 23,000 US dollars for his work. He'd be staying around the hanger to await their return.

Elena plugged the USB stick into her laptop and began running the GPS locator program. She sat in the second row of the truck. Her window rolled down to expel the smell of Lev in the back.

Branislav drove and Viktor sat in the front passenger's seat. Viktor was furious at Lev for getting drunk, but more at himself—he should have seen it. A private jet with a full liquor cabinet was all a drunk like Lev could ask for. While they slept, Lev finished off two bottles of Cognac. A Camus Vintage, and a Camus Prestige. Viktor shook his head. The guy went through at least 6,000 Euros worth of booze that would be added to their bill. Viktor was surprised Lev hadn't drunk himself to death.

Viktor looked over his shoulder at Elena, "Do you have anything yet on their location?" He wanted to get this mission back on track.

"Yes," Elena said, staring down at the laptop. "Looks like their last position was a place called Merida; it's about a three-hour drive from here."

"Good, keep tracking their movements. We'll have them soon," Viktor said.

"Shit," Elena said.

"What is it?" Viktor spun his head around to look at Elena.

"This program only downloads once a day. It's a piece of antiquated shit! The Mexican sold us crap! This is for imbeciles! Elena spat the words out. Her fingers were flying over the keyboard, desperately trying to get more information that the program wasn't willing to offer.

Viktor turned back to face the front. He gave a sideways glance to Branislav. He could not believe how badly this mission was turning out.

Chapter Twenty-Eight

Four pelicans skimmed the surface of the waves just off the beach as McAllen watched from the balcony of the rented beach house. Only a few clouds dotted the horizon, and in an hour, there would be a green flash over the ocean. He usually marveled at it, putting everything aside just to watch it. Not tonight.

The laptop on the table in front of him streamed a video of the FBI agents breaking into his house in Merida. Just before he'd left his villa, he'd activated a motion-sensitive camera hooked up to a wireless IP Network.

He couldn't help the feeling of fear that gripped him as he watched the agents in their black coveralls, bulletproof vests and helmets storming his place. They entered in textbook fashion, guns pointed, squatting low, and hands signaling to one another as they cleared each room. McAllen admired them—they were good. He was thankful he'd left. He could see himself flat on the floor with hands cuffed behind his back—an agent at his side had he stayed 24 hours more.

He felt lucky, but stupid at the same time. The very moment he'd learned about Goodman's death was the time he should have left Mexico. Every Mexican checkpoint would now have his picture. He'd passed two Mexican military checkpoints just driving from Merida to where he was hiding. He'd been lucky and got through. He didn't expect to be that lucky again.

He picked up his cell phone and dialed a number. The number rang four times before the familiar voice of Sebastian Germaine answered, "Hey Mac, we knew you'd be calling. Is it time for the cavalry?"

Sebastian and McAllen had served together in Vietnam. Sebastian Germaine was mid-sixties, wiry and short in stature but long in paranoia. He wore his long gray hair in braids, Willy Nelson style, and wore Navaho amulets and beads to ward off evil spirits.

He'd been a crack sniper in McAllen's unit in Vietnam and later a sound engineer for Janice Joplin and the Grateful Dead. Years of hallucinogenic drugs made him paranoid. If there was ever someone to have at your back, it was Sebastian. He could assess all manner of danger—real or imagined.

Sebastian was with McAllen's two other lifelong friends, Percy Stronach and Theo Martin. They were all Vietnam vets who had immigrated to Canada to find their own peace after the war in Vietnam ended.

They'd all settled close to McAllen on Vancouver Island in British Columbia. McAllen was a chemistry professor, Sebastian a sound engineer for rock musicians, Percy an oyster farmer, and Theo a boat builder.

If McAllen got in trouble, they all got in trouble. McAllen had developed a formula for something called polywater that made water like plastic. He'd sold the formula to some Wall Street guys who tried to double cross him. Percy, Theo, and Sebastian were at his back then. They helped save McAllen, and they'd even gone on the run with him to Mexico.

McAllen chuckled, "Yeah, I guess I do need the cavalry. Where are you guys?"

"We just arrived at the Merida Airport."

"I thought you guys were on a road trip to Ecuador." McAllen sat up in his chair, his lanky body unfolding as he clutched the phone tighter.

Sebastian laughed. "Look, as soon as we saw all this news with these Bio Bugs attacking pipelines in Alaska and Russian, and about ships sinking in the Mediterranean, we knew your ass would be in a knot. The boys and I ditched the van in Panama and high-tailed it back here."

McAllen sighed; he loved hearing Sebastian call his other guys the "boys," as they were aged 63 to 75. There was a time when they'd been boys together, but that was so many years ago.

"Any ideas on how to get me out of here?" McAllen asked. "My face is all over Mexican media. They say I'm the bandito who'll destroy their beloved PEMEX Oil, their national oil company, and they have a price on my head."

"Well, I'd say the roads are out."

"Affirmative, I think my face is at every Mexican checkpoint. I was lucky to make it here."

"I suggest we use a boat, then a helicopter."

"How do you figure?"

"Simple," Sebastian said. "We hire a boat in Campeche and pick you up at your dock. There are no checkpoints on the ocean. We'll be just some guys on a fishing trip, and then we get you back to Campeche where there's a whole bunch of helicopters flying around for the offshore oil rigs. We'll hire one to get us the hell out of here. Sound, okay?"

McAllen nodded his head as he spoke, "Hey, sounds fine to me." Campeche was a small port city west of his location. "What's your ETA?"

"Should be by tomorrow morning, but I'll let you know when the boat is in the water. The helicopter will take a good chunk of cash, but we still got lots. We should be able to get to either Guatemala or Belize with a few hours of flying time."

"The Margaritas are on me when we land," McAllen said. He heard Sebastian say, "Roger that," and put down his phone. He watched the sun set and caught the green flash just before it disappeared below the horizon.

He wondered how close the FBI and the Mexicans were to finding him. He went into the kitchen and pulled a Corona out of the fridge. He sat back on the balcony to watch the waves as he took a long pull out of the bottle. If his friends didn't arrive in time—this would be one of his last nights of freedom.

Chapter Twenty-Nine

Bernadette sat at the far end of the boardroom and watched an FBI agent set up a laptop and hook up a data projector while a hotel staffer pulled down a movie screen in the front of the room. This announced their evening briefing by Senior FBI Agent Lance Cooper.

Cooper was mid-forties, tall, with a rectangular face, brush cut, and heavy eyebrows that gave him a serious look. His gravel style voice made him sound like he stepped out of a 1950s crime drama, and J. Edgar Hoover, the originator of the FBI, was somewhere in the room.

Bernadette glanced at her watch; it was 9:30 p.m. The day of investigation and searching for the professor had led from the villa he was not into the search of countless other villas he was not in. They turned over one small rental unit after another, and then proceeded to check every hotel in the downtown core.

Someone in the senior FBI force called it quits for the evening. They came back to the hotel, downed a quick dinner, and came to this room for the briefing. Bernadette felt the movement in her stomach of the nightly fare of rice and beans mixed with pork that swam inside of some kind of grease. Her stomach was negotiating the mass, and not really liking the result. She wondered if she would succumb to the dreaded "Montezuma's Revenge" of Mexico, which resulted in a bout of diarrhea. Her stomach did a small flip; she burped softly and drank some water. "*So far so good*," she thought.

Agent Cooper cleared his throat, a signal that he was about to begin. "I want to bring your attention to recent events that have transpired around the globe today to give you some idea of the gravity and the importance of our search for the person named Professor Alistair McAllen." He cleared his throat again, drank some water and motioned toward what was appearing on the screen.

The thirty-some agents in the room lifted their heads up from their own laptops and cell phones and watched the screen come into view. The first image was a satellite shot. The title underneath the picture showed the latitude and longitude of the position and the time of the shot, which was the day before.

"What you are looking at is an image taken by a US Naval Intelligence satellite over the Aegean Sea. Two days ago, a supertanker from a Russian oil company came apart approximately 100 nautical miles from the island you see to your left. It's called Mykonos. The tanker had three million barrels of oil on board, and our information is that the entire cargo of oil is in the ocean and floating toward that island." Cooper pointed with a laser showing the small island that was about to have its beaches coated in oil.

An agent near the front of the room that Bernadette only knew by the first name of Hillary spoke up. "How is the cleanup operation going?"

Cooper expelled a sigh. "That is a good point; here is a view of this morning in the same area." He hit a button and the satellite image came up. There was not one sign of vessel traffic in the area.

"I don't get it. Where are the clean-up vessels and salvage ships?" Hillary asked.

"There are none, as any ship that has ventured into this area has been sunk by a wave, comprised of what our analysts believe to be whatever sunk the tanker." Cooper went back to his laptop, and brought up a series of pictures of ships. "We have reports that this cruise ship was sunk, as was this Coast Guard Cutter, as well as several small freighters. We have no idea on the number of lives lost, but our estimates are in the thousands. The only thing able to survive in this area is a wooden boat." He brought up a series of pictures of the ships that had been sunk.

"Do the analysts think this is the work of the Bio Bugs released by the Chechen Terrorists?" Hillary asked.

Cooper punched up some more images on the screen. "That is exactly what they think. Just this morning, the Russian Security force identified the names of two men from the crew manifest, brothers named Anzor and Kerim Kadyrov. Both are linked to this man . . ."

"This is Adlan Kateav," Cooper said, bringing up the picture on screen. "Who the Russians think is their leader, and also responsible for the attack on the pipeline in the Samara region of Russia a few days ago."

Bernadette nudged Anton who was sitting beside her, and said in a whisper, "That looks like the guy driving the car we saw early this morning."

Anton whispered back, "Are you sure about that?"

"Oh yeah, I . . ." Bernadette stopped in mid-sentence as

Cooper's glance arched its way in her direction. Agent Winston was across the table and gave her a frown.

Cooper continued with his briefing. "Now, with the recent events in Europe, the problem of finding this professor has taken on an entirely new scope of international proportions." He paused for effect, cleared his throat while he took a sip of water. Bernadette could see what he was about to say was bothering him.

"As of tomorrow, this search is being taken over by a combined detail of the CIA and Military Intelligence, with the aid of both the Mexican police and military." Cooper took another sip of water, as if just saying the words had left a bad taste in his mouth.

An agent named Tony King spoke up first. "We're being sent home?"

Cooper shook his head, "No, we stay in place, our mission is the same, but the search will be run by a CIA head with several Military Intelligence liaisons. Look, I know none of you like this, but at this point this thing has escalated. As you can see from the picture behind me, if these Bio organisms grow unchecked, all shipping traffic in the Mediterranean Sea is in jeopardy, as well the lives of those on board the ships. At this very minute, the entire US Navy's Sixth fleet is weighing anchor and setting sail to get out of range of these things."

Bernadette nudged Anton again, and whispered, "It's about to get very crowded here very quickly."

Cooper shut off his laptop, and an aide unplugged the data projector. The FBI agents rose up, took their laptops, and left the room. Bernadette and Anton followed.

Anton walked behind Bernadette and when they were away from the other agents, he tapped her on the shoulder. "Okay Bernadette, here's the deal. I brought you along on this search for McAllen not only for your instincts, but also for your ability to share information. If you think this Chechen terrorist is here in Mexico, don't you think that needs sharing with the FBI, especially Agent Winston, whom you promised you'd be on your best behavior?"

Bernadette shook her head. "You know Anton, I'm sorry if you don't like my methods, but here it is. If I tell these guys I think this Adlan guy is here, it's going to put everyone on high alert. They'll go in with guns out and shoot the first thing that moves. I don't want McAllen killed; I want to capture him, and I want his formula to stop this crazy bug that his student invented—does that sound too much off the team for you?"

Anton's head was down, staring at the floor and measuring her words, "No, now that you put it that way, I see your point. But this puts us both in danger without any back up."

"Hey, I got your back, and you got mine," Bernadette said and smiled. "We head out of here at 6:00 a.m. tomorrow morning, do a little recon of this fishing village, and if we find evidence of McAllen we call for backup, if we find nothing . . . well we rejoin the main task force back here in the city. Does that sound fair?"

"Sure, but why do I feel like I'm going to be in big trouble if I go along with you and worse if I don't?"

Bernadette patted Anton on the shoulder. "Ah, the magic of dealing with a woman. Get some sleep; I'll meet you down in the lobby at 6 bells." She turned and headed for the elevator. Once again, she hoped her instincts were right.

Chapter Thirty

Bernadette did not fall asleep until midnight. She tossed and turned until then, trying to get the temperature right in her room. The hot, humid air seeped into everything. She had wanted to keep her window open, but finally gave up, turned up the AC and got under the covers.

The first dream she had, she was in a clearing in a forest. The forest looked familiar. The trees were like the ones in northern Canada, where she grew up as a child on the reservation. A stand of dark green Jack pine was interspersed with the soft green of the poplar trees. The poplar leaves waved in the wind, while the Jack pines swayed.

There was nothing unusual about the dream. Nothing fearful or scary as the woods seemed so familiar. A crow flew overhead, and then another. When she looked up, a flock of crows was circling overhead. They cawed a few times as they flew, but the wind in the trees was the main sound she heard.

A dark form appeared at the line of trees. The form moved into the clearing and became a bear. Bears rarely scared Bernadette. If she didn't surprise them, she knew they wouldn't bother her, but just go on their way.

This bear swayed back and forth. It sniffed the air; it stared at her. The crows cawed more loudly then swooped down toward her and flew away. She felt their wings beat past her hair. The bear gave her one long parting glance, then turned and made its way back into the woods. She was all alone in the clearing again . . . just the sky, the trees, and the wind.

She woke up. Her clock glowed 4 a.m. Her t-shirt was drenched in sweat. She got out of bed and threw water on her face in the bathroom sink. She stripped off her underwear and t-shirt and got into the shower. The water was a tepid mix between hot and cold. She let it run over her face and down her body.

The dream of crows and a bear would be nothing to anyone, Bernadette thought. Unless you were a native North American like she was, imbued with her grandmother's storytelling. Crows and Bears were good spirits; the Natives learned from them. But why did they both appear in her dream. Was it a warning?

If Bernadette was back on the reservation, back in her grandmother's house, she would have curled up beside her and Grandma Moses would have told her about legends of the Bears, and how they helped the Dene people. And the Crows, how their feathers were entwined into lances and hung from teepees. The wisdom of the crow was revered in stories around the campfire during hunting parties. Elders would tell stories long into the night while the children sat in awe of the tall tales.

Now, in this Best Western Hotel room in Mexico, Bernadette was somewhat confused by the two images of these creatures coming into her dreams. She was not superstitious. But the dream had given her an eerie feeling. Was she afraid of what she had put Anton and herself into for the next day? Was she wrong to pursue McAllen with just the two of them? With no back up, as Anton suggested. But she convinced herself it was always best to go hunting on her own—it was her way.

She doubted herself for a moment, and then shook her head. There was no time to second guess or reevaluate the avenue she had chosen. That was her way. If she were wrong about something, she would do it differently next time. But the thought entered her head, *"Would there be a next time after this?"*

She shook herself violently, toweled herself off, put on fresh underwear and a t-shirt and went over to the window. Large clouds floated overhead. They piled high into the sky, full of moisture that they would be dropping on the city in the morning. The moon made a fleeting appearance; it peeked from behind the clouds, and then disappeared.

Bernadette got back into bed, pulled up her covers and watched a lone gecko inch its way across the ceiling. She smiled. "Hey, a least I got some company." She turned over and tried to sleep. Sleep never came.

Chapter Thirty-One

At 5:45 a.m. Bernadette made her way to the hotel lobby. Anton met her and handed her a coffee he had found in the hotel kitchen. Her eyes stung from lack of sleep. The coffee with double sugar, double cream, peeled her eyes back. "Thanks Anton. Let's get going before this place gets too busy."

"Copy that," Anton said as he led the way to their car outside. "I told my roommate, Valdes, that we were running down some addresses in the suburbs."

"He bought that?" Bernadette asked getting into the car.

Anton threw his jacket into the car's back seat. "Hey, Valdes seems to have got some bug, you know that Montezuma revenge thing, and he was up all night. He didn't look like he wanted much conversation this morning."

"Great, that'll keep him occupied and out of our hair," Bernadette said, settling back into her seat. The air outside was warm and humid. The heat in the car was making her drowsy. She shook her head, rolled down the window, and forced herself to focus. "I think it's going to be a long day, Anton," she said as they pulled away from the curb. "Who knew we'd be on a case to find a chemistry professor before he's found by some Chechen Terrorists?"

"You think they're after McAllen and the formula, don't you?"

"Absolutely. This situation is getting stranger by the minute."

Anton swerved the car around a taxi. "You know I read this thing about Mark Twain saying that truth is stranger than fiction because fiction is obliged to stick to possibilities and truth isn't. I wonder what Mark Twain would have to say about a bunch of Bio Bugs roaming the sea and eating ships?"

Bernadette laughed, "Yeah, I think Gene Rodenberry may have even put this into one of his Star Trek episodes. Or at least had Captain Kirk do battle with some Chechens, which he may have called Klingons."

Anton looked over in amazement, "Since when have you become a Trekkie?"

"Hey, this case has been so crazy that I figured anything to get me up to speed on what we were dealing with would be helpful. I'm up to Star Trek the Next Generation in my reading. I'm amazed at how much of what is in Star Trek is now part of everyday life."

"Like the nanites in the Bio Bugs we're dealing with in the Mediterranean Sea?"

"Yeah, exactly like that. Look, last year I was fighting McAllen as he tried to place a plastic expanding thing called polywater into the oilfields. This year, I'm trying to track him down for a Bio Bug that is wreaking havoc in pipelines and anything containing iron, plus attacking people," Bernadette said.

"So, what are you saying, you want to go back to chasing old-fashioned criminals, like crack heads and car thieves?"

Bernadette winced as she said. "Hell, no! This is way too much fun."

They beat the heavy morning traffic, and made their way to the countryside by 7 a.m. The concrete of the city turned to sparse jungle, flat fields, and rows of ramshackle houses, some painted in bright hues of color that dotted the landscape like someone had dropped Lego blocks from the sky.

By 8 a.m., with only a few wrong turns and a few questions to locals, they entered the small fishing village of San Crisanto.

Bernadette said, "My God, this place is small, even by the standards of small."

Anton stopped the car at an intersection with three shops that looked like they might constitute the town center. "Yeah, there's not much here. You wonder why McAllen chose this place to hide out."

"I think we start by asking that guy who just opened his shop," Bernadette pointed to a green metal awning that swung open. Two chairs and four tables sat beside the dusty road. A Corona Cerveza sign, bleached by the sun, promised this place might have food.

"You think they might have seen McAllen?"

Bernadette smiled, "Sure, that and I can see a pot of coffee brewing in the window."

"Always looking for your next coffee fix," Anton said, climbing out of the car.

"Hey, the army travels on its stomach, the police force travels on caffeine—didn't you ever hear that?"

Anton bought two coffees from the man in the shop. He produced a picture of McAllen and asked him in Spanish if he'd ever seen him. The man looked at the picture, looked at Anton, then out at the car with Bernadette in it. "No," was his sharp answer. He disappeared into the back of the small shop.

"I see that went over well," Bernadette said, taking a coffee from Anton. She sniffed the coffee, took an exploratory taste, added another packet of sugar, and tried it again. She made a face on the second sip. "Man, they make some harsh coffee here."

"Hey, it's caffeine. Now our little guy in there, I think he's seen McAllen, and made us for cops."

"Which means, you think he's in the back room calling everyone he knows in the village to tell them some strange Gringo cops are in town?" Bernadette asked.

"That's about right." Anton put his sunglasses back on, took a sip of his coffee, and poured the rest into the street. A door opened a crack on the other side of the street. A face peered out, and went back in. The door slammed shut.

"We're getting nowhere here. McAllen is smart. I'd say he has a villa somewhere outside of town and sends his housekeeper to pick up supplies," Bernadette said.

"I agree, let's get started," Anton said. He drove the car down the narrow street. In the rearview mirror, doors opened, and shop owners stood to watch them drive away.

"You know if you weren't such a tall, dark and handsome . . ." Bernadette stopped as she said the last words. They sent a chill down the back of her neck.

"A tall dark and handsome what?"

"Ah, just that they made you for a cop right away . . ."

Bernadette finished her coffee and threw the empty cup into the back seat. Her Grandmother's dream was there below the surface of her consciousness. "*A tall, dark man will not be able to defend you in bright sunshine.*" Bernadette put her sunglasses on and tried to shake the thoughts out of her head.

"Any idea where I'm heading?" Anton asked as they left the small village and drove down the narrow highway beside the sea.

Bernadette said, "Yeah, I've been looking at Google Earth and scanning several of the villas beside the ocean." Her finger slid down the phone. "I've been looking for places that are somewhat removed from other villas with access to the sea. I've found fifteen that would be a good match for a hiding place."

Anton looked over at Bernadette and sighed, "Just fifteen?"

"Hey, if this job was easy, everybody would want to do it." Bernadette slid down her phone again. "Now, I do have another way of doing this."

"And that is?"

"Call a friend." Bernadette hit dial on her phone. "There is a real estate agent named on a bunch of these villas, a guy called O'Connell. I'm thinking a little local knowledge might help."

"Is this Mr. O'Connell?" Bernadette asked into the phone with a wink at Anton. "Yes, Mr. O'Connell, this is Bernadette Callahan, um yes, sorry for calling so early, but I'm driving out here in San Crisanto, Yucatan, and we're looking for something rather large to rent on the ocean. You know, four to five bedrooms, with pool, that sort of thing. I don't see anything that large listed from the signs I'm seeing out here."

Bernadette took a piece of paper and pen from the glove compartment, "I see, you only have the two and three-bedrooms available. Was there anything in that size that rented recently? We just wanted to perhaps view it from the road." She threw in a giggle, "You know just to see what we missed, and perhaps book it for next year."

Bernadette started to write as the realtor spoke to her, "Uh-huh, that's great. Now you'll have to take my number down, and if something this size comes up, you make sure to call us, because we love this place and want to rent for six months next year." Bernadette ended the call. "I just narrowed it down to three places."

"Why do you think McAllen would want such a big place?" Anton said.

"Because he has his friends coming back from South America, just like the post card said. And he's a creature of habit. The last time I tried to capture him, he was with his friends. I think he's got some patterns we can follow, and this is one of them."

Anton shrugged. "Okay, I'll go with anything right now, pattern, hunch, and a bit of blind luck thrown in."

The first place on the list took a half-hour to get to. The large villa could be seen through the white wrought iron gate from the road. A Mercedes SUV and three sports cars were parked in the driveway. A group of Mexican children played on the lawn.

"I'd say a no to this one," Bernadette said scratching it off the list.

The next location was a half-hour in the other direction. They crossed back through the little village and made their way past sparkling white villas and condos looking out to sea. The road narrowed until dense foliage began to brush both sides of the car.

The road came to an end. White adobe walls hid the villa. A large blue gate, paint peeling in the sun was open on one side. Dusty tire tracks showed recent entry. They got out and peered into the grounds. A blue Chevrolet Malibu was parked beside a red Jeep.

"That's the same car I saw the people who looked like Zara Mashhadov and Adlan Kataev in yesterday," Bernadette said.

"How can you be sure? There are a lot of blue rentals like that one in Mexico," Anton said, trying to remain as inconspicuous as his tall frame would allow.

"I remember the license plate."

"You remember the license plate from yesterday?"

"Uh-huh, I used to memorize license plates while on highway patrol in northern Canada; it's how I beat the boredom. That is the exact same plate as the car I saw them driving yesterday. I'm positive."

"Okay, if you're right, we're going into a very dangerous situation," Anton pulled out his cell phone. "I'm calling for backup, and we sit on this entrance until it arrives."

Bernadette pushed Anton back behind the gate, and placed her hand on his phone. "Look, Anton, if you call for backup, it will be at least an hour before they get here. Even if they scramble a helicopter—you know the drill. They have to go through all kinds of hoops with the Mexican military . . . and by then . . ." Bernadette pointed in the direction of the villa, "McAllen could be dead and only chance of finding the formula or a way to stop the Bio Bugs could be gone." Bernadette took a breath, "You heard what the scientist said, it could be months before they find any kind of antidote to these things and McAllen was the next best thing to Goodman when it comes to knowing what Goodman was thinking when he made these things."

Anton put his cell phone back in his jeans, "Damn it, Bernadette, I hate it when you make sense." He hit the trunk release and pulled out two side arms. He handed Bernadette a Glock .40 pistol and put a Ruger ultra-compact pistol in his pocket.

Bernadette took the side arm Anton handed her. "Now how did you get hold of these? I was informed we Canadians were strictly observers, and not allowed firearms."

"Hey, I talked nice to the FBI liaison, and just like that we got some weapons on loan," Anton said.

"Okay, that doesn't sound right . . . how did you really come by these?"

Anton shrugged, "Well, I told you Valdes was sick all night, and he looked really bad this morning. I asked him if he wouldn't mind if I used these today, and he mumbled something like . . . sure okay . . . and I took them."

"You mean you stole these from Valdes, my God, when he finds out he'll kill you?"

Anton looked almost hurt. "Stole is a harsh word, Bernadette. Let's say borrowed for an indefinite period . . . and it's not like I didn't ask" He winked at Bernadette. "Looks like my Sicilian ancestry is showing—just a little."

Bernadette chuckled. "Yes, obviously the Sicilian blood is beating strong in your veins." She checked the safety and looked down the sight. "I thought guns scared the hell out of you."

"They still do. I was hoping we could wave these around and get these Chechen terrorists to put their hands up. And I did give you the big one."

Bernadette shook her head. "God help us! Okay, stay close to me, and watch my hand signals. I think we can get close to the house without being seen."

Anton stayed behind Bernadette. They walked up the

driveway and past the two cars. Bernadette did a quick check of the cars, and they moved on. One window looked down on the driveway. A curtain blew in the breeze.

The main entrance was on the side. Four low windows rose above the sidewalk. They crouched and came up to the first window. Bernadette scanned the interior. "There's no one there," she whispered to Anton.

Bernadette moved to the next window, scanned the interior, and moved forward. Anton followed. The main entrance door was a large double wide with heavy metal hinges. Bernadette pulled her gun, motioned for Anton to watch her back and opened the door.

The door swung open. The heavy hinges groaned in protest. Bernadette froze. They had just announced their presence to anyone in the house. She waited to hear footsteps. There were none.

A wide stairway led to the upper floor. She motioned for Anton to follow her. She made her way up the stairs. Her heart sounded like a drum in her ears. Her breathing sounded like a bellows. She was sure anyone within two city blocks could hear it.

The upper floor led to a series of hallways. They took the left and headed down it. Bernadette, her gun in front of her scanning for targets, expected to see someone jump out of a room and begin firing at any moment. There was nothing. *Maybe they'd gone . . . escaped by boat.* The thought crossed her mind.

The hallway led to an outside balcony. The balcony led to a larger one. A two-story guesthouse was joined by a walkway. A series of windows looked onto the ocean. Bernadette motioned for Anton to stay and give her cover. She made her way across the bridge and to the first window.

Bernadette peered into the first window. A man was in a

chair. Feet and hands tied. His head hung down. A small stream of blood dripped from his head and pooled on the white tile floor.

Bernadette felt pressure at her back. She turned to see Anton. She turned back to the window. She knew it must be McAllen in there. She whispered to Anton over her shoulder, "Look, I told you to stay back across the bridge to cover me."

The next sound Bernadette heard was a thud. She whirled around to see Adlan standing over Anton with a knife in his hand. Anton's eyes rolled back in his head as he fell to the ground. A red stain appeared on his shirt.

Bernadette's hand came up with her gun. It never made it. Zara was at her side. A blunt object came down on her head. She dropped to the ground.

Viktor paced back and forth outside the Suburban. Branislav leaned against the truck, blowing smoke rings into the humid air. Elena was in the back seat staring at her laptop.

Viktor stopped at the window. "How long now?"

Elena rolled her eyes, "It's still two minutes to upload, just like I told you 10 seconds before, and just before that . . ."

Viktor stomped away and threw a glance at Branislav, who shrugged and blew another smoke ring. There was nothing they could do until the GPS tracking device gave them an upload. It was at 1000 hours every day, and they were at 0958 and counting.

Elena shouted out the window, "I have them."

Viktor ran back to the Suburban, pounding his hands on the hood, "Let's go—let's go—let's go."

Branislav jumped into the driver's seat, started the Suburban and they tore down the dusty highway. Elena shouted directions to him.

Viktor pounded the dashboard, "We've got you—you bastard, Adlan, and I'll have your whore Zara as well. Ha, this bullshit will be over, and I'll have both these shitheads in Moscow by tomorrow. Ha."

"How far are we Elena?" Viktor said, looking back at her.

"We are 20 kilometers."

"Good, good . . . Lev, get your weapons checked and ready . . . stay sharp." Viktor yelled to Lev in the third-row seat.

Lev sat up straight and gave a thumbs up sign and a toothy grin to Viktor. No one had seen him pick up the bottle of Villa Lobos Platinum Vodka at the last store they were in. He'd stolen it. As he reached down to check his weapon, he took another gulp. Lev was getting himself ready in his own way.

Sebastian glanced at his watch. They'd cast off at 0730, and he knew it should have been sooner. Getting the boat without the Mexican captain was the problem. He had to pay extra, a lot extra.

He'd finally negotiated a 37-foot boat with a 5.7 liter inboard. He should have been cruising at 50 miles per hour. The engine was giving poor compression, and he was averaging 37. Sebastian was pissed. There was nothing he could do. They'd been cruising for 2 hours, and another 2 to go. It would have to do.

Percy and Theo sat in the chairs on the deck. They'd slung some fishing rods to make them look like a bunch of gringos out for tarpon. They were cleaning the weapons they'd purchased in a tavern. Sebastian had given strict orders; don't shoot any American FBI or Mexican police. They had enough of a price on their head for supposed sabotage of oilfields. He would not have murder added to it. Nothing was worth that.

He pushed the throttle and listened to the engine. It still wasn't responding properly. He shook his head and eased back on the throttle. In the last hour, he'd tried McAllen's cell phone three times. There was no answer. He wondered if they'd make it to McAllen before the FBI and Mexican police.

Chapter Thirty-Two

The first thing Bernadette tasted was blood. Her tongue rolled round her mouth searching for saliva. She swallowed hard and opened her eyes. The right side of her head pounded. Her hands and legs ached. She was tied to a chair.

McAllen was tied to the chair beside her. He looked passed out; his head rested on his chest. Bernadette could see his chest rising and falling. A ceiling fan paddled the air above, gently blowing his hair.

She tried the bonds of her hands. They cut into her wrists. Too tight to even try to maneuver out of, and the bonds around her legs were the same. She looked around the room. It was a large guest room. A refrigerator and sink were on one end of the room, and a few chairs. A single bed was pushed against the wall.

Zara and Adlan were nowhere in sight. An open window let in a stream of bright sunshine. Bernadette turned her head to shield her eyes. She realized at that moment the situation she was in. The FBI in Merida had no idea where she and Anton were. If they did, they could run a GPS locator on her cell phone. She could see her cell phone. It was smashed beside the door. So was Anton's. Then she remembered—Anton.

Nausea rose in her stomach. She breathed in heavily and swallowed hard. Tears formed at her eyes and burned hot streaming down her cheeks. The realization hit her that if she had listened to Anton, they would still be outside this villa waiting for the FBI backup. Now, Anton was dead. And she would suffer the same fate at the hands of these terrorists.

Bernadette realized she should have listened to her Grandmother Moses. The dream last night was of a bear and crows. They were telling her of her death. A door opened and Adlan walked in, followed by Zara.

"Ah, it is good to see the RCMP Detective is awake." He took her badge from his pocket and read her name. "Detective Bernadette Callahan of the Royal Canadian Mounted Police." He took a chair from the room, placed it backwards in front of Bernadette and straddled it. "I have never met one of your kind. The legends say you are fierce, and never give up." He laughed, pointing to McAllen. "It seems you have found your man—yes."

Bernadette rolled her tongue around her mouth, seeking saliva to speak. Her voice sounded hoarse as she did. "Let's say he is a person of interest."

"Ha, I like that," Adlan turned and winked at Zara behind him. "You know, I have been a person of interest for some time with the Russians." He chuckled at his own joke.

"Now, we are very glad of your arrival, Detective Callahan. This professor . . ." Adlan turned his head to look at McAllen, "has been most uncooperative."

Bernadette looked from Adlan to McAllen. "Perhaps you were not being friendly in your methods."

Adlan grabbed Bernadette's chin in his hand. His large fingers and thumbs squeezed hard on her jaw. "In Chechnya, the Russians would torture our women to give up information about the resistance."

He brought his face close to Bernadette's. His breath was hot on her face. "I was told my children were tortured in front of my wife, and still, she would not give me up. Then they tortured her." Adlan brought a large hunting knife to Bernadette's face. "They inflicted intense pain on her for hours. She only cried out my name as she died."

"Zara!" Adlan shouted. "Wake up the professor!"

Zara grabbed a bucket of water and threw it over McAllen. He sputtered, shook his head, and looked around. "Ah, I see we have company." He looked at Bernadette, eyeing her up and down, and then looked to Adlan. "You should have warned me. I would have made some tapas, or maybe one of my special Margaritas."

"You can see this professor has been very flippant with us. We have been asking . . . perhaps somewhat aggressively . . ." Adlan looked at Bernadette and let out a soft sigh, "for the password to the computer program that holds the formula for the lovely bugs his students created."

McAllen said nothing. He looked at Bernadette. She saw him assessing the situation. There was a calculation going on his brain. The expression in his eyes said there was a plan forming. His eyes darted from Adlan to Zara. Like someone calculating distances.

Adlan let go of Bernadette's face. "The professor here has been quite impervious to pain. He seems unconcerned that we could hasten his death. I regard him as a true warrior . . . but I wonder how he can withstand the pain of a woman?"

He brought the hunting knife up to Bernadette's nose. The large blade reflected the light onto the ceiling. She felt the sharp edge of the blade on her skin. "You see professor . . . with one flick of my blade this lovely nose is gone . . . do you want to be responsible for this?"

"I don't know who this lady is. How can I feel responsible?" McAllen said, throwing a shrug of his shoulders to bracket his words.

"Ah, that is true, but you will hear her scream. As I do my work, she will die right here . . . right here in front of you . . . for that you will be responsible," Adlan moved the blade from Bernadette's nose. The hot blade trailed along her skin until it reached her neck, and then rested on her collarbone.

Bernadette was trying not to tremble. She looked over Adlan's shoulder and focused on Zara. It was Zara who was trembling. The gun in her hand was shaking as she watched Adlan move his knife over Bernadette's face as he made threatening gestures.

Zara had just watched Adlan torture McAllen for the past two hours. McAllen was tough. This policewoman looked tough as well, but she also looked at lot like Zara's dead mother. She'd been tortured to death by the Russians. Zara had heard her screams so many years ago and she trembled to think of another woman suffering that same fate.

"You know Professor, the Russians were fascinated with Chechen women—they excelled in slicing pieces off of them until they bled to death." Adlan move his blade back to Bernadette's nose, ". . . perhaps if were started here . . . this might . . ."

"Adlan no!" Zara screamed from behind him. She stood with a gun in her hand, pointed at his back.

Adlan stood up slowly and faced Zara. He towered over the tiny Zara. "Zara . . . shut up."

Zara faced him; she shoved the gun in his chest. "You will not torture this woman to death . . . I will not allow it."

Bernadette could see the punch coming. Adlan's right hand clenched tight. The sinews of his arm corded like a spring. The punch was a classic right cross. It caught Zara under the chin and lifted her off her feet and sent her flying against the wall. She lay there; her head drooped over to the side, her mouth open. Bernadette couldn't see whether Adlan's powerful punch had killed her or just knocked her unconscious.

Adlan turned back to Bernadette. He shook his hand, clenching his fist. A few drops of blood appeared on his knuckles. "Sometimes, you see . . ." He motioned to Zara's crumpled form, "we all have problems with our people . . . and now, I will perform a few surgeries on you for the benefit of our professor friend . . . and see if he feels responsible."

Bernadette's body trembled uncontrollably as Adlan's knife came beside her nose. He let the blade rest there, and then looked over at the professor. "Such a shame to remove so beautiful a nose . . ."

Bernadette breathed deeply and closed her eyes. If she could have willed her face to back up from the knife, she would have. There was no way out. The knife felt razor sharp, and she tried not to think of what would happen next.

The gunshot was loud. Her ears rang. The sound reverberated around the room in a wave that crashed over her several times before she opened her eyes. Adlan's body was falling forward. Half his head was gone.

Anton stood behind him. The gun in his hands smoked. A slow curl rose from its muzzle as he trained the gun on Adlan's crumpled body. The pool of blood from Adlan's head spread out onto the white tile floor.

"Anton, my God . . . I thought you were dead," Bernadette said. He looked like a vision, something surreal that had risen from death. She shook her head to make sure he was real. His white polo shirt was a mass of red blood.

Anton picked up the knife from Adlan's body. "Hey, didn't I tell you I have Sicilian blood in me . . . it takes more than a knife to kill a Sicilian." He moved around to Bernadette and cut the bonds on her hands. In bending down to cut the bonds on her feet, he stumbled, and fell to the floor.

Bernadette knelt by his side. "Anton, hold on, we'll get you some help . . ." She looked around for a cell phone; both their cell phones lay smashed by the door. Adlan didn't have one, and she checked on Zara . . . nothing.

Bernadette looked at McAllen, "I need a cell phone to call for help."

McAllen stared at her for a long few moment, "Sure, I can get you a cell phone . . . but you need more than that. You want to call your federal agents in Merida, that's going to take them scrambling a chopper to get here. Your friend there . . ." He motioned to Anton with his head, "has got maybe twenty minutes of life left in him . . ."

"What do you suggest?"

"I suggest you untie me, and I will call a doctor who lives 10 minutes from here, and I do some triage on your friend with my medical kit. I promise you I've done a few knife wounds in my Vietnam days—and after that—you let me go . . ."

"I can't do that. You have to come in for questioning . . . to solve this thing with these Bio Bugs."

"Stop being such a tight-assed Mountie, for Christ's sake . . . your friend is dying, damn it . . ." McAllen lowered his head. "Okay, look, here's what else I'm going to do, I'm also going to give you a USB stick that has the formula to reverse the effects of the Bio Bugs."

"You have this?"

"Yes, I have it, I was going to send it to the FBI once I was out of Mexico, but as you can see," he motioned his head to Adlan, "I was detained."

Bernadette looked down at Anton, his breath was shallow, and his eyes were glazing over. She needed to act. "Okay, but if you don't attend to my partner immediately, I will shoot you." Grabbing the knife she cut his bonds.

McAllen rubbed his wrists, "I'm sure you will." He went to the bed in the room, and grabbed a cell phone from under the mattress and smiled, "Too many people never look in the obvious places—I stash my money there too." He dialed a number, spoke in Spanish, and snapped the phone shut. "The doctor is on his way—10 minutes—now your turn." He threw the phone to her and pulled a medical kit from a cupboard.

Bernadette called the FBI emergency number she memorized before they left Merida. She told them to triangulate the helicopter on her cell phone, then left it on and placed it beside Anton as she watched McAllen attend to him.

McAllen unwrapped a large gauze pad and applied it to Anton's wound. "It looks like there were no internal organs hit. I think we have trauma and loss of blood. I told the doctor to bring some units of plasma."

Anton's eyes started to roll back in his head, his breathing shallower. Bernadette started to slap his cheeks. "Anton . . . stay with me . . . Anton . . ." She heard footsteps running towards the room.

Chapter Thirty-Three

Bernadette looked up at the door. She expected to see the Mexican doctor there. Four people entered the room. Three men stood with submachine guns, and a woman with what looked like a stun gun in her hand filled the doorway.

No, Bernadette realized, *these aren't Mexicans. From their looks, not American either, she had a feeling that things had made a turn for the worse—if that were even possible.*

The square-looking one with dark features stepped forward, motioning with his machine gun at Zara. "I see you have captured our Chechen's for us."

"Yes," Bernadette said, "That is Zara Mashhadov, and the late Adlan Kateav is there on the floor. And you are?"

"I am Viktor Lutrova of the Russian Security Force. We have been chasing these suspects for some time."

Bernadette stood. "I am Detective Bernadette Callahan of the Royal Canadian Mounted Police. My partner here," she motioned to Anton, "is with the Canadian Security and Intelligence Agency—I have the FBI on the way. I'm sure they'll turn Zara over to you once she's been questioned by the FBI and the Mexican Police." Bernadette couldn't believe her tone. The Russians still trained their guns on her.

Viktor turned to the woman; she said something to him in Russian, the word McAllen was at the end of her sentence. She pointed to him with her stun gun.

Viktor nodded his head, and turned back to Bernadette. He advanced a few more steps. His machine gun leveled at her chest. "My associate informs me that you have Professor McAllen in our presence. We will take him back to Russia with us; we understand he knows the formula for those little Bio Bugs that have been a problem for all of us."

McAllen didn't look up from where he was applying a large gauze pad to Anton's knife wound, "I'm not going anywhere with you. Russia, the USA or any other country will not be getting the formula. I only have the antidote; I destroyed the formula."

The man behind Viktor said something to him in Russian. Viktor seemed deep in thought. Bernadette sensed the tension in the room go up a notch. The third Russian standing beside the fallen form of Zara took the safety off his weapon. Bernadette sensed there was something unsteady about him. He weaved as he stood.

Viktor looked back at Bernadette, and down at McAllen, "That was a nice speech, professor. But you will come with us, and one of our associates in Russia will extract the formula from you, with a small amount of persuasion." He smiled. A set of perfect white teeth framed in tense lips.

"I can't let you do that," Bernadette heard herself saying. She stepped forward towards Viktor. His gun barrel was touching her chest *"God,"* she thought, *"first a knife, now a machine gun . . . not my day."*

"Professor McAllen is in my custody, and a Canadian Citizen. If you leave here with him, I'll have you stopped by the Mexican Police."

Viktor laughed, "My dear RCMP lady, with one burst of this gun, we will have your silence."

Bernadette didn't see Viktor take the safety off his machine gun. She heard the click. The click was loud—it reverberated into her solar plexus. Her body shuddered in anticipation of what it expected next—a hail of lead.

Something moved by the door. Zara leapt up and grabbed the machine gun from the weaving man beside her. Bernadette could see what was coming. She hit the floor.

Zara put a full round into the drunk Russian. She swept the weapon across the Russian woman and the other two men on fully automatic. Viktor had only seconds to return fire. He caught Zara with a burst to the chest, but she kept firing.

Zara, badly wounded, grabbed a fresh clip from one of the fallen Russians, and walked from one Russian to another, firing a shot to each of their heads. Bernadette could see the hatred in Zara's eyes as she put a well-aimed burst into each of them as they lay on the floor.

Zara collapsed by the wall. She dropped the smoking weapon. Bernadette rushed to her side. She could see there was no saving her; a sucking sound was coming from her lungs. Bubbles foamed in the blood. She was fatally wounded.

Bernadette knelt by her side and put her mouth to Zara's ear. "Thanks for saving us."

Zara could barely speak. In a whisper she said, "It was all about the hatred . . . the hatred for the Russians . . . you just got in the way . . ." Her head dropped to one side. She was dead.

A Mexican stood in the doorway. A stethoscope around his neck, a black bag in his hand, he muttered, "Ay, dios mio," as he surveyed the carnage of bodies.

Bernadette motioned him to look after Anton. A young Mexican lady came behind the doctor with a bag; the doctor got her to assist him. They broke out plasma and syringes and began triage on Anton. McAllen gave the doctor instructions in Spanish, and then walked over to Bernadette.

"Looks like this gun fight is over," McAllen said looking around the room. He reached into his jeans pocket and produced the USB stick. "Here's the antidote I promised. Tell them to administer the formula, just as it's written here. You can tell the scientists that I neutralized the God Gene; they'll understand that. Most others won't. The world will be fine in the morning."

Bernadette heard a boat outside. A sleek white boat tied up alongside the pier. A man that looked like Willy Nelson, with long grey braids falling out either side of a faded baseball cap, was running towards the house, a gun in his hand. Two others followed him. Bernadette knew it was Sebastian, Percy and Theo.

McAllen went to the balcony and waved. He shouted, "I'll be right down—no need to panic."

"We heard gun shots—is everyone okay?" Sebastian asked. He stopped in mid-stride.

McAllen looked back into the room and smiled at Bernadette, "Yeah, all those who matter are just fine . . . I'll meet you at the boat."

He turned back to Bernadette, "Well detective, looks like we cross paths again, nice seeing you."

"You need to know that the American and Canadian governments are offering you a complete pardon, and immunity if you're implicated in any way with the Bio Bugs," Bernadette said.

McAllen paused for a moment then touched her arm and squeezed it gently. "That's mighty nice of them, but I don't trust either of them. When it comes down to it, they're probably just as bad as the Russians. If they give me a pardon it would mean they'd want to see if I could recreate something else as a biological weapon. I think I'll take my chances with my boys and me being on the run."

He smiled and turned and jogged down the steps and onto the beach where he met his friends and got onto their boat.

She stood at the balcony railing watching the boat disappear into the horizon. When she heard the rotors of the FBI helicopter coming toward the house, she went back inside to check on Anton. His color was coming back. The Mexican doctor said he was doing fine.

Bernadette looked at the USB stick in her hand and at four dead Russians and the two dead Chechens. She had a hell of story to tell the FBI when they landed. She wondered what she'd come up with.

Chapter Thirty-Four

Senior CIA Agent, Maxwell Crowley, stood in the conference room of the Best Western Mayan hotel and looked down at Detective Bernadette Callahan sitting in the chair. Sitting across from her was FBI Agent Cooper and an US Army Captain dressed in fatigues. She assumed the captain was part of the Military Intelligence Corps sent to look for McAllen. Agent Carla Winston sat on a chair away from the table, by the far wall.

Agent Cooper looked at her with an expression that could not hide how pissed off he was at her. Anton and Bernadette were supposed to be observers and consultants. They had defied orders, taken guns from another FBI officer, and gone hunting McAllen without requesting backup, or informing their liaison agent Carla Winston. Cooper's hunched shoulders showed his anger.

"Now, Detective Callahan," Crowley said, "Your report is that you found McAllen, and that he gave you the formula to reverse the damage of the Bio Bugs." He held the USB stick that McAllen had given Bernadette, "and that somehow, you were not able to detain this man. Even when he was being offered a full pardon. Is that what you are telling this room?" Crowley swept his arm in a wide arc to show Bernadette the total breadth of her story.

Bernadette looked directly forward, straight into Crowley's eyes. She could see he knew she was lying. But a thing about a lie is if you keep it right there and constant, it remains what it is—a lie that must be proven false. "Yes, that is what my report states. As I was attending to my partner, our suspect, Professor Alistair McAllen, disappeared in the confusion."

Crowley looked down at the paper in front of him. "Your report also states that four Russians engaged in a gun battle with two Chechens, resulting in the death of all six of these people." He looked up from the paper. "This is what you want to state in your report . . . you're stating the facts the way they happened?"

Bernadette held Crowley's gaze. "Yes, those are the facts."

"And you could not find the formula that this Professor McAllen had for the creation of the Bio Bugs?" Crowley asked. He looked in the direction of the Army Captain. Their disappointment was evident.

Bernadette said, "Yes, sir, McAllen had only the antidote, he said the formula had been destroyed somehow . . . he did not elaborate on that."

Crowley, Cooper, and the Army Captain engaged in a whispered conference. Bernadette thought about Anton. She'd spoken with him just that morning. There were several nurses in his room, all looking after him. He'd been airlifted to Houston, and then again to Edmonton, Canada, once he was stabilized. His mother was flying from Toronto to be by his side.

"Just what I need," Anton had said. "My mother will be overseeing all the nurses and bringing me soup."

Bernadette told him she would see him back in Canada on her return, once the FBI, CIA, and American Military Intelligence debriefed her. Her attention came back to Agent Crowley. He was looking for something more from her—was there something she was hiding?

Of course there was. She'd let McAllen go in exchange for her partner's life. Would she do it again? Of course she would.

"Detective Callahan, are you with us?" Agent Crowley asked.

Bernadette shot her head up. She looked around her. The men in the room where looking at her. She had fallen into a trance. There was a fly feasting on spilled sugar on the conference table.

Crowley looked pissed. He was trying not to show how Bernadette was annoying him in front of the others, but it wasn't working. The harder he tried to hide his displeasure the more it showed. "Do you want me to repeat the question then . . .?"

"Yes, if you wouldn't mind," Bernadette said, now fully aware of the room.

"I said, was there anything else we should know about this USB stick you say you obtained from Professor McAllen . . ." Crowley looked at his peers in the room, "before he disappeared by some sort of miracle?" The others at the table nodded their heads in agreement to his statement.

Bernadette understood the question, but knew they would not understand the answer, "Yes, Professor McAllen said he neutralized the God gene in the formula."

"And what may I ask, is that supposed to mean?"

Crowley looked at her, while he rolled the USB stick between his fingers.

"The professor said you wouldn't understand, and actually I don't either, but he said our scientists would understand it," Bernadette replied.

Ramón Martin waited at the private airport until they closed, then he went home. He returned the next day to wait for the Russians. They did not show up. 24 hours had passed since they'd left. He was worried. He called the Russian Embassy in Mexico City, he told them, his *guests were late*—the code for this mission.

The contact at the Embassy was abrupt with him. Even by Russian standards, Ramón found it odd. He was told to go home and wait for a call. Two days later, Ramón received a call to go to the airport. A white Suburban drove up followed by two white vans and Mexican police.

A Mexican Police Captain approached Ramón. "Senor Martin, I have four coffins to return to Russia. The Russian Embassy said you would take care of this . . ."

Ramón Martin fainted on the tarmac.

Chapter Thirty-Five

Agent Winston took Bernadette to the Merida Airport for her flight back to Canada. The ride to the airport was quiet. Winston said nothing but cleared her throat several times like she wanted to. Bernadette sat in the passenger seat waiting for the tongue-lashing she knew this compact little black lady looked capable of.

Winston parked the car in front of the terminal and turned to Bernadette. "You know, Detective, that shit you pulled out in San Crisanto almost got you and your partner killed, but God dam it girl, I can't fault your instincts. You found McAllen and ended up with the antidote. You keep falling in a bucket of shit and come up smelling like a rose —I hope this keeps working for you—because one day relying only on your instincts can get you killed."

"They almost did, Agent Winston. And look, for whatever it's worth, I'm sorry for getting you in trouble. My instincts get in the way sometimes, and I just act." Bernadette said looking squarely at Winston.

Winston chuckled, "I've been in worse than this, and

you getting the antidote helped big time. Sometimes the biggest screw-ups can be rectified with a good ending."

Bernadette grabbed her bag and started to get out of the car "By the way, I've been out of the loop . . . you know . . . being interrogated by your bosses and all. Did they get the antidote from McAllen over to Europe?"

Winston grinned, "Yeah, they did, the combined Air Forces of Europe bombed the ocean with the antidote yesterday. A few boats tested the waters, and all metal-hulled boats are safe on the waters. And the Bio Bugs are now happily digesting the oil spill and dying out when they've had their fill."

"I guess that's a relief."

"Sure is, and you'll never guess what the antidote was," Winston said.

"Beats me," Bernadette said, "What was it?"

"McAllen recommended in his antidote to decrease this thing called the God Gene, or VMAT2, I believe that is its scientific name, by forty percent. He gave instructions to use a vaccine called FUNVAX, and even gave directions where the US government had the vaccine stored in the vaults of the Pentagon."

"I've never heard of it, what's it supposed to be?"

"FUNVAX is short for fundamentalist vaccine. It was supposedly developed by the Pentagon to vaccinate religious fundamentalist, like terrorist. I thought it was a hoax, you know one of those things put on YouTube to scare us all. Well, it turns out the government had the vaccine all along. But the strange thing is McAllen knew where it was."

"Bernadette shook her head and laughed, "Damn if I'll ever understand science, or how McAllen got his information. I don't think I want to know." She grabbed her bag and headed into the airport.

Bernadette flew to Edmonton to visit Anton, before driving back to her home. He was already up and walking. Two nurses were trying to help him, although it was unnecessary. His Italian mother watched them like a lioness ready to pounce. She gave Bernadette a steely cold glare, before she reluctantly left them. There was almost a snarl on her lip as she walked out of the hospital room.

They only had a short moment alone. Anton took her hand, "You know my mother thinks you'll be the death of me and has forbid me to work with you again." Anton laughed and grimaced in pain from his stomach wound.

Bernadette squeezed Anton's hand, "Hey, I understand her anger, the rest of the RCMP and your department might have made that happen if we hadn't had solved the case. The Bio Bugs are no longer a threat, and both your department, the RCMP and even the Americans are willing to forgive us."

"My god Bernadette, you do come out smelling like a rose."

"Yes, Anton, but only after falling into a large bucket of crap."

Bernadette gave him a gentle hug and made her way home as fast as she could. The highway back to Red Deer reminded her of coming up for air while being on a long dive. Every road sign home relaxed her a little more. By the time she reached her home street, she was humming a tune.

Turning the corner to her house, she saw her grandmother's truck parked in her driveway. She drove up beside it, grabbed her bag and went inside. Grandma Moses was in front of the television with Sprocket nestled at her feet.

"Hey Grandma, good to see you. How was the Sundance Ceremony?" Bernadette asked, dropping her bag at the door, and crouching to greet Sprocket. The dog nuzzled her face. She wrapped her arms around the big dog and felt the warmth of his fur. His breath panted on her, warm, moist, smelling of the outside.

"It was good," Grandma Moses said, her head moving only slightly from the show she was watching.

"I just got back from Mexico, Grandma . . . you know that dream you had . . . well the tall, dark man . . . he did save me . . ." Bernadette pushed Sprocket away, patting his behind as she walked by.

Grandma Moses switched off the television and turned to face Bernadette. "I know. In Montana we had an all-night session to take away your friend's bad medicine of fear—we gave him courage." She rose slowly from the chair. "We sent a bear and crows to your dreams to let you know everything would be okay."

"I . . . I saw them . . . the night before we went out on our mission . . . I thought they were a bad omen . . ." Bernadette stammered.

Grandma Moses smiled, "Bernadette, you need to study your Indian lore . . . bears and crows are good." She walked into the bedroom and closed the door.

Bernadette bent down, scratched Sprockets' ears, "Damn it, dog, if I'll ever understand half of what that woman says or dreams about. But I'm so glad for whatever medicine she sent my way."

There were many things she needed to do. She needed to call Chris, and tell him she was okay, and yes, she had feelings for him, but her feelings of duty to the RCMP just kind of pushed everything else in her life to the edges. Was he going to be happy living on the edge of her life?

She changed into her running gear and with Sprocket loping beside her she hit the pathway and settled into a long easy run. As they ran by the river a large hawk swooped down and picked up a rodent and started to flap with its prize into the sky.

Bernadette watched the scene and smiled, "You see Sprocket, that's what a hawk is supposed to do."

McAllen, Sebastian, Percy and Theo sat around a table in an outside café in Antigua, Guatemala; the light was starting to fade in the square. The church bells chimed the hour, and a group of small children finally started to disperse after their attempts to sell the men trinkets made of beads had failed.

Sebastian looked over the menu. "Looks like the specialty is pescado a la plancha." He looked at Percy who didn't understand Spanish. "That's fish sautéed in garlic and butter with citrus—you'll like it."

Percy nodded in Sebastian's direction. "Sounds good to me." He turned to McAllen. "Well Mac, looks like we got your ass out of the fire—and you didn't even start the thing."

McAllen dug a nacho chip deep into some fresh guacamole and shoved it into his mouth. He chewed thoughtfully for a moment. "You know boys, I've been thinking about that since we got here. There are lots of people after us for something they think we did. So, let's do something that will get their attention."

"Like what?" Theo asked.

"Just give me some time. I'll come up with something," McAllen said. He smiled and raised his glass of beer. "Here's to science—Salud!"

Next in the Bernadette Callahan Series

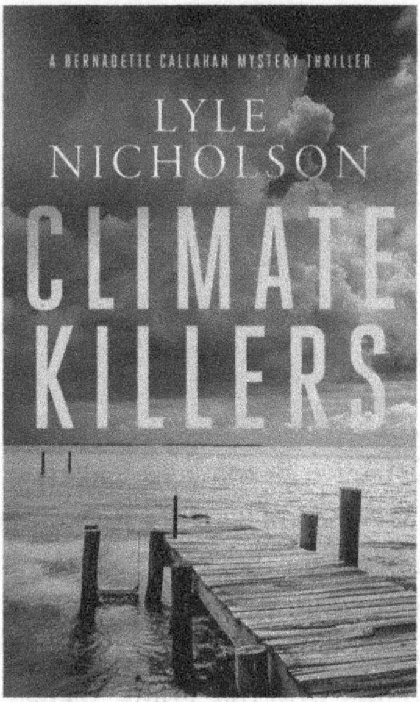

vinci-books.com/climate-killers

A race against time. A detective pushed to her limits.
The fate of the world hangs in the balance.

Detective Bernadette Callahan embarks on a journey to find the one man who might hold the key to North America's climate crisis. With help from unlikely allies, she must navigate a world of mysterious clues, cutting-edge science, and government upheaval. But with a mole inside the FBI leaking information Callahan must stay one step ahead if she hopes to succeed.

Turn the page for a free preview…

Climate Killers: Chapter One

The heat hit Detective Bernadette Callahan as she stepped out of her RCMP Jeep. The sun's rays made her skin itch, the hot air grabbed the back of her throat. A rivulet of sweat began its way down her chest. Her bra would be soaked in minutes. She hated that.

She walked towards the crime scene—an old house frequented by drug dealers. The oppressive heat wasn't stopping the dealers from killing each other. She took a drink of her water bottle. It had been filled with ice a half hour ago but was turning tepid already.

Yellow police tape wafted in the hot breeze. An officer at the door shifted uncomfortably as the wind blew in his direction. He was young and tall with rippled muscles in places where most men didn't know there were places.

He looked up at Bernadette. "Hey, Detective, looks like I won the heat wave pool—it's been fifty-eight days above 35C."

Bernadette smiled. "Yeah, Stewart, you won. Hope that gives you enough for some cold beer." She stood beside him at the doorway. The heat from inside the house was worse than outside. The smell of decomposing bodies hit a gag reflex in the back of her throat.

Constable Stewart saw her discomfort. "There's no need to go in. The CSIs have been here for the past hour, they've taken all the pictures. A pretty clear gang hit. All the victims are known, long lists on their rap sheets… but if you still want to check it out…"

Bernadette paused for a moment, and then donned a pair of gloves. She walked in, took a quick look around and nodded at the CSI team. They looked in pain. It was 37 Celsius outside; it must have been high forties inside.

When the bile in her stomach started to move upward, she knew she'd had enough. She backed out of the room, avoiding the knowing look of Constable Stewart.

"Yeah, you're right. Pretty straightforward," Callahan said. "I'll catch the photos and report at the detachment. She walked straight to her Jeep, started it, and hit the A/C on high.

The stench of death started to clear from her nostrils. The bile receded in her stomach as she sucked in cool air. She sipped some water. She looked down at her bra. She cursed, "Damn it, soaked again."

Her phone rang, it was Chief of Detectives Jerry Durham, "I need you back here," he said when she answered. He was always direct. He was a good guy to work with—but direct.

The RCMP Detachment was only minutes away in the small city of Red Deer, Alberta in western Canada. The city was on a flat prairie in sight of the Rocky Mountains with over one hundred thousand people, but there was enough crime there to keep an RCMP detachment and Callahan's serious crimes division busy.

This was Bernadette's second year in the city. She liked it there. The people were straightforward, most working for the oil service companies and the criminals were just as dumb as anywhere else.

Bernadette was in her mid-thirties, a red head with Irish and Native Cree ancestry and definite ideas of right and wrong that made her the perfect candidate for the Royal Canadian Mounted Police, except when she bent the rules, which was too often for her superiors.

Her instincts and work ethic were excellent which kept her one step ahead of reprimand. She put on the radio as the news came on. The announcer went over the latest death tolls from the heat. Eastern Canada had over 500, western Canada had just under 200 hundred—for the month.

The worst news was the American states. The deaths were hitting the thousands in the mid and southwest USA where temperatures were over one hundred Fahrenheit.

This heat wave had started in mid-August. It was now late October. The Canada Geese should be flying overhead. Instead, they were hanging around up north. Maybe they knew something no one else did.

Everyone was talking about this as climate change. Some people were loudly proclaiming the heat wave was the result of all the world's misdeeds and misuse of the planet, but Bernadette had a gut feeling there was something more happening. She couldn't put her finger on it. It just felt weird.

She reached the RCMP headquarters and ducked into the women's changing room for a quick shower and change of bra and t-shirt. She carried several changes with her. This was her second one of the day.

She found Chief Durham in his office. He was beginning to look older than his mid-forties. The job, or his three kids had managed to recede his hairline and add a multitude of wrinkles to a once unblemished face.

"Sit down, Callahan." Durham motioned her to the chair in front of him.

"Am I in some kind of shit again, Chief?" Callahan asked.

He shook his head. "No, but if something comes up—you always come to mind." He swiveled his laptop and punched some keys. "We got a Skype conference with Canadian Security and Intelligence Services. You're just in time."

The screen came on. Agent Anton De Luca was in front of them. "Good afternoon, Detectives." He greeted them with a beaming smile, looking his usual well-put together self. Bernadette thought De Luca could have been the star of a half dozen Italian soap operas or commercials. He had drop dead handsome looks with a silky voice that sounded like you'd just been placed in a vat of tiramisu.

"What's up, Anton?" Bernadette asked. "You run out of serious international espionage that you have to call up us little city folks? I only got dumb ass drug dealers—but you're welcome to them."

Anton shook his head. "Always with the sense of humor, Bernadette. I hope you keep that as I tell you what mission I have for you."

Bernadette felt her insides take a small loop de loop, like the roller coaster ride that flips upside down and has you screaming for it to come back up. "You got my attention."

"Good, a group of scientists in Canada and America think this latest heat wave cannot be attributed to what we've experienced in normal climate change," Anton said. His demeanor was solemn now.

Bernadette stopped herself from blurting out *I knew it*, instead, she sat forward and said, "Really? Why do they think that?"

"The heat wave has come on too quickly," Anton said. "Several scientists think this is a manmade event."

"I don't get it. How do you heat up a region of the planet like what's happening now?" Bernadette said. She looked up at Durham. "You know, I've been thinking this is crazy odd myself. What are the scientists thinking?"

"They think someone is messing with the ocean currents," Anton said.

"Wouldn't we see something like that?" Durham asked. "I mean… it seems like you'd need something significant to affect a body of water."

"Well, yeah," Anton admitted. He paused for a second as he read from his notes. "Professor Bjarni Sigurdsson, from Iceland, came up with a theory of how we could turn the temperature down or up just from adjusting the amount of heat generated under the ocean floor."

"Where is the good Icelandic professor now?" Bernadette asked.

"That's the problem. He's gone missing. He was supposed to present a paper in Stockholm on how North America could change the currents and temperature of the Pacific and provide more rain or drier conditions when needed. He never showed up. He vanished without a trace."

"How long ago?" Bernadette asked.

"Back in June of this year," Anton said.

"I take it you want me to go out and look for him?" She cocked her head to one side. "You know, I'm pretty good at finding people, but asking me to head to Sweden on a five-month-old missing persons case is kind of pushing it."

"No. I'm not asking you to go to Sweden. I need you to go to Nicaragua."

Bernadette sat back in her chair. "You found this Sigurdsson guy in Nicaragua?"

Anton shook his head slowly. He looked straight into the screen. "We found Alistair McAllen there. We think he can lead you to Sigurdsson."

"How is McAllen linked to Sigurdsson?" Bernadette asked.

"The Stockholm police found Sigurdsson's cell phone. He had numerous calls to McAllen." Anton said. "There's also some history between the two. They go way back in their university days. The bright boys in intelligence think McAllen's our way to Sigurdsson, and your name came up as the way to get the information."

Bernadette dropped her arms to her side. She looked at her Chief of Detectives then back to the screen at Anton. "Are you serious about this? You really want me to meet up with him again? Why do you think I could convince him to find this missing professor?"

"Because you let him go last time you met. Remember?" Anton said.

Bernadette cleared her throat and sat up straight in her chair. "If you read my report of when we met in Mexico, you'll see I was helping you, Anton. Remember, you were injured, and I aided you… then he got away."

Anton smiled into the screen. "Yes, Bernadette, that was a wonderful report. The FBI and the CIA had to swallow hard to digest what they knew was a total fabrication of the facts—now listen," Anton put up his hand, "I know you want to throw out a whole lot of rebuttals but we don't have time."

Bernadette closed her eyes, and then opened them

again. There was no way she was getting out of this. "Okay, let me have it. When do I leave?"

"You're booked on the 6:55 am flight from Calgary to Houston tomorrow morning. There's a layover in Houston where you'll be met by your partner from the FBI," Anton said.

"Who is?" Bernadette said.

"Agent Carla Winston."

"Oh—my—god, this keeps getting better," Bernadette said.

"You know her?" Chief Durham asked.

"We were in Mexico together, helping in the hunt for McAllen," Bernadette said "She was supposed to be my minder there, you know, look after me so I didn't step out of line… I sort of stepped out of line…"

"Here's your chance to make it up to her," Anton said. "You're on strict orders to find McAllen, see if he has knowledge of where Sigurdsson might be, report that information and head home. This is seventy-two hours tops—you'll be back by the weekend."

"Let me get this straight. Everyone in the intelligence community in North America knows where Alistair McAllen is, and you want me to go see him and not arrest him—is that correct?" Bernadette asked.

"You got it. He's on an island in Lake Nicaragua. Intelligence says he's heavily armed. If we send in the FBI there'd be a shoot-out and an international incident. Nicaragua doesn't like the USA very much; they are getting friendly with China right now. We need you do this quietly. You got that?" Anton said.

"Yup, I got it, Anton." Bernadette smiled at Anton and threw him a salute. She looked at Durham, "I'll turn my file over to my partner and go home to pack a bag."

Durham nodded. “Are you going to be okay with this? I remember you having some history with this Professor McAllen.”

Bernadette swallowed hard and looked at Durham. “Yes, he escaped from me once off the coast after he tried to damage world oil, and I kind of had to let him slip away in Mexico…” She dropped her eyes and cleared her throat. “Anyway, you’re right, we’ve had some history—”

“And you’re going to be okay with meeting him again?”

“No worries, Chief. I’ll handle this with care and be back in time for our weekend barbeque.” She got up and headed out the door, a knot growing in her stomach. Was it foreboding of the mission or what she had to say to her fiancé when she got home?

Climate Killers: Chapter Two

The knot in Bernadette's stomach hadn't gone by the time she reached home. She saw Chris's truck there. She'd hoped he'd be off fishing somewhere, so she could have packed, and headed to the airport in Calgary, and just left a note. That would have been easy. This was going to be hard.

She put the engagement ring back on her finger. She told him she didn't wear it during work as she was afraid, she'd lose it in a take-down of a felon, but what she didn't admit to him was that it made her feel like she was caught in a trap.

It reminded her of the traps her grandfather used to set back on the reservation in the far north. They'd find fox, rabbits, and weasels with one leg caught in a steel trap on her grandfather's trap line. The animals would gnaw on their legs to try to get away. She felt the ring burn on her finger sometimes like it was caught in something.

She walked in the door. Her dog, Sprocket, a big lop-eared German Shepard with a semi-obedient personality met her at the door. She bent down and nuzzled her face in his fur.

"You may not want to get too close to him," Chris said from the kitchen. "I think he was rolling in a dead squirrel this afternoon."

Bernadette patted Sprocket and gently pushed him away. "Way to go, big fella, I'm sure you think you'll smell like a star to all the lady dogs out there."

Chris stood at the doorway of the kitchen. "Well, star detective. How'd your day go with the bad guys?" He was dressed in shorts and tight t-shirt, his muscles stretching the shirt fabric to its limits. His hair was wet from his shower. His curls hung down in rings over his brown eyes. Holding a bowl and whisk he announced, "I'm making your favorite dinner tonight, beef wellington and for dessert I whipped up a key lime pie."

"What's the occasion?" Bernadette asked. She felt a foreboding of the storm that was to come with his answer.

"It's been one year since I asked you to marry me—it's also a year since I left the RCMP to be your house husband," Chris said.

Bernadette crossed the room. She embraced him and put her head on his chest. The words *househusband* had been their joke, at first. Chris had left the RCMP on his small island detachment off the coast of British Columbia so they could be together. They wanted to make this work.

He was going to find work in oilfield security, but it never happened. There were only security guard positions in their small city. The corporate security jobs were in Calgary, or up in the Oil Sands in the far north. He had offers for Dubai and even a lucrative one from Afghanistan, but they were all three- to six-month stints.

Their relationship felt fragile. Both of them had been total loners before, no dependents. Now, they had to be there for each other. It was hard to get used to.

"I have to drive to Calgary tonight, Chris," Bernadette said. She kissed his chest and looked at him. "I have to go to a Latin American country, get some intelligence for CSIS and the FBI and I'll be back by the weekend, I promise."

"Are you going to save the world again?"

Bernadette shook her head. "No, nothing so earth shattering. I just… I need to go down there to meet with someone… get some information on a missing person."

Chris held Bernadette's face in his hands. "I hate to give you the third degree, but can you tell me who you're going to see, or is this the hush, hush shit?"

"Yeah… it's that kind of shit… sorry," Bernadette said. She could have told him it was McAllen she was going to see. She didn't have time for the blow up.

Chris kissed her on the forehead, picked up his bowl and whisk and walked back into the kitchen. "You, know," he said over his shoulder, "maybe this is good, you going away for a few days."

"What do you mean?" Bernadette asked. She stopped in her tracks. She was about to head to the bedroom to start packing.

"Maybe it will give us some time to think. I got an offer for a security detail in Afghanistan. Some American corporation wants their people kept safe over there. The gig pays real well, and I get free medical."

"Does that free medical include the body bag they send you home in?" Bernadette said.

They stood and looked at each other. There was so much more to say, but the words had to be careful. They each knew they didn't have the time for the depth of conversation they needed to have. Chris went back into the kitchen and Bernadette went into the bedroom.

She grabbed her carry-on bag, threw in her usual four to five changes of underwear, t-shirts, and jeans with a few pairs of shorts and runners. She stood over the bag, feeling that something was missing. Chris and her were drifting apart.

She went into the kitchen and kissed him hard on the mouth, "Look, big guy, I know things haven't been great with us. But how about you wait until I get back. We'll head out somewhere. Maybe go to Banff, have wild sex in some classy hotel and go hiking along the glaciers."

"Sounds good. How about if I save this dinner for when you get back as well?"

"What's a hungry girl going to eat?"

"How about key lime pie—after we have a shower together."

Bernadette grinned. "You always have great ideas…is that one for the road?"

He pulled her tight, his hands slowly moving down her back, resting on her buttocks. He massaged both cheeks, pulling her into him. She felt how hard he was. "You know, I am feeling a little hot and sweaty, a shower is a great idea."

A few hours later, Bernadette was in her Jeep, for the two-hour drive to the airport in Calgary. She felt better but unsettled. The sex was always great with Chris. It was sometimes what held them together. She wondered if it was enough.

She stayed in a hotel that night near the airport and boarded the 6:55 am flight to Houston the next morning. Just as she was getting on the flight and about to shut off her phone she read a text from Chris: *Sorry, Bernadette, I decided to take the job in Afghanistan. I leave for Kandahar tomorrow. We'll talk soon. Love you, Chris.*

A flight attendant came by her seat. "Sorry, ma'am, you'll have to turn off your cell phone. We're about to take off."

Bernadette nodded, and shut off the phone. This felt like their relationship was ending. Could she get it back? Would she fight for it?

She slept for much of the morning flight. On her arrival she looked around for Agent Carla Winston in the airport terminal. They'd agreed in a text to meet in front of Hugo's Cocina in terminal D.

Bernadette saw Agent Winston. She looked the same as when she'd seen her last in Mexico. She was African American. A trim little package, all of 5'5" with short black curly hair that showed signs of grey. She was dressed in a light blue casual pantsuit. It still said FBI, but on vacation. Bernadette thought she'd been uptight when she met her previously. It seemed nothing had changed.

Carla Winston turned and saw Bernadette. Her facial expression was one of recognition, then disapproval. The scowl that formed over her eyebrows threw a line of wrinkles all the way up to her forehead. It was obvious to Bernadette that Agent Winston was not happy with her choice of partner.

"Detective Callahan, I trust your flight was alright?" Winston asked in a monotone. She didn't extend a hand for a handshake. She looked Bernadette up and down. Regarding her t-shirt, jeans and black boots as if she'd been subjected to a scan—and failed.

"Ah, yeah, okay flight. But the food was awful. They got anything good here?"

"Best tacos in the airport," Winston said as she walked towards the restaurant.

Bernadette watched Winston walk into the restaurant and muttered, *"My, aren't we the frosty little thing?"*

They took a table away from other diners and let their eyes peek at one another other over the menus. Winston put her menu down and stared hard at Bernadette.

Bernadette cocked her head to one side. "Okay, Winston, let's have it. You want to give me a big piece of your mind about something that's pissing you off. I could see it from across the concourse. So, let it fly so I can enjoy my taco in peace after you get done your speech."

Winston's lips went into a thin line. Her eyes narrowed. Her hands clenched and unclenched. "Okay, I'll tell you what's on my mind. I got a son, a hell of a good one. He's studying to be an Engineer at the University of Virginia. And I have a nice condo in Fredericksburg, Virginia. I'm married to an okay man—no I lie, my marriage is on the rocks…but that's not the point. I got an okay job with the FBI and I intend to retire in twenty years. You get me?"

"Okay, sure. Nice bio by the way. But what exactly are you getting at—?"

"What I'm getting at is the shit you pulled in Merida, Mexico, almost got your partner killed. I know I told you I couldn't fault you for going by your instincts. You did get the antidote that saved the pipelines, but that could have gone the other way. So, here's what I'm saying," Winston leaned forward, and her voice was a fierce whisper, "Don't pull any of that crazy shit with me. I intend to go back home to my wonderful son and my useless husband—you hear me?"

Bernadette picked up a nacho chip from the table and dipped it in pico de gallo sauce. "You've made yourself very clear. Now, how about we order lunch? That breakfast sandwich I had in Calgary is long gone."

Winston snapped her menu back open. She ordered the fish tacos and Bernadette ordered the Carnitas de Pato. It was duck with tomato sauce and tortillas. She thought about ordering a beer. She wasn't on the clock, as they were just travelling, but from the cloud she could see over Winston's head, she decided not to push it.

When lunch was over, a quiet affair, with little conversation, they went their separate ways. Boarding time was several hours away. Bernadette decided to find somewhere quiet to see if she could send a text to Chris and Winston said she had some correspondence to catch up on.

When Bernadette came out of the restaurant she noticed a crowd milling around the departure lounges. The departure screens for many flights showed CANCELLED. A small script below said *due to excess heat.*

Bernadette pulled out her cell phone and punched up the local Houston temperature. It read 125 Fahrenheit. She'd read a report those smaller jets like the Bombardier CR7 couldn't fly past 118 F. The flight to Managua was on a Boeing 737-800. Its heat limit was 126F.

Bernadette looked at the time. It was 2:00 pm. Hopefully, a thunderstorm would develop and cool things off before they took off at 5:30 pm. Excess heat made it impossible for the jets to get lift off on the runway. As North America was heating up, more planes were being delayed or cancelled for days on end until the heat waves passed.

She didn't know if she could stand being delayed for hours, or days, with the frosty Agent Winston. She went in search of a newspaper and coffee. Maybe find a quiet place to send a text to Chris. She wanted to write it when she was more composed. Her first response had been to send him a WTF! She needed to rethink that.

Carla Winston watched Bernadette make her way down the concourse before heading in the other direction to make a phone call. She needed to report in. There was nothing about this mission she liked. That she'd been chosen to accompany Bernadette Callahan was strange, the person who was her superior on this mission was stranger still.

Adam Morgan had been in the office of Congressional Affairs, and then was transferred over to the Counter Terrorism group. FBI agents normally didn't drop down into the trenches where Winston was. They rose up the chain.

She'd met Morgan a week ago when this mission was discussed. He'd said he'd receive word from the 'highest level,' how this had to proceed. But what was strange was all their meetings had to be away from the J. Edgar Hoover Building.

Their meeting had to be kept secret. There were leaks in the department he'd said. He gave her a separate burner phone that couldn't be sourced back to the FBI.

Morgan wasn't an easy man to like. He made furtive movements with his eyes. They bounced around when he spoke, never looking at her directly. Slim, with a thin face and pointed chin that did nothing to instill any confidence in the words that came from his small mouth, he dressed well, almost too well for the FBI and always had manicured fingernails. Maybe that's what put Winston off the guy. Who in the FBI would get a manicure? Who had time?

She dialed his number. He picked up right away. "Agent Winston. Have you met with your contact?"

"Yes, I've made contact. I'm in Houston, we board in a

few hours for our next destination," Winston said. She couldn't believe how much this man annoyed her.

"Good… listen, there's been a slight change of plans."

"How slight?"

"You are authorized to eliminate Professor McAllen once he's given you the location of Professor Sigurdsson," Morgan said. "Detective Callahan may be eliminated as well."

"Who authorized this?" Winston said, looking around to see if anyone was listening in.

"This comes from the highest levels," Morgan said. "Professor McAllen has been deemed a high value target. Detective Callahan let him escape FBI custody in Mexico. She's believed to be working with McAllen."

Winston couldn't believe what she was hearing. She'd never had this briefing before she left Washington, despite reading the file on Callahan from the Canadian Security and Intelligence Service. Why hadn't they seen anything criminal in her activities? There was no mention of a connection between Callahan and McAllen.

"Okay, I understand what you're asking, but you realize I have no weapons on this trip. The Nicaraguan government would not authorize either of us to have any firearms in our luggage."

"The person you're meeting in Managua will have a weapon for you. He will be discreet in handing it to you."

Winston sighed quietly. "Okay, I got that." She was hoping the lack of weapon would have scrubbed the command to kill Callahan.

"Winston, I can't stress how much this will advance your career if this mission is a success. If you fail… well let's not talk about that…"

"Yes, sir, I understand," Winston said. She ended the

call and headed for the ladies' washroom. The elimination of Professor McAllen was understandable. Detective Callahan's kill order was outside her pay grade. What if she didn't do it? Would they fire her for insubordination? She felt sick.

Adam Morgan smiled when he hung up from Winston. Maybe they could get this back on track after all. Sigurdsson should never have escaped. But then, he was dealing with a group of bunglers and half-wits who could barely follow a proper order.

When Sigurdsson was brought back in and the operation was brought back on line, he'd get rid of those who didn't meet his standards. This list was long. Agent Carla Winston would be one of the first to go. That was already planned in Nicaragua.

He dialed a number and heard the long-distance exchanges click in. Matvel Sokolov picked up the phone. "Adam, you have things ready for us."

Morgan winced. He hated to be greeted informally by someone who he considered beneath him, especially this Russian.

He'd found him when he was in the Office of Congressional Affairs. Matvel was working hard to entice members of Congress and the Senate to give favorable contracts to Russian companies, all owned by the Russian Mafia.

Matvel was good, but Morgan had been better at finding the collusion and bringing in several congressmen who'd swelled their bank accounts. One such congressman was Lawrence Derman. He rolled over so quickly he couldn't get his information out fast enough.

Derman and Sokolov were what Morgan needed. He added a retired and unhappy Admiral Fairborne to his mix, and he was set. North America had no idea what they were in for.

"I have everything ready for you, Matvel. Take them all out. You understand. I want no one left to make a report of what happened."

"I have hired the very best," Sokolov said. "There will be no survivors."

www.ingramcontent.com/pod-product-compliance
Lightning Source LLC
Jackson TN
JSHW031117260725
88309JS00006B/9
9781036703622

About the Author

Lyle Nicholson writes crime and mystery books you will find hard to put down. His first book in the series, *Polar Bear Dawn*, takes place in the high Arctic of Alaska in the unforgiving winter.

The series is based on Detective Bernadette Callahan, who readers love for her hard-nosed style, and failure to follow the rules. As a female detective, she is a phenomenon in Canada's Royal Canadian Mounted Police. You will enjoy her style as she solves crimes that will take you on a world journey.

He lives in Kelowna, British Columbia with his wife, and spends much of his time cooking, enjoying fine wines and writing novels. Somehow, he calls this work!